To Savanna
may you only experience
Best in Life

Gravesend

Smile often

By

Stay Beautiful

Phil Farina

June 2016

1

ISBN 13-978-1511855204
10-1511855207

SECOND EDITION 2016
Published in the United States of America

Dedication

Writing a book is never an easy task. A successful book requires nurturing and support from a whole team of folks that often are not properly recognized for their contribution. To all of those folks who   put up with me while writing this book I want to express my heartfelt Thank You. There are too many to mention but you know who you are!

I would also like to offer a special thanks to my wife Cathy, who helped with the grammar, and whose patience and support were an integral part of the writing process. Thank you for all your help and influence.

I would also offer my deepest thanks to my cousin Linda, who not only played an integral part in the writing of the book but was also my inspiration for the character of the same name.

A book is nothing without an editor and my editor Cristen Bartus, who gave freely of her time and experience and was constantly supportive throughout the process. For this I thank you

And finally, I save the most sincere THANK YOU to my literary agent and "son" Scott who took on this project when no one else would and gave life to the book.

To all of my friends, relatives and supporters who bought a copy and shared my story with others, THANK YOU. Without your support and encouragement this story could not have been told.

Phil Farina
April 2015

Gravesend

Prologue

My name is Roberto Mauro, but my friends, if I had any, would call me Robbie. The story I am about to tell you is true. I promise you, I will tell you no lies; only the truth. I will make every attempt to tell you the story exactly as it happened without embellishment or interpretation. The events that shaped my life are presented as best as possible directly from my memory vault. Where necessary I have checked the facts against historical events to make sure my memory was not embellished. Telling the story of one's life is an amazing adventure in itself. It forces the storyteller to not only remember the events, but requires him to evaluate the course of his life in such a way that it becomes cathartic as well as enlightening. It is also a difficult task to tell this life story, especially if the life has been guided by a series of strange events. I will do the best I can to present to you the story of my life, a life that continues its journey although unsure of the direction or the final chapter.

People say that every good story has a beginning, middle, and an end. Mine doesn't. Oh sure, it has a beginning and a middle; quite the complicated middle actually for one who has spent only twenty-five years on this mortal coil. However, I'm not really sure there's an end. Perhaps I'm writing this story to find the end or at least to begin to see if there even is one. Or, maybe, I am telling my story just to help me understand everything that has happened. This is not a story designed to teach some ultimate moral lesson. Quite the contrary, perhaps it is a story told to warn others, or at least to educate others, as to the "possibilities" that life can offer. The energy that is my life is presented here not only to share with you, but to help me understand that energy and what it all means. If by the written end of my story you have been enlightened by my experiences and understand its meaning, then I hope that you are the richer for it. I, who has actually lived this life, am still struggling to find its meaning and final direction. I hope we can both benefit as the story unfolds.

As a person who likes to study people, I have noticed that in everyone's life there is an event; a life-changing event; a cataclysmic moment that changes a person forever. You didn't plan for it; you didn't see it coming; but it changes your life in such a way that nothing is ever the same again. With most people, they don't even know that the event has happened until years later when they're looking back on their life and say, "What happened on that day really changed my life." The event could be a chance meeting, kind words from a mentor, or a horrifying accident.

For me, however, I knew exactly when the event happened. In fact, I was told well in advance the exact time and place that my life would be changed forever. Problem was I didn't believe it then, and I'm not sure I believe it now. But there it was the event that changed my life from what it once was to what it soon became. However, in order for you to fully understand the entire story, I need to tell it to you from the beginning. So here it is, my life story.

Chapter 1

I was born on June 18, in Misericordia Hospital in Harlem, in what was then the Italian section of New York City. The hospital was run by the archdiocese of New York and was administered by the Sisters of Misericordia. The locals called them the "Gray Sisters of the Sacred Heart" because they wore a simple gray habit covering them from head to toe. Covering three quarters of their face, each wore a pure white wimple with a trifold of linen above their forehead to symbolize the Holy Trinity. Five sisters of the order came to New York on September 1, 1887. The sisters were to assist Rev. McQuirk in caring for women in a maternity shelter for the poor. The original five sisters first settled on Staten Island, then moved to Harlem where they ran a hospital and also taught midwifery to other young sisters. The sisters ministered to hundreds of young women and, by 1893, 717 unwed mothers had been given free medical service and all the general medical and surgical services that were offered at the time. The sisters were a blessing to those poor immigrants who came from Italy and Ireland to settle in this new land.

Both of my parents were born in Italy. My father was born in Sicily in the town of Piazza Armerina, in the foothills of Mt. Etna, while my mother was born in the large city of Naples. They both came from intense Roman Catholic backgrounds. Therefore, my deeply religious Italian parents would not have their firstborn child come into this world in a place that was not run by a Catholic institution. So there I was, the first generation American son born to Dante and Vincenza Mauro, surrounded by nuns, priests, and doctors. This was my first introduction to the religious life. It would not be my last.

It was a warm June morning the day I was born. My mother went into labor before sunrise and the proud parents-to-be arrived at the hospital around six a.m. The nuns whisked her away to the delivery room while my dad was sent to the waiting room. The hospital staff was old fashioned to say the least so my father was kept far away from the delivery room. This was the purview of the doctors and nurses; to them the father had no place in witnessing the mess of birth.

So while my father waited in the comfort of the lounge, Mom was prepared for the delivery room. Mom was in labor for only a few hours and I was born at five minutes before noon based on the timestamp on my birth certificate. I always tell people "I was born at lunch time because I craved real food. After nine months of eating my mother's delicious cooking through a tube, I couldn't take it anymore. I wanted my first real Italian meal."

Unfortunately, my first real meal came in a bottle at the hands of one of those miserable Gray Sisters. Can you only imagine what must be going through a newborn's mind swaddled in a pristine blue blanket, when he looks up to suckle on that first warm bottle and all he can see are the eyes, nose, and mouth of a stranger covered completely in gray? Assuming my eyes could focus, I would guess this had to be a little traumatic.

After my first bottle at the hands of a nun, I was finally introduced to my mother. After a short visit I was whisked away back to the nursery. I hear it is normal for babies to cry and fuss when they are taken away from their mother to be brought to the nursery. I guess I wasn't normal. I didn't make a peep. In fact, the nuns and student nurses were quite concerned about this silent baby.

Years later, my father told me that when he came to the nursery to look at me through the nursery window, he noticed that I seemed to be different. Most of the babies were crying and fussing but I was not. He told me that I seemed to be looking around attentively, watching the hubbub around me. My Dad said it was eerie to say the least. The nuns were fussing among the other babies and whatever they were doing, I was watching, staring even, following their every movement. The other babies cried and fussed in the nursery so they were held and cuddled. I was quiet, so I was unnoticed, but I seemed to notice everything.

When a nun or student sister nurse did pick me up to change me and wash me, I just stared, watching her. Usually, the sister would stare back and, in that voice reserved for cherished pets and other people's children say, "You are a strange little one, much too quiet."

On the day I was to leave the hospital for the first time, Sister Marguerite, the head nurse in charge of the nursery, came in to check on the student nurse, Sister Teresita, to see how things were going.

"Good morning, Sr. Teresita. May God's blessings be upon you."

"And also with you, Sr. Marguerite," chimed the good, young sister.

"And how are things in the nursery today? Are all God's little babies happy and healthy?" the older sister said laughing, while bending to pick up one of the crying babies.

"All of the cherished ones are very happy. Thank you for asking Sister. They're all laughing and cooing. All except that one, Sister, the Mauro baby. He just looks around staring, as if he knows what's going on around him. Sister, I'm afraid for his very soul. I think we should pray for him," said a genuinely worried Teresita.

"We should pray for them all, Sister. Every day we should pray for them all."

"Yes, Sister, we should pray for them, we should pray for them all every day and always. But I must confess to you, Sister, I will be much pleased when the Mauro baby goes home with his new parents later today. I will pray for him so that the Holy Spirit follows him home."

"Yes, Sister Teresita, we shall pray for him."

If they only knew how much I would need those prayers later on.

And so it was, glad to see me go, the good young Sr. Teresita swaddled me in my new blue blanket and handed me to my mother as the new proud parents prepared to take me home to meet the rest of the family.

We left the hospital five days after I was born. My mom held me in her arms as my father and she walked from the hospital's 86th St. exit to my new home on 107th St.

I spent the first few years of my life growing up in a tenement building on the fifth floor in a corner apartment. I was constantly surrounded by family. My maternal grandmother, Philomena, and my mother's sisters, Genevieve, Dominica, and Elizabeth, all lived in the neighborhood. A few blocks away in a similar tenement building, my paternal Grandmother Lily lived with her youngest son, Phillipo. My father's sister, Emanuela, and his oldest brother, Conrad, lived over in Brooklyn, in what must have seemed to be another part of the world. We were a very close-knit family: the first generation to leave poverty-stricken Sicily looking for a better life in what my family called "La Terra Della Libertà."

8

Some – well many – went on to say I was a rather strange child, quiet and observant. I would often sit for hours listening to the conversations of other people, hearing their words in broken English, piecing together the stories of their lives. There was a genuine energy in our family. You could feel it as they spoke in animated form, waving their hands to emphasize what they were saying, sitting around the kitchen table hearing them telling stories of the good old days in Sicily, and sharing the hopes and dreams of what their new lives will be here in America.

But more than peering into the past, I could sometimes tell just by looking at someone that something was going to happen. I could just see it in my mind. Almost like a daydream, full of color and sound. I didn't know what it meant at the time, but it seemed that I had the ability to see when something bad was going to happen. It's not at all that I could see the future; it's just that sometimes I could just "see" that something bad was going to happen. And more often than not, it did.

I can barely remember the first time something like this happened. I was about five years old. I was sitting in the living room playing with my stuffed dog. Since we lived in the city on the fifth floor of a tenement building, it was not very likely that my family would get me a real dog, so this little stuffed dog was always at my side.

So there I sat on the overstuffed couch with Dog, yes, I really did name him "Dog", when my Uncle Sonny, aka Phillipo, walked in and patted me on the head.

"Hey Roberto, how are you and Dog doing today?" he called as he knelt down and rubbed my head. Before I could say a word, as soon as he touched me, I knew something was going to happen. I saw it. I saw it in my mind's eye, clear as day. The vision just came into my brain as if were happening right there in front of me.

What I could "see" was everyone in the family dressed in their finest clothes, the clothes they reserved for Sunday mass: black suits and dark ties, subdued dresses and plain skirts. They all looked sad. There was crying. Especially my Grandmother Lily. I could hear her wailing deep in my mind. The agonizing sound reserved for a mother at the loss of a child. It was frightening. But, like a burst of lightning that brightens the dark night sky for a second and is gone, so was the vision in my mind. I didn't know then what it meant.

Later that evening, as my parents were putting away the dishes from supper there was a knock at the door. Grandma Lily, who was visiting with us at the time, answered the door.

"Allo, oo dere?" she called in her best English.

"It's Officer Colin. Mrs. Mauro, please open the door."

A policeman at the door! A great deal of panic erupted in the kitchen. My mother began to ring her hands on the dishtowel she was using to dry the dishes. My father ran his hands through his hair as though trying to pull thoughts from his temples. And poor Grandma stood by the door not knowing what to do.

Fortunately, Officer Pete Colin was a friend of the family. He was the beat cop from 105th St. to 110th St. so it was not unusual to see him walking patrol in the neighborhood. Since my dad worked in the same neighborhood that Officer Colin walked every day, they got to know each other. So it was a little bit more comforting to let him in rather than some unknown policeman.

Why is there a policeman at the door?" my father said to no one in particular. "Open the door and let's see what's going on." My grandmother opened the door and in walked Officer Colin in that stiff gait reserved for policemen.

As soon as my grandmother opened the door, you could tell that Officer Colin was there on official business. Officer Colin was a broad figure standing at least a head taller than my father. Even though he was a friend, that night, in his crisp blue uniform, he was quite frightening. No pleasantries were exchanged; he got right to the point.

"I'm sorry to inform you that your son, Sonny, was found dead in the alley behind the old tavern on 108th Street about two hours ago."

The family was in shock. Uncle Sonny was my father's youngest brother and the baby in the family. He never seemed to look for trouble, but trouble always found him anyway. Grandma began to cry hysterically, as

10

all Italian grandmothers are wont to do. My mother quickly put her hands to her mouth stifling a cry. She gently put her arm around my grandmother and led her sobbing into the bedroom. My father and Officer Colin stayed in the kitchen to talk.

"What happened?" my father questioned, as fear and concern were evident in his dark brown eyes.

"We're not really sure. Someone reported a body in the alley. Officers were sent to investigate and they found Sonny shot in the back of the head, execution style," reported Officer Colin rather matter-of- factly.

My father was noticeably taken aback. Officer Colin offered to take him to the morgue in order to claim the body and to prepare for the funeral. My father went with the officer while my mother tried her best to console my sobbing grandmother.

No one noticed me sitting at my place at the kitchen table quietly observing the entire ordeal. I thought about whether this was what I had seen earlier in the day when Uncle Sonny rubbed my head. No, this couldn't be what I saw earlier. My childish mind reasoned that the events were unrelated; that is, until the next evening.

Early the next evening all of my family was gathered in the parlor, dressed in their Sunday best, mourning the passing of Phillipo Mauro. Everyone was there talking quietly, trying to understand what happened. In the middle of it all was my Grandma Lily wailing, crying as only a mother can do when she has lost her youngest baby. I could deny it no longer; my vision was complete.

Chapter 2

Living on the fifth floor in a rundown tenement house in a walk-up apartment was not easy. Whenever you left the building, you had to have a plan. It wasn't easy to come and go as you pleased. Living on the fifth floor, you had to walk down five flights of stairs just to get to the main entrance. When you returned from wherever you had been, it was another five flights of stairs back up. Every time you left and came home, you had to walk up 200 steps! So before you left the apartment to do anything, you had to make sure you had a good plan because you did not want to walk up and down those steps all day.

When you did finally make it to the fifth floor hallway you were greeted by dull gray walls, chipped linoleum floor, and bare incandescent bulbs, most of which didn't work. The janitor was rarely seen, so the burnt bulbs were often left unchanged for weeks at a time. The halls were dark and, to a five-year-old, scary and filled with monsters. I rarely, if ever, went out into the hall by myself. Frankly, I was terrified. I knew even Dog couldn't protect me.

Each floor of the tenement building consisted of fifteen apartments. Some were one-bedroom; most had two bedrooms and one apartment on each floor had the extreme luxury of three bedrooms. We enjoyed a cramped two-bedroom apartment affording me the luxury of my own space. Although only a space of seven feet by nine, it was still my space. Our apartment number was 513 and was at the far end of the hall.

There were actually some advantages to living on the fifth floor of a five-story tenement building. The most obvious advantage was that no one lived above you. You didn't have someone stomping on your ceiling all day and all night making noise. You only had to worry about the people pounding on the walls on either side, or yelling and threatening in the hallways as fights between drunken residents continued deep into the night. Unfortunately, a tenement building in old Harlem did not attract the high end of American society.

Most of the residents in our building were Italian immigrants who came from the old country to escape poverty, and sometimes the law. But since most of us were Italian, there was a kind of a kinship among our fellow tenement dwellers. You could almost say we protected one another. If you did not live in our building, you were an outsider. If you were not Italian, you were viewed with suspicion. We were kind of a large, somewhat amorphous, family trying to make a living, trying to get ahead the best we could to provide for our families and enjoy life in America.

Unfortunately for us, Italy was not the only country sending their tired and their poor and huddled masses yearning to breathe free. Other countries were sending the wretched refuse of their teeming shores, their homeless and criminals to the golden door that was America. Yes, there were immigrants from Ireland, Germany, China and, most hated of all, the Jews. These teeming masses escaped their countries in ships by the millions, crossing the great Atlantic Ocean in wretched conditions. Many did not survive the journey, succumbing to seasickness, pneumonia, diarrhea, and other vile diseases. Those that survived the journey arrived with a few dollars in their pocket and the clothes on their backs, their fair share of lice and fleas, and an empty belly. Yes, New York was a dumping ground and, as such, was a dangerous place to live.

Things changed rapidly for the Mauro family after the death of my uncle Sonny. Officer Colin assured my father that they would find out who killed his younger brother, but, of course, they never did. There were murders, robberies, rapes and other hideous crimes to deal with in the streets of old New York. One more dead Italian just didn't matter that much to New York's finest. Uncle Sonny was murdered, we all knew, but no one was ever caught or punished and the grief exhibited by the Mauro family never truly went away. A little bit of my grandmother died that day. She was never the same again.

Chapter 3

As time went on, although hard to imagine, the difficult living conditions for the Italians were soon to get even worse. The reason: Irish were coming ashore.

The Irish considered themselves a better class of people than the lowly "guineas" or "meatballs" who were crawling around the streets of New York. This was going to be their town. They could sweep these meatballs in the gutter; take their jobs, move into their homes. The Irish thought they were a better class of thug and would soon be ruling the Harlem environs. Unfortunately, the Irish underestimated the Italian Mafia.

The somewhat safe streets in the Harlem section of the great city of New York became a war zone. The Italians and the Irish were slugging it out in the streets, the alleyways and every dark corner of the neighborhood possible. The bars and taverns became meeting places for each of the gangs to decide what they were going to do next. Fistfights, stabbings and shootings, gang beatings; every day something else. It just wasn't safe in the old neighborhood anymore. But what could we do?

Our family didn't have any money; my father was a common laborer. He was good with his hands. He could build anything, fix anything. Often, if we had a little extra money, he would replace the light bulbs at our end of the hallway to try to bring a little light into our home. He often had jobs that would last for five days and then, when the job was finished, he would be out of work for five days sometimes longer. There was never an assured supply of money. It was virtually impossible to save any money as everything we had went to our day-to-day living expenses.

The year after Uncle Sonny died, Grandma Lily came to live with us. She couldn't live alone anymore; she was frightened and still in mourning. When she came to live with us, I had to share my monk's cell of the room with her. There was no place else for her to go. So now, there we were: the four of us living in an apartment on the fifth floor of a tenement house in a dangerous neighborhood with no apparent avenue of escape. Until one day a messenger came.

It seems that although Grandma Lily lived in America, she had a husband who still lived in Italy. His name was Pietro Mauro and he lived in the mountainside village of Piazza Armerina near the city of Enna on the island of Sicily at the foot of Mount Etna. And, apparently, he was a wealthy man.

I found out in later years that Grandma Lily was what kids these days would call a "player." She was a beautiful young woman who enjoyed the company of men – more importantly – the company of rich men. She was probably considered quite "loose" in her day and called worse behind her back. Yes, Grandma Lily definitely enjoyed the company of men, many men.

When she was a very young woman of nineteen and still living in Sicily, she married her first husband. Well, married is not exactly what happened. It was more like an agreement. You see, her first so-called husband was actually a prince in the ruling Sicilian family at the time. Since she was a peasant and he was destined to become a leader in Sicilian society, they could not be seen together, but they certainly could sleep together. From this first clandestine union came Conrad, the oldest son of the Mauro clan.

Unfortunately, the prince could not possibly claim this child as his own, so a large sum of money was paid to the young Lily to keep quiet. She also had to agree to never see the Prince again. So dear sweet young Lily left the prince behind to meet her next lover, and so on, and so on.

Six children and four "husbands" later, the now older and wiser Lily met her last husband, Pietro Mauro. Pietro was actually Lily's second cousin, and they shared the same last name. Since all of Lily's bastard children bore her last name, with her legitimate marriage to Pietro, all of the children had the appearance of legitimacy.

As was often the case in Sicily and other parts of the old country, not all of the children lived to become adults. The Mauro family was no exception. By the time her youngest son was born, there were only four surviving children: my father Dante, his oldest brother Conrad, his middle sister Emanuela and, of course, the baby Phillipo.

Once again, it was a knock on the door around supper time that brought the news to the Mauro family. This time, however, the news was much more pleasant. It seems that Grandpa Pietro had died back in the old country leaving Grandma Lily with what amounted to a small fortune. However, in order for her to claim her inheritance, she would have to go back to Italy, prove who she was, and claim her newfound wealth. And that's exactly what she did.

It took over two months for Grandma to make the round trip journey to Sicily to claim her inheritance. Grandma Lily left New York Harbor aboard a Cunard Lines passenger ship bound for Naples. Strangely enough, it was the same ship that had brought her to America the first time. From the port at Naples, she took the ferry to Sicily and arrived in the port city of Messina where she then traveled overland to Piazza Armerina.

As luck would have it, when she stood before the magistrate to prove her identity, the magistrate was one of her Biblical husbands. He remembered her fondly and immediately awarded her the full inheritance. In the eyes of many, Grandma was now "rich." Having been awarded her handsome reward, she decided to stay a little longer and visit with the rest of her family.

When Grandma finally returned from her transatlantic crossing, we met her at the port of New York at the same dock where the Mauro family had first arrived in New York so many years ago. My mother and father, my aunts and uncles, and I were all there to greet Grandma as she stepped off the ship and was enveloped by her family's loving arms. Things were going to be different now, much different.

Chapter 4

In the two months that passed since Grandma left for Italy to collect her inheritance, the old neighborhood continued to change, and not for the better. Before she left, there was significant, sporadic fighting between the "Goombas" and the "Micks", but now the trouble was more concentrated and constant. What was once an uneasy coexistence between the Italians and the Irish degenerated into more violence, as jobs became scarce and it was harder to put food on the table.

The Irish thugs seemed most intent on taking over the neighborhood and displacing us Italians. What started out as threats progressed to beatings and then moved on to killings. Violence had become an everyday affair. The Italians felt they were protecting their turf; the Irish felt it was their turf to take. It wasn't safe for either side.

Since my father was a day laborer, unless he was hired for a period of time, he would have to leave the apartment on 107th Street and walk to 115th St. every day and stand on the corner with the rest of the day laborers hoping to be chosen for that day's work. My father was not a very big man standing only 5' 2", but he was very strong and a hard worker.

He was very good with his hands, and the people who would hire the day laborers knew how good a worker he was soon enough. He went from being chosen last to chosen first when any jobs were available. My father was often chosen to do the finishing work because of his skills and craftsmanship. The Irish saw him as taking bread from their tables and made him a target.

The New York Public Library was building a new branch of the library system at the corner of 115th St. and 7th Avenue, an easy walk from the apartment. The library construction project was funded by a gift from the Andrew Carnegie Foundation. The building would soon become a three-story edifice with a distinctive façade and enduring elegance that enabled the building to be designated as a New York City landmark in the future. The completed three-story building was described as having "an uncommonly rugged and handsome elegance designed by McKim, Mead and White in the rustic Italian palazzo style." The construction project would not be completed for several years, so this was an excellent place for the day workers to congregate in order to be chosen for that day's work.

And so, it was to this site that my father would travel when he left the apartment around sun-up with his toolbox in one hand, his lunch bag in the other, and a spirit of hope that he would be chosen to work another day. Unfortunately, life can sometimes be a double- edged sword; while one edge brings luck, the other edge brings grief.

My father and I had a little ritual that we came to practice every day. I would wake up in the morning when he did and join him for breakfast. We would sit at our little metal kitchen table and I would have my bowl of cereal. I often chose a bowl of Cream of Farina, served warm with a little milk. Sometimes my father would add some sugar to sweeten the taste. He would lean over and say "Don't tell mama." and wink conspiratorially. He would enjoy his cup of morning espresso and a fresh- baked chocolate biscotti made with fresh almond. The sweet smell of which lingered long after we were finished. On his way out the door, he would tousle my hair, give me a hug, and tell me that we would play catch in the hallway when he came home after work.

My father would come home from work most days just before supper time. And there I would be in the hallway, sitting in front of our open door, waiting for him with my little pink ball that we bought for ten cents at the pharmacy down the street. No matter how tired he was or how difficult the day he had, before he would come into the house and greet my mother with a kiss and a soft, "Buona sera, mi'amore," we would play catch in the hallway for at least fifteen minutes. These were the most glorious fifteen minutes of my day because I had my father all to myself. He would throw the ball, I would miss it, and it would go rolling down the hallway. We both would be laughing while I chased the ball and tried to throw it back to him. Sometimes my throw was so bad that the ball would go under the banister and start heading down the steps. My father would make a big show of running down the steps to get the ball. He would come back up huffing and puffing causing me to laugh so hard that I knew it was time to end the game. He would then pick me up on his shoulders, duck my head safely under the door, give my mother a big hug and kiss, put me down, and go to our tiny bathroom to wash up for dinner.

One morning, after we'd sat down to our ritual breakfast, dad got up to leave and I felt something was wrong. He kissed my mother goodbye and went to tousle my hair as always, but I looked him right in the eye and said, "Papa don't go, please don't go today."

He just looked at me with a strange expression, and then smiled and said, "Roberto, you know I must go to work today. I need to bring the money home so that I can buy you a new ball, and we can play in the hallway. Don't worry. Everything is fine. Be ready in the hallway today and maybe we will have a new ball to play with."

I just knew everything would not be "fine", but without the words to beg him to stay, he started the eight block walk to work.

Chapter 5

Dante

I loved my son Roberto more than anything in my life. He was everything to me, my firstborn son who would carry on my name; he was the future of our family and the reason I worked so hard to make for him a new life, a good life. But sometimes I would look at his large brown eyes and not see a little boy but the soul of someone much older, much wiser. It was strange, very strange. As I walked to work that morning, I thought about him telling me to stay home. I could see in his eyes he was worried, but he was only a little boy of five. What could he possibly know?

What I didn't know was that day was the day the Irish thugs decided that none of those "damn Goombas" were going to get a job at the library construction site. As I was walking along to 115th St., I noticed a crowd on the corner that seemed larger than normal. Usually, there are ten or fifteen of my fellow laborers with their toolboxes in hand waiting for the bosses to make their choices for the day, but I could see a much larger crowd. As I got closer, I knew something was wrong because at our usual corner were twenty five or thirty Irish thugs with baseball bats, clubs, and chains.

Across the street from the construction site was the Italian work crew. Some of them were from my building, men I worked with. They were gesticulating wildly and throwing verbal taunts back and forth between themselves and the Irish mob. It seemed none of my compatriots individually wanted to face the Irish gang. They knew there was strength in numbers but, without a leader to organize them, they didn't know how to proceed. I knew something needed to be done, so I headed straight across the street to try and help decide what we were going to do about this intrusion on our turf. Now, I am not the kind of a man who enjoys a fight, but I knew then that if we did not stand up for our rights here and now, we would have no rights tomorrow. If something were going to happen, it was going to happen today.

"Who the fuck do these Irish bastards think they are, trying to keep us from getting a job?" my neighbor Mario shouted to me as I came closer. "We were here first and, besides, there is plenty of work for everybody. There is a no reason to fight," said Mario to one of the many workers gesticulating wildly with his hands. "There's just no Goddamn reason for this."

"Mario's right. We can't let them take away our work. We've been working on this project for more than a year. They just can't come in and take away our jobs. If we don't stand up to them now, we'll have nothing," argued Salvatore, another neighbor from the floor below me. .

Back and forth, back and forth with the comments. As the words became louder, the men's anger rose. They began to exhibit a mob mentality. Whatever one of them was going to do, all of them were going to do. They were past the point of reason. I knew then that there was no preventing this mess.

The Irish across the street could hear the shouts from the Italian mob, and they were itching for a fight. Pretty soon the Irish were starting to shout back, "Yeah, you fucking Goombas, what are you gonna do about it?"

"Come on over. You want a job? I'll give you a job. I'll give you a job stitching your fucking skull back together."

At this, I put my toolbox on the ground next to me on the right and my lunch bag on the left. Sighing a slow, steady breath, I led my fellow Italians across the street to take back what was rightfully ours.

Chapter 6

Robbie

That evening, as it got close to suppertime, I was in the hallway waiting for my father to come home. I was very excited about getting a new ball when my father came home but something was bothering me.
Somewhere in the back of my head, there was something niggling at me. I could see something in my mind's eye, but it wasn't clear; it was foggy, and it wasn't good. I could see my father holding his hand and what looked like a bandana on his head. I had no idea what it meant so I waited and waited in the hall, but my father still hadn't come home. My mother called to me in the hallway, "Supper's almost ready, you two."

"Mama, Papa's not home. I've been waiting for him in the hallway, but he's not home."

At this, my mother came out into the hallway and saw me there by myself. She knew it was very unusual that my father had not come home by suppertime, and she became a little concerned. She decided to take a walk down to the construction site to see if my father was working late and earning some extra money, something we seriously needed.

So, she asked Grandma Lily if she could watch the food on the stove and keep an eye on me while she went to investigate

Chapter 7

Vincenza

It was most unusual that on a Friday night the men would be working overtime at the construction site. After a long week of hard work, the men needed to rest. No one wanted to work late on a Friday night unless it was absolutely necessary. So, since it was a nice evening and supper was almost ready, I decided to walk over to see if my husband was working late.

It was a short walk from the apartment to the worksite. In less than ten minutes, I got to the site and was surprised at what I saw. Instead of seeing men working or leaving to go home, all I saw were a half dozen uniformed policeman walking in and out of the construction site or standing on the corner. I thought this was most unusual and didn't know what to do, but then I saw Officer Colin.

Frantically I rattled off, "What happened? Where is everyone? Where's Dante? Please, please tell me what happened!"

"Slow down, Mrs. Mauro, slow down. There has been a fight. From what we can tell, a group of the Irish immigrants tried to prevent the Italian workers from coming to the construction site and the whole thing degenerated from there. We are still trying to sort things out." Officer Colin tried to calm me down and walk me away from the area.

"Where is my husband? Where's Dante, my husband, where is he?" I pleaded as the information began a process in my mind that there was a fight and a fight means someone got hurt. "Tell me, where is he, what happened. Tell me."

Looking a little exasperated, Officer Colin once again tried to calm me down and said to me, "Hold on a minute. I have a list here of the people we arrested or were sent to the hospital. Let me see if Dante is on either list."

Now I was really scared. Arrested! He can't be arrested. What will we do if he was arrested? But then I thought, if he wasn't arrested and he wasn't home, that means he must be in a hospital. That was no better. What if he was seriously injured or dead, what would we do? I was now beside myself with worry.

Officer Colin took the notebook out of his uniform pocket and looked down the list and told my mother, "It looks like he's okay. They took him to the hospital to get some stitches on his forehead and to look at his hand, but he seems okay. I will walk with you over to the hospital if you would like, Mrs. Mauro."

"Oh thank you, thank you. I don't know what to do," I replied without any wasted breath between my words. "Thank you."

So together we began to walk to Misericordia hospital, the same place where my son was born. We never actually made it to the hospital however; as we crossed 96th St. on the walk over to 86th St., I spied my husband walking slowly towards us. I did not recognize him right away because the man I saw was a little bent over and had some bandages wrapped on his head and his arm was in a sling. But, as soon as I noticed it was him, I let out a scream and ran the other block and a half to greet him.

"I'm fine, really. I'm fine. It was just a little beating. A few stitches. A sore hand. I need to sit down, have a hot meal, a big cup of espresso, a good night's sleep, and I'll be fine"

"O my God, look at you. Your hand, your head. You okay; are you okay?" I said crying and hugging him at the same time. "I was so worried. I didn't know what to do. I was so worried. Come, let's go home. Let me take care of you. Let's go home. Roberto will be so worried."

And so together hand in hand we slowly walked the rest of the way home. Soon we arrived home to find Robbie, still sitting in the hallway, watched over by his grandmother. When he saw his father he showed no surprise. If I had to guess his feelings (which I often did), I would assume it was regret on his little face. It was as if he knew something no one else could know and he was powerless to prevent it.

Chapter 8

Robbie

Sunday in our family was always a special time. My mother would wake me early and force me to put on my Sunday best, and together we all walked to church to give thanks for our bounty and our health. After church, my mother would buy me a pretzel from the corner push cart as a reward for going to church. When we returned home, she and Grandma Lily would prepare a huge Sunday dinner to be shared by everyone in the family.

This Sunday was even more special: Grandma Lily had come home from her journey to Sicily and my father, although still sore from his altercation on Friday, was alive and would recover. My uncle Conrad and my aunt Emanuela were also coming to visit. Yes, this Sunday was going to be very special; we had much to be thankful for.

When we returned home from church, my mother and Grandma Lily began to prepare our traditional Italian Sunday meal. Eating a well-prepared Italian meal is one of the great pleasures of being a part of an Italian family. Each region, and sometimes even within each city, there are specialties. The preparation of these special delicacies is considered an act of love, for Italians believe that food comes from the heart and not from the kitchen. So, being a weekly affirmation of love, the Sunday meal could last for several hours.

The traditional Sunday meal would consist of five selections. Even though she was fresh from her trip abroad, my grandmother could not resist making her gastronomical delights for her family. On this very special Sunday, my mother and grandmother outdid themselves. We made ourselves comfortable at our normal places around the table while my mother put the finishing touches on the plate of antipasti she was preparing in the kitchen. With great fanfare, my mother brought out a platter filled with choice delicacies of Italian cold cuts, prosciutto ham, and delectable cheeses surrounding the center of the plate, which was piled high with fresh calamari. My grandmother carried in a basket filled with fresh hot homemade breads and a bottle of Chianti. These were placed in the middle of the table to the sound of much lip smacking as we prepared to dig in.

After the antipasti came the first course of homemade pasta. Once again, my mother outdid herself by placing before us, not one choice, but two choices of fresh pasta. First, it was ravioli stuffed with ricotta cheese and spinach in a fine marinara sauce. Next to that was placed a bowl of homemade ziti covered in a homemade Bolognese sauce. You could feel full from the smells alone.

As the plates from the first course were cleared, my uncle Conrad asked my father how he was feeling.

My father replied, "I feel okay, a little beaten, a little weak," in a resigned voice. "The doctor tells me it could be several weeks for my hand to heal and that it may be difficult to continue my day job. I don't know what to do about the bills," he lamented.

Uncle Conrad was the oldest son of the family and, since his father passed away, he was viewed as our family's patriarch. Uncle Conrad had an agenda on his mind that he was not quite ready to share with the rest of us, but I could see that there was something yet to come. He was waiting for the right moment to share it with everyone. But, he was not prepared to ruin our Sunday meal with heavy discussions. He waited patiently for the right moment.

Our secondi was a mouthwatering presentation of chicken baked to perfection with bread crumbs and Parmesan cheese. The meat was so juicy and so tender that it literally fell off the bones. To this was added the side dish of a garden salad with fresh ripe tomatoes laced with fresh buffalo mozzarella cheese and, of course, homemade Italian dressing. Delicious.

After this came the traditional basket of nuts. This was accompanied by the challenge of who could get the nut out of the shell without breaking the nut inside. Uncle Conrad was the family champion. He never used a nutcracker but could crack open the largest walnut with his bare hands and remove the meat completely intact. Finally, presented for our enjoyment came the dolce, which consisted of fresh fruit and cheeses. We all enjoyed a cup of espresso while my father and his brother and Uncle Rosario, Emanuela's husband, enjoyed a digestivo of Limoncello kept freezing cold in the family ice box.

To show his appreciation for the fine meal that my mother served, my father would laugh as he loosened his belt and pushed back from the table, "It is good that Sunday only comes once a week for if we ate like this

26

every day I could not fit into my pants! My dear Vincenza, as always, it was a wonderful meal." Everyone agreed passing along the compliments to my mother and grandmother.

Soon, the dinner dishes were cleared from the table and we were all seated around the table idly chattering when my uncle Conrad finally made his move and said it was time for a family meeting. Now a family meeting is traditionally where the important members of the family gather to discuss important decisions or to solve a problem. My uncle had a very specific agenda when he called this meeting. So there we all sat, at the table, my two uncles, my two aunts, my mother and father and grandmother as the family meeting began. Once again, being a very quiet child, no one even noticed I was present.

Aunt Emanuela was married to Rosario Pinello, and they lived with Rosario's mother and father in a beautiful home in the Gravesend section of Brooklyn. They had a daughter three years older than I named Linda. Uncle Conrad and his wife Sandra lived in the Sheepshead Bay section of Brooklyn because Uncle Conrad worked on the waterfront, and this area was close to where he worked. They had two children Lillian and Annette.

My uncle Conrad began by telling my grandmother of the changes that have been happening in our neighborhood since she departed on her trip to Sicily.

"Mama, we are so glad that you have come home to us safely from your journey back home to Sicily. But, while you were gone, things have become very dangerous in the neighborhood, and I am afraid things will only get worse. Look at what happened to my brother. This time he was lucky, maybe next time not so lucky. The Irish mob wants to move in and take from us what little we have."

Now, when my Uncle Conrad spoke, people listened. He was the oldest male of the family, and he also stood six feet two inches! He cut an imposing figure, but he always spoke to his mother with respect and love in his heart, and she knew that he only wanted the best for his mother and that it was good to listen.

"I have heard the stories. I cried when I came home to see my poor baby beaten. What can we do? This is our home, we live here," lamented my grandmother.

"Emanuela and I have discussed some ideas and feel it is best for the family to live closer together. If we live closer together, we can protect each other and help each other when something bad happens like it did to Dante. We think you should move to Brooklyn to be close to us. There is a beautiful home not five houses away from where Emanuela and Rosario live that would be perfect for you and Dante and his family. That way we would all be close together as a family should be," proclaimed Uncle Conrad in an authoritative but pleasant voice. "Dante and Vincenza would be there to take care of you and you would be safe, and that is most important."

"But move. How can we move? Where would we go?"

"Mama," began Uncle Conrad, patiently explaining to his mother once again, "I will take you to Brooklyn this week – you and Dante and Vincenza, even little Roberto – we will all go. It will be an adventure. You will see. The house is only a short walk from your daughter's home and is on a very safe and quiet street. It will be like we were back in Sicily, all together."

"But how can we buy a house?" Grandma countered, "We have so little."

"Mama, when Papa died, he left you money. He left you money so you would be safe. He would want you to use the money to buy a home in a safe place, to be happy so that he knows that he protected you," Conrad explained, playing the "Papa card."

"Yes, he would want me to be safe," reflected Grandma. And so the decision was made: we would go on an adventure to Brooklyn.

Chapter 9

The next day was Monday, March fourth, a beautiful, nearly spring morning. The day dawned bright and sunny with a nearly cloudless, blue sky, a perfect day for an adventure. We all woke up quite early and placed before us at the kitchen table was a hearty breakfast of eggs, homemade toast and a bowl of Farina. My mother and father also enjoyed a cup of espresso and fresh homemade biscotti. Grandma was a little nervous about the day ahead so she didn't really eat that much. After breakfast we all washed up and put on our traveling clothes and departed the apartment for the train station.

The closest train station was located at the corner of 110th St. and Lexington Avenue. This was also known as the Lexington Avenue subway station. We took the short walk from our apartment at 107th St. and entered a dark hole in the ground also known as the subway system's underground entrance. We traveled down below the streets of New York to board the Lexington Avenue subway southbound toward our destination in Brooklyn.

The subway train station was a sight to behold for a five-year-old. Noise, smells, throngs of people all filled my sights and senses until they were nearly overloaded. First, we left the bright sunny streets of New York and went down into the dark bowels of the station where my father purchased our tokens, fifteen cents per passenger, which we then put into the turnstiles and entered into the station itself. The walls of the station, as well as the ceiling, were covered in white, square ceramic tiles while the floor was a dirty gray poured concrete. The overhead glow of the lights cast an eerie yellow aura against the bright white tiles, giving one the feeling that they were truly in a wondrous place. Below our feet and above our heads you could hear the sound of trains thundering over the tracks or screeching to a stop as metal wheels were breaking against hard metal rails, squealing a high-pitched scream as the train thundered into the station. Before each train rushed into the station you could feel the wind pushing in front of the train announcing the arrival of the next the electric horse. It was truly amazing.

We walked along seemingly endless corridors until we reached the platform for the southbound Lexington Avenue subway. My father held my hand to keep me from crossing the yellow safety line, preventing me from falling onto the subway tracks. After only a few moments of waiting, we heard the train coming and felt the rush of wind as the subway cars screamed into the station. The train came to a stop, the doors magically opened and people rushed both in and out of the subway car without making a sound. We were thrust forward as the crowed platform moved as one onto the train. In less than twenty seconds the doors closed and the train lurched forward.

We only stayed on the Lexington Avenue subway from 110th St. down to 59th St. where we left the train and had to walk across the station to the IND line, which was also known as the Culver line. Built and financed by Andrew Culver, the Culver Line ran from Park Row in Manhattan, across the Brooklyn Bridge, to Sands St, in Brooklyn. It continued onto 36th Street, then via the 5th Ave El to 36th Street. From 36th Street and 5th Ave, the line ran to 9th Ave, and then switched to surface tracks running along an alley to Gravesend Ave (McDonald Ave). From there it went along Gravesend Ave along a private right of way to Culver Depot at West 5th Street and Surf Ave where the line came to its terminus.

After a short wait at the IND platform, we boarded our second train, the F line, to complete our journey into Brooklyn. I loved everything about riding the train. First, it was noisy. Screeches and squeals from the wheels filled my ears as the train moved into tight right or hard left turns or came to stops to at the various stations as the brakes were applied to slow the train down. The banging of the cars against each other as the train pulled out or slowed down added to the cacophony of sound. The lights would also flicker on and off as the train would make turns, disconnecting the power for a few seconds. It was like my own private light show. Finally, there was the rhythmic clicking and clacking of the metal wheels against the metal rails as the train's wheels bumped over the track connections. The smell of hot bodies pressed close together in the closed cars added to the experience. But the best was yet to come.

As we moved into Brooklyn, a most amazing change took place. From the time we had entered the Lexington Avenue subway earlier that day, we had been traveling underground in the dark, twisting- and- turning subway tunnels. When we got into Brooklyn and we were approaching 59th St., the train suddenly burst from its underground tunnel onto an elevated section of railway thirty feet above the ground! It was absolutely amazing to see buildings and people flashing by as the train roared high above them. Looking down through the window, I saw sparks spilling from the wheels as they rode along the metal track high above. We soon exited the train at the Avenue U station. This time, instead of taking the stairs from underground up to street level, we climbed down through twisting girders to the streets below. The rest of our journey would be on foot.

The train let us off at the corner of Avenue U and W. 8th St. We had to walk east on Avenue U, 13 blocks to E. 5th St. To a young man who is used to seeing only tall tenement buildings, Brooklyn was certainly a sight to behold. Most of the buildings were no taller than five stories and many appeared to be well kept, unlike the dirty façades in Harlem.

Avenue U represented the shopping district and, as such, there were many large, bay shop windows filled with men's trousers women's dresses, pharmacies touting the latest pharmaceuticals, and, to my delight, every color and kind of candy store. The people walking the streets seemed friendly. Many would tip their hats, or wave hello as we walked by. The shop owners were sweeping their sidewalks and bidding us good morning. This was a far cry from the dangerous streets of Harlem.

When we arrived at the corner of Avenue U and E. 5th St., we turned right and proceeded south to my Aunt Emanuela's house. As we turned the corner, the commercial avenue morphed into a quiet residential street. Instead of multi-storied tenement buildings like those in Harlem, the street was lined, on both sides, with identically built duplex homes. The street was a wide avenue lined with beautiful Sycamore trees. It was quite the park- like setting, or at least it appeared so to a five year old used to the narrow treeless streets of old New York Harlem.

We arrived at my Aunt Emanuela's house in time for lunch. We were met at the door by my Uncle Conrad who led us into the kitchen where a sumptuous lunch of Italian cold cuts and fresh baked bread awaited our arrival.

After lunch, we all walked, led by Uncle Conrad, to the home that my uncle had wanted us to see. The two-story home at 2190 E. 5th St. was identical to all of the other houses in the neighborhood. It was a frame construction, two story, duplex house with a cement sidewalk out front and a shared driveway leading to a garage out back. From the street, there were three steps up to a small porch, framed by a wrought- iron gate. From the porch, there were another five steps to the front door. The inside consisted of an entranceway followed by several large rooms, leading into a kitchen and dining room and then a short hallway to two bedrooms and a bath. The second floor, a duplicate of the first-floor, could be used as a rental property, ensuring a small, additional income for the homeowner, if they chose to do so.

Grandma Lily was very pleased with what she saw: quiet neighborhood, close to her daughter and oldest son, and a home big enough for all of us to share with rental income to boot! She was sold, and soon so was the house. Using a little less than half of Grandma's inheritance, she paid for the house in cash, and soon the Mauro family owned a small piece of America. We moved in less than a month later. Two years later I would meet my first ghost.

Chapter 10

By late April, we had fully settled in to our new home. I was fortunate enough to have my own bedroom, no longer sharing one with my grandmother, who had her own room at the front of the house. Things couldn't be better. It is an Italian tradition to believe that, if things get too good, tragedy will strike. Unfortunately, this tradition is all too accurate.

In front of our home was a beautiful, mature sycamore tree also known as a London plane tree. The tree stood taller than our house and was marked with spotty bark with wide growing limbs. Large, green leaves provided shade but would also teach me a lesson in the near future.

All during that spring and summer I would play out front under the shade of that beautiful tree. I even watched a robin build her nest in one of the lower branches. Since I didn't have any friends, being the new kid in town, that tree was quickly becoming my best friend.

In late July, my mother told me that it was time for me to register for school in September. School! I was going to a new school. I remember being rather excited and a little terrified.

Of course, my parents were going to enroll me into a fine Catholic school, Our Lady of Grace, which was located on Avenue W and E. 2nd St. just a short walk from the house. My mother and I walked to the school and we met with Mother Superior.

Mother Superior was an older nun and was confined to a wheelchair. She was dressed, like all of the nuns at Our Lady of Grace, totally in black from head to toe. Covering most of her face was a black wimple with a white interlining across her forehead down her cheeks and under her chin. She looked like pumpkin, only in black! Soon we completed the registration program, and I was fully registered to become a new student in first grade that September.

The school was run completely by priests and nuns and was dedicated to a strong Catholic education. Once again I was surrounded by people dedicated to a religious order. The school also had its own church dedicated to the Virgin Mary. We were required to attend mass every morning before class and were expected to attend mass every Sunday followed by Sunday school. The church once again was going to play a very important role in my life.

As summers often do when you are young, that summer seemed to have passed very quickly. I did make some new friends before the end, however. Next door to me lived two brothers. One was my age, Mark, and one a year older, Roger. We would soon become lifelong friends. Next door to my Aunt Emanuela lived the girl who would become my first girlfriend: Yolanda, but everyone called her Yolie. The four of us attended Our Lady of Grace School and as such, we soon became inseparable.

September came and it was time to go to school. Yolie, Mark, and I were in first grade, while Roger was in second. Since he was a year older, he was going to teach us all the ins and outs of our new school. It was like having an older brother.

As late summer progressed into early fall, I noticed something strange happening to my Sycamore tree. The leaves were starting to fall. I didn't think about it as a problem because the wind would sometimes blow leaves off the tree, particularly during a rainstorm. Soon, however, more and more leaves were falling from the tree. One late autumn day I came home from school and, much to my shock, all of the leaves had fallen from the tree! Being a city boy, and not knowing much about trees, I thought my favorite tree had died. I ran into the house and called to my mother, "Mama, Mama, come quickly. There's something wrong with the tree!"

My mother came rushing out of the kitchen wiping her hands on the dish rag, "Roberto, what's wrong?"

"Our tree – it's dead. All the leaves have fallen. Come see. It's dead."

My mother looked at me for a moment, and then a smile came across her face. "Roberto honey, the tree is not dead. It is fall. It's the time of the year when all the trees lose their leaves so that they can rest for the winter. Then, in the spring, they come back to life and grow a new set of leaves."

"No Mama, it is dead I tell you. It is dead. There are no leaves. They are all on the ground. Come see, please come see."
"Roberto honey, believe me. The tree is fine. It only looks like it's dead. Sometimes a tree will look dead, but will not be dead. It is only resting. This is a form of energy. Sometimes it is necessary for a living thing to

rest. Unlike you, a tree does not sleep each night to renew its energy; instead, in the fall after the tree has bloomed and protected a new flock of nesting birds, it will drop its leaves and rest. The winter rest will restore its energy and soon, in the spring, the life energy will return and the tree will bloom and be alive once again. As long as there is energy, there is life. It is not time for the tree to die. You will see. It will be as strong as ever, come the spring."

And sure enough, at the end of a long winter the Sycamore tree grew a new set of leaves. So something that is once dead, if it's not it's time to be dead, can come back. Soon, I would learn that it's not only trees that can come back from the dead.

Chapter 11

A few years later, tragedy struck. Fortunately, it did not strike the Mauro family, but was close enough.

Yolie, her mother, father, and grandfather lived next door to Aunt Emanuela and Uncle Rosario. Mark, Roger, Yolie, and I were constantly together. One summer day, I was walking from my house to Yolie's house, to see if she could come out and play. I was about twelve years old at the time and was beginning to develop quite a crush on Yolie.

Her grandfather was working on a ladder, close to the second story of the house, painting the windows. I knocked on the front door, and Yolie answered.

"Hey, Yolie do you want to come outside. Maybe we can find something to do?"

"Sure, give me a minute I just got a new Spalding ball and we can play hit the stick."

"Great, I'll meet you outside, in front of my aunt's house. I'll find a stick." I turned around to walk down the steps and go find a stick.

Yolie and I were playing out front for about a half an hour, when we heard a strange sound. It sounded like wood scraping against the side of the house, followed by a muffled scream and a thud, as if something had fallen. We rushed around towards where we thought we heard the sound and stopped horrified at what we stumbled across.

As we entered the driveway between the two houses, we saw the ladder that Yolie's grandfather was using while painting the windows, laying on the cement driveway. There was paint all down the side of the house culminating in a large splash at foot of the ladder. Also, at the foot of the ladder, lay Yolie's grandfather in a pool of what looked like red paint. Unfortunately, it wasn't paint; it was blood.

We didn't know what to do. Yolie ran to her front door to get her father, while I ran to my Uncle Rosario's front door to get him. We all arrived back in the driveway at about the same time. My Uncle Rosario took one look at Yolie's grandfather and knew that something terrible had happened. He quickly gathered up Yolie and me and brought us to the front of the house so that we couldn't see what was happening to her grandfather.

A few minutes later, Yolie's father came to have a word with my uncle. We couldn't hear what they were saying, but based on the look on Yolie's father's face and my uncle shaking his head and looking at the sidewalk, we knew it couldn't be good news. Uncle Rosario came back to where we were sitting, sat down next to Yolie and told her the horrible news. Her grandfather had fallen from the ladder and was killed when his head hit the hard concrete driveway. There was nothing that could be done; it happened very quickly.

Yolie looked for a moment at my uncle with her large brown eyes, and quickly got up from where she was sitting, ran to her front door, and into the house. My uncle looked at me sitting there and said, "It was an accident, Robbie. He must've stretched too far on the ladder, lost his balance and fell. It was over very quickly; he did not suffer. Maybe you should go into the house while I help Yolie's father cleanup."

Instead of going into the house, I told him I would walk home. And so I did. Uncle Rosario waited with Yolie's father for the morgue wagon to come and take away the body.

A couple of hours later, I went back to Yolie's house to see how she was doing. I went up to the front door and rang the bell. Her mother came to the door; it was quite evident that she had been crying.

"Good afternoon Mrs. Grimaldi, I was wondering if I could speak with Yolie."

"I'm sorry, Roberto. Yolie's pretty upset like we all are. It was a terrible thing that happened. I'm sorry for you and for her, that you had to see that. I'm sure she will be okay. Perhaps, tomorrow – hmmm. Maybe you could come back then and talk with her." At which time, she bid me goodbye and closed the front door.

I decided to go back to my Uncle Rosario's house next door and see how he was doing. But, before I could get to the front door, I noticed something shining in the street. It looked like a marble. From a distance it was dirty, but as I got closer I noticed there were not one, but two of them.

As a bent down to pick up the marbles, I heard a familiar voice. "Roberto, don't touch those. I'm going to need those later."

I looked up to see who had spoken. To my shock and amazement, there stood Yolie's grandfather. He was dressed in a black suit, white shirt and black tie. I know it couldn't be him because he was dead; I saw him die. But nonetheless, there he was, standing not three feet in front of me, looking down at me with a smile.

I looked down again and had a closer look at the marbles, and saw they were not marbles and all. They were his eyes! It seemed that the force of the fall, when his head hit the cement driveway, must've knocked his eyes right out of his head. When my uncle took up the garden hose to wash the blood down to the street, his eyes must've rolled down into the street with the blood. I didn't know what to do so I looked up and he was gone. I took off for the house as fast as I could.

A few minutes later, after calming down and trying to figure out what I just saw, I went to the front window overlooking the street. There I saw another man dressed in a gray suit with gloves on his hands bending down in the street picking up "the marbles." I called my uncle right away, and told him there was a man in front of the house. He came to the window and looked out and told me, "That's just Mr. Dimitri. He is the funeral director. He is probably coming to the house to talk to Yolie's family about the arrangements for the funeral.

I never told anyone what happened. But I knew that it was Yolie's grandfather who was standing there and told me not to touch "the marbles" in the street. So, much like my Sycamore tree, what was once dead, might, even for a brief moment, come back to life if it was not their time to be dead.

Chapter 12

The next few years were very good for the Mauro Family. Our tenant upstairs was an elderly spinster who paid her rent on time and never complained. In fact, we never saw her leave the house. This provided a steady income for my grandmother and allowed her to feel very secure in her new home.

My father got a great job working for a manufacturing company in New York City. Every morning, he would walk to the EL train station, the same one we took when we first came to Gravesend, and take the express train to the city. Every evening, he would return via the same route and be home in time for a fine family meal. He was very happy. We had a steady income and were soon able to buy some of the newest household appliances to make my mother's life easier and happier.

My mother was also very happy in her role as housewife and manager of our household affairs. She would clean the house, wash our clothes and prepare exquisite Italian meals, all the while smiling and doing her best to make a bright and happy home for all of us.

I was doing well in school. I had excelled in my classes in grammar school and was preparing to enter high school next year. Yes, things were going well for our family but, as always, things changed, or almost changed.

Chapter 13

Every summer, my father and I enjoyed a little tradition. Once a month, we would get up early, and take a walk along Ocean Parkway to spend the day at Coney Island Amusement Park.

Coney Island was the local hot spot for New Yorkers who wanted to leave the city and enjoy a day or a week at the beach and the amusement park. The area was filled with some of the finest hotels including the famous Coney Island House and the competing Manhattan Beach Hotel, among many others. It was also here, at Coney Island, that in 1871 Charles Feltman invented the hot dog and sold them to hungry visitors from his hot food wagon. He soon became a multi-millionaire from selling the tasty treats.

Coney Island was noted for its pure sand beach and fresh salt water swimming. The water in Gravesend Bay was usually calm and could be quite warm in the summer. Unfortunately, sometimes the undertow could be dangerous, especially by the rocks at the northern end of the beach. Several people would drown every summer, mostly those who were showing off to the ladies, or had a little too much to drink before swimming by the rocks.

Despite these dangers, Manhattanites flocked to Coney Island beaches in the summer to get away from the oppressive heat of the city and the heavy traffic of the Long Island beaches. Although the beaches were a draw for many visitors, my father and I would spend the day at the amusement park located at the end of Coney Island Pier.

The amusement park was known as the Steeplechase Funny Park and featured twenty-five rides of various degrees of excitement. For only a small fee, one could buy an entrance ticket to the park and be given a large white cardboard button with a blue line drawing of a clown's face. Around the perimeter of the ticket were twelve small blue circles. As you went on a ride, one of the twelve holes was punched out by the carnie operator. When all the blue circles were punched, you were done for the day. It was a great way to spend an afternoon with my father.

My father and I would normally arrive in time for lunch, a fresh hot dog, of course loaded with mustard and sauerkraut on a soggy white bun, washed down with a bottle of ice cold Coca Cola. My father was not much for the rides, but he would walk with me from ride to ride while smoking a fine cigar, a guilty pleasure frowned upon by my mother.

So it was, once a month, my father and I would spend the day together at the park; me on the rides, him smoking a cigar, and each of us enjoying the other's company. Sometimes my father would sneak off, while I was standing on line for the next ride, and get himself a cold beer sold at various beverage stands throughout the park. He was only out of sight for a minute or two and quickly returned to make sure I was safe.

It was on just one of these occasions, while my father was getting his beer that something strange occurred.

I was on the line for my favorite ride, the Flying Swings. On this ride, you would get into a chair suspended from four chains attached to a rotating overhang. As the overhang rotated, it would also lift higher, bringing the swinging chairs high off the ground and out to the side. It was like the feeling of flying round and round. People would scream with feigned fright as we flew faster and faster, higher and higher for a full five minutes. You could see most of the park from this vantage point and even could see the ocean at the end of the pier. Since it was my favorite ride, I always saved it for last. When the ride was done, my father and I would walk home and excitedly tell my mother all about our adventures.

As usual, the line for the ride was quite long and my father had more than enough time to take a short walk to the beverage cart and get his cold beer, I waited patiently in line until I heard a familiar voice call my name.

"Roberto, Roberto over here," I could hear someone calling.

I looked around. I could see my father in line at the beverage cart talking with someone else so I knew it wasn't him calling, yet the voice was very familiar.

"Over here, Roberto," came the voice again.

This time, I did see who was calling. It was my Uncle Sonny, the uncle that was killed so many years ago. He was standing there waving at me and calling my name.

"Yes, Roberto, it's me. I am sorry to frighten you, but you must not go on the ride. It is not your time," said my uncle.

"Not my time." What did that mean? I know it is not my time; there were at least two more turns before I would get to the head of the line. What was he talking about and why was he here? I couldn't understand, but then it came to me. Just like Yolie's grandfather, my uncle was here to tell me something.

"It's not your time, Roberto. Leave the line. Find your father and go home. It is not your time."

I still didn't understand, but I ducked out from the line and walked to the beverage cart where my father was just getting his beer and I told him "I'm real tired, can we go home now?"

"Are you all right, Roberto? You look like you have seen a ghost!" my father chided.

"Just tired and a little hot."

"Okay then, let me buy you an ice cream cone to cool you off. I will finish my beer and then we will go home."

The ice cream cone, vanilla covered with chocolate, went a long way in soothing my sorrow for not going on my favorite ride. It also gave me a moment to think of why my Uncle Sonny was there. I found out why the next morning.

On Sundays, my father had his own tradition: he would sit in the parlor with a cup of espresso and a fresh biscotti, chocolate and almond, of course, and read the paper. Sometimes, I would sit with him and read the funny papers. That Sunday was no different, but the news was.

The headline read "Tragedy at Coney Island." The paper told the story like this:

"Yesterday, tragedy struck the joyful visitors to Coney Island's Steeplechase Funny Park. At 4:20 PM the Flying Swings went from joy ride to death trap as riders went crashing into the ground when a gear in the mechanism locked, throwing the riders to and fro like rag dolls. Seven

42

people lost their lives and many were injured as people flew through the air hitting many others on the ground. No one knows the cause of the accident but the local police are investigating the incident."

The memory of what I thought my uncle said came rushing back to me: "It's not your time." I was wondering, if I had gone on that ride, would I have been killed or injured? I know, either way, my uncle saved my life. I wish I could thank him somehow.

Chapter 14

After eight years of strict religious education, I was finally ready to leave religion behind and move on to the concept of non-secular education. Next fall Mark, Yolie, and I were to join Roger in attending Sheepshead Bay High School. SHBHS was located on Avenue X in the Sheepshead Bay section of Brooklyn. Sheepshead Bay was the border neighborhood to Gravesend and only a two-mile walk from home to school. The Four Musketeers, as we were trying hard to be called, were planning to march into school in the fall as the new leadership. It was not to be.

As we are all too well aware, the economy moves in cycles. We were entering a time of the next down cycle and many fathers working in New York were losing their jobs. Unfortunately, the first casualty in our little group was Yolie. Her father lost his job early that summer, right after our eighth grade graduation. She and her family moved away to live with her maternal grandmother the day after my birthday, June 19th. It was one of the saddest days of my young life as I was smitten with Yolie, my first puppy love. We never saw her again. Saddened as we all were, we passed that summer in kind of a fog and returned to our first year with the big boys as the Three Musketeers. We would soon learn that leaving religion behind and entering the "dark side" would have its own consequences.

Chapter 15

Despite how different it was, high school was actually a great time. We would never admit it at the time, but the quality of the education we received from Our Lady of Grace was an excellent preparation for high school. Many of our classmates went from OLOG to SHBHS. There we were pooled with many graduates from the local New York City public schools. It is said that "the cream always rises to the top" and we did. The OLOG students were far better prepared and soon became the leaders of each grade level. With leadership, however, comes responsibility. Soon Mark and I learned that our teachers expected much more from the OLOG graduates than from the public school kids and we had no choice but to buckle down and work harder.

Unfortunately, this was not the general attitude of the PS students and, from time to time, we were bullied or pushed around, especially after a test when Mark and I would get an A and the big city boys didn't. But we learned to live and let live; the threats were mostly verbal and really childish, not like today where schools are plagued with gang violence or even guns. Gangs and guns were not a threat. So Mark and I, with help from Roger, breezed through academia in our first year of high school. That summer, however, things began to change.

Chapter 16

That summer, Roger and Mark's maternal grandmother died. She lived to the very ripe old age of ninety-two. She had a long and wonderful life and died quietly in her sleep. The boys' mother was an only child and, as such, she was tasked with the responsibility of going through her mother's belongings and settling the estate.

Since Grandma lived only a few blocks away, Roger, Mark, and I were enlisted to help go through the apartment and remove everything. Our job was to provide the manpower to either bring things back to their house or dispose of the unwanted junk in the large dumpster in the back of the apartment building. We had no idea what we were in for. How much junk could an old woman of ninety-two have? As it turned out, a lot!

It seems that Grandma was sort of a hoarder. Not one who kept everything, mind you. She kept only the oddest of things. We soon learned that Grandma was kind of a gypsy. Not in the sense that was deemed negative at the time, but more in the sense of someone who practiced the occult.

She had a rather smallish apartment by today's standards. There was a small entrance hall stacked to the ceiling with paper magazines and old books. The hallway had that "old lady" smell. You know the one, a combination of musk, dust and antiseptic. It hit you as soon as you entered and stayed with you all the way home. From the entrance hall, there next came a small living room in which she had statues, glass balls, strange dead animals, and about a thousand glass jars of various shapes and sizes filled with various colored liquids, some with something strange and mysterious floating in them. Roger's mother seemed to know what to expect; we did not.

We later learned that Grandma was sort of a spirit person back in the old country. Before she moved to America from Naples, she developed a reputation for healing the sick using strange potions and elixirs. She communed with the dead through glass balls; later, we found out these were crystal balls. She told fortunes and generally was considered "gifted" in a way that allowed her to earn a living as a spirit adviser and quack doctor. When she came to America, she brought most of her important items with her and must have continued to collect more and more unusual items, filling the apartment with the strange and wonderful.

When we all arrived at the door and entered the room, Mrs. Donato told us, "Boys, this is going to take some time so let's dig in, but be careful; I don't want to break anything and spill something all over the place."

"Okay," we said in unison, "Where do we start?"

"Let's start here in the living room," she directed. "We can put all the jars and bottles into boxes and haul them down to the trash bin. Be careful, I do not want something disgusting spilled on any of us." Neither did we.

So we got to work picking up bottles with different fluids and floating objects. There were deep reds and blues and a few green and clear liquids. Some had what looked like flowers floating in the liquid. Some had small animal parts.

"Yuck," exclaimed Mark horrified. "I think this is a jar of eyeballs, disgusting"

Roger and I ran over to inspect the jar and sure enough the jar was filled with eyeballs of every size and hue.

"Hey, Mom, can we have these?" Roger called out to his mother.

"NO!" Came the immediate reply from across the room. "All of the jars go into the trash directly and nothing is to remain. Understood?"

"Yes, Mom. Understood." Roger muttered, obviously disappointed.

So that first day we collected bottles, looked into each one and reluctantly put them in a box and hauled them down four flights of stairs to the alley dumpster in the back. Throwing out a jar of eyeballs was hard for any young man, but not obeying was even worse (the Old Catholic guilt trip). So, jar after jar of wonders soon found their way into the trash.

Later that day, after a lunch of grilled cheese and milk, we were still hard at work at the task of cleaning the living room. The glass jars were all in the dumpster. Now we concentrated on the rest of an odd assortment of various items.

First, came the glass balls. Some were clear and some were colored red and blue and yellow. These Mrs. Donato wanted to keep as a memory of her mother, so these we carefully packed away wrapped in old newspapers we found in the hall and put them carefully into boxes for later transportation back to the house on Avenue U.

So for the rest of that Friday we packed, hauled, boxed, and dumped as instructed for all of the items in the living room. Soon the only thing left was a couch, two lamps, a small table and a chair or two.

"Enough for today, boys; tomorrow we can finish the rest."

So we locked the apartment door, hauled the last of the trash to the alley and headed home, a little worse for wear. Mrs. Donato saw how tired we were and how hard we worked and came up with a great idea.

"I know we have not had dinner yet but on the way home we pass the corner soda shop. How about I treat all of us to a nice lemon ice for all the hard work?"

"Great idea," came the reply as we quickened our pace and headed right over to the soda shop.

"Dessert before dinner," chided Mark as we all laughed and ran to the front door to be the first in line.

The next morning, we all got together early and headed out once again to finish the job of emptying the apartment.

While Mrs. Donato was busy going through drawers and cabinets looking for anything important or worth keeping, Mark, Roger and I were assigned the task of clearing out the closets. In the hall, we found mostly "old lady clothes," the kind of long smelly coats that all grandmothers seemed to have. Black lambskin or heavy cloth predominated the collection in the closet. These were headed for the resale shop where we assumed they would be bought by some other "old lady."

The hall closet finished, we were next directed to the bedroom closet where we would come across an item that would change our lives forever. Now anyone who has been fortunate to be in an Italian family knows that "old Italians" smell funny. I do not know what it is but it seems all grandmothers share an old person odor. It is perhaps a mixture of mothballs, perfume, body odor, and hair spray with an added touch of smelly soap. As soon as we entered the room, boom there is was; "Old lady smell."

Most of the drawers were already cleaned out and the contents either destined for the dumpster or to be taken home later that night. The bed had already been stripped and the sheets prepared for the resale shop. The only thing left was the closet, so we set right out to work. Since this was the last project of the day, the sooner we finished the sooner we headed home with the hope of another "dessert- before- dinner" treat of Italian ice.

So, with the thought of fresh sweets on our tongue, we tackled the closet with fervor. Out came the few dresses and nightgowns. These were quickly prepared for the resale shop. When the hanger bar was empty, we came across some boxes on the floor. We quickly pulled these out and rummaged through them. There were some strange figurines made of wood and stone. They looked like creatures with large heads and horns. Some were red and some were black. They all looked a little creepy so, of course, we wanted them. These we quickly put into our pockets so Mrs. Donato would not banish them to the trash bin in the alley.

Our job in the closet almost done, we looked around once more and made sure there was nothing left to do before we headed out for lemon ice. As we were getting ready to leave, we noticed that above the clothes bar was a small shelf.

I asked Roger, "Don't you think we should look on top of the shelf to make sure there is nothing left?"

"No, Grandma was real short and there is no way she could reach that shelf. Besides it's getting late and I am really hot and tired. Let's head home."

"Come on, one look and we are out of here. Pull over the chair and I'll check, and then we are gone." I should have listened to Roger and never looked on the shelf.

Roger pulled the chair over and I jumped up and looked into the dark recesses of the closet. There in the far back right hand corner was a box. "Hey, guys, look at this. I told you we needed to check up here. There is another box".

"Bring it down and let's dump it in the trash and get out of here"

"Hold your horses. Help me get this out and let's see what it is before we toss it."

Carefully, I stepped off the chair. There in my hand was a box made of red wood. It was polished to a brilliant shine and you could see it was handmade and must hold something of value because in the front center of the box was a small lock. No one locks a box unless there is treasure to protect and this treasure was all ours.

"Look, guys," I said excitedly, "a locked box. There has got to be something in here."

"Well, I think we should tell mom what we found," Roger murmured a little hesitantly. "We have no idea what is in the box and it doesn't belong to us."

"Well, actually it does," I tried to explain logically. "We found it. It belonged to your grandmother and she passed away, so you can say you invented it."

"That's inherited it, you dope," Roger said, slapping the back of my head. "Anyway, whatever is in the box, unless we open it, we will never know, right? So let's take it home and open the box and then we can decide what to do. Agreed?"

"Agreed."

So we added the red wood box with the small lock to the bottom of the box of items heading home with us and prepared to leave. The plan was once we got home to bring the box to the basement, quietly remove the red wood box, and store it away from sight until we could find a way to open the box and see what was inside.

On the way home, we didn't want to stop for Italian ice for fear that the red wood box might somehow be discovered, so we passed up Mrs. Donato's offer and headed home with our treasure.

Chapter 17

The next morning was Sunday, and we were all expected to go to church. So early Sunday morning my father, mother, aunt, uncle and older cousin Linda and I all walked to church together. Well, somewhat together. Linda was older and more mature than me, so it would be an embarrassment to be seen walking with me so she had to walk ahead of the family, but not too far to appear unescorted. Linda and I had a mutual love/hate relationship. She loved to hate me and hated to love me. Alone we were the best of friends but, out in public, she didn't admit I existed. That was okay by me, as having to be around a self- centered, teenage female was no fun for a self- centered, teenage male, so we went our separate ways together.

That Sunday at Our Lady of Grace Church the sermon was all filled with talk of hellfire and brimstone. I never saw Father Murphy so worked up about anything in all the years I knew him. The gospel reading was taken from Matthew 28:34 . It was the story of when Jesus banished the devil from the possessed man and cast the spirits out into a herd of pigs.

"And when he was come to the other side into the country of the Gergesenes, there met him two possessed with devils, coming out of the tombs, exceedingly fierce, so that no man might pass by that way. And, behold, they cried out, saying, what have we to do with thee, Jesus, thou Son of God? Art thou come hither to torment us before our time? And there was a good way off from them a herd of many swine feeding. So the devils besought him, saying, if thou cast us out, suffer us to go away into the herd of swine. And he said unto them, Go. And when they were come out, they went into the herd of swine: and, behold, the whole herd of swine ran violently down a steep place into the sea, and perished in the waters."

Now when father came to the part about the evil spirits being cast into the herd of pigs, some of us good Catholic boys just could not help laughing. Unfortunately, Father did not find the story quite as funny as we did and that probably set him upon his discourse in the sermon how "we were all going to suffer the fires of hell if we did not forsake the devil and worship the one true God, the Father, through his son Jesus Christ." He really poured it on heavy that Sunday and somehow he knew exactly which boys in the pews laughed and which did not. As we all got up to leave, as was custom, Father left first and opened the doors to the outside. This was done so no one could leave until Father gave permission. Father would stand on the right side of the exit and would shake hands with the gentlemen and the boys; and tip his head to the wives and young ladies. But today he added a new action, to smack the back of the head of each and every one of the boys who laughed at the pig story. How he knew who laughed must have been by divine revelation because he was nearly 100% accurate in his head slapping!

With mass over, we headed home. Linda, of course, lit off once again ahead of the family and arrived home soon enough that she was already out of her Sunday best when the rest of us returned home to share the traditional Sunday repast.

Later that afternoon, I found an excuse to head over to the Donato house to meet with Mark and Roger so that we could finally get into that red wood box and discover our new found treasure.

Chapter 18

As soon as I arrived at the house next door to mine, the three of us headed down to the basement. The basement at the Donato house was a large unfinished area that had a few lights and a work room but no real furniture save a few old chairs that the family no longer used. It was not the most pleasant place, as the basement windows rarely let light in after early afternoon and most of the lights in the ceiling were burned out or of low wattage. It was kind of dank and a little dark, the perfect place to hide our treasure.

So down we went. We opened the box in which we had our treasure only to find that opening the red wood box would turn out to be a little more complicated than we first thought. Since we had no key and it was not a combination lock, we really did not know where to begin.

"Let's just break the lock off," the ever impatient Mark urged.

"No, dummy, what if the box is empty and we ruin the box completely? Or what if what is inside gets broken? There has to be a better way," informed Roger.

Well, we tried a few ideas. First, we simply pulled on the lock, just to see if it held at all. After all it was old and most likely not very strong. But no, it held fast.

Next, we used a screw driver to try to pry the lock off, but once again, nothing, except a few new scratches on the pristine red wood box.

Next we tried to slip a knife behind the clasp holding the lock to see if the screws would let loose and fall apart allowing us to open the box. Again, nothing close to success.

"Come on. Think, you guys," mumbled a frustrated Roger. "This can't be that tough."

So we sat there staring at the lock, when suddenly I noticed something really strange.

"Hey, guys, look at this." As they came closer, I pointed out to Mark and Roger, "There is no key hole for the lock! How the hell can anyone open a lock with no keyhole and no combination? It makes no sense."

"Move aside, of course there is a keyhole," exclaimed Roger as he pushed me to one side.

"Okay, genius; show me."

Well, look as hard as he could, Roger couldn't find a key hole either. Now we were stumped. Could whatever was inside have been purposely locked in such a way that no one could get inside the red wood box? If so, then there must be something extraordinary inside and now, more than ever, we had to break in. Little did we know how extraordinary the contents of a simple red wood box would be.

Chapter 19

The next afternoon after our chores, there we were back in the basement still stumped with the riddle of the locked box.

"Okay, look, maybe we are going about this the wrong way. Maybe the lock is there to throw us off. Maybe there is a panel or something that slides open the box open like one of those puzzle boxes," proposed Roger.

"Not a bad idea. Turn over the box and let's look at the back side and see if there is a panel or something," I suggested.

At first glance, the back of the box looked just like the front and appeared to be made of a single sheet of highly polished red wood. But, upon very close inspection, I began to see a possible thin fault line in the otherwise single sheet of wood.

"Guys, look here, does that look like a split or a crack?"

Roger took the box and inspected it closely. "I think you're right," he said excitedly. "Maybe it slides or pushes in or something and the box comes apart."

Sure enough, after fifteen minutes of pushing, prodding, and sliding, we suddenly discovered the secret to open the box. You needed to press your finger in the dead center of the box and a spring loaded panel popped open when you released the pressure. Then you turned the panel counterclockwise and the entire back of the box came off.

So, with the top now off the box, we all three peered inside to finally gaze on our treasure.

"It looks like some old lady scarf. What good is that?" quipped Roger with disappointment as we all looked in the box to see what looked indeed like a fine red silk scarf.

"Come on, really? Do you think someone would go through all that trouble to hide a scarf? Remember all the weird stuff your grandmother had all over the apartment. There has to be something more," I said.

Mark was the first to reach in and pulled out the scarf to discover, to our amazement and excitement, the scarf was just a cover. There was something wrapped inside the scarf.

"Look at this. What is it?" Mark removed the red silk scarf from around another piece of wood. "It looks like some old piece of wood."

We began to examine the wood but, as we turned it over, we soon discovered it was not ordinary piece of wood.

"Holy hell, what's that?" exclaimed Roger when he turned over the board. "I have never seen anything like this before. Have you guys?"

Shaking our heads, we agreed there was nothing like this in our experience.

What Roger held in his hands was unique indeed. It was a single highly polished piece of dark brown wood, maybe walnut. It was about one quarter inch thick and a little more than one foot wide and about two feet long. The front was covered in weird black markings.

First, on the upper left corner was a picture of what looked like the sun, but no ordinary sun. There was a face on the sun that looked like a jack-o-lantern mixed with a skeleton with black rays coming out of the perimeter. Next, across the top from left to right was the word "YES" followed by a skeleton head with a pair of wings. Next, came the word "NO" followed by the depiction of a half-moon in a circle where the moon had a face like a witch. And that was just the top of the board.

Under this, in three rows, came the letters of the alphabet. The first row was A – K, the next row was L – U, and the last row was V – Z. On the left side of the third row was the word "Hello" and on the right side was the word "Goodbye." Under the two words were strange icons. It was a circle, inside of which was inscribed a five-pointed star.

Under the letters came the numbers 1 – 0. Finally, at the very bottom of the board was a pair of wings looking like they were clipped from a bat. Around the outside border were more strange depictions of stars and comets.

"What the hell is this thing and what does it do?" asked Roger as he turned it over and over again in his hands. "I have no idea what this is; do you, guys?"

Shaking our heads in unison, Mark and I whispered, "No."

As we continued to look at the board, I noticed something else was still in the box. There was another red scarf. This one also appeared to contain something; only this something was much smaller.

"Guys, here. Look at this." I pulled out a small red package and began to unwrap it. A small wooden object, the same color and type of the wood that made up the board, fell into my hand. This object was about six or seven inches long and was in the shape of a heart with a small clear circle in the end that came to the point of the heart.

"What do you think this is?" I asked, turning it over in my hands.

As I did so, I noticed some writing on the back side. It looked like one word "OUIJA"

I tried to pronounce the word in my head but all that came out was "'oou- gee- iI- jaa',"

Now we were truly perplexed. We had some kind of a board with strange markings and a heart shaped piece of wood with a strange word on the bottom.

It was getting close to suppertime, so I suggested we wrap everything up the way we found it and put it all back and close the box. Tomorrow we could get back together and see if we could find out what this was. We all agreed and I headed off next door thinking, what the hell did we find?

Chapter 20

For the next couple of days we didn't have much time to dig further into what we found. My father decided it was time to clean the basement, or rather it was time I cleaned the basement.

"In the back corner there are some old boxes," my father instructed. "There are some old clothes and junk we have not used for many years so haul it upstairs and throw it in the trash."

I looked at where he was pointing and in the darkest, dingiest corner of the basement, behind the boiler was about five boxes of junk. If that was all there was this would be easy. "No problem I'll get started."

So I crawled into the dark corner and started hauling out boxes. Ever the inquisitive one, I pulled out the first box and dumped it on the floor to see what was there. Some real old and smelly clothes spilled out of the box at once filling the room with the stench of mold and mildew. They were covered in mold from the damp basement. I started to sneeze as the dirt and mold entered my nose and throat. "Not a good idea" I thought as I piled the junk back into the box and hauled it up the stairs and out into the trash.

The next boxes were similar, filled with musty, old dirty clothes. Out they went. I made one more trip behind the boiler to make sure I had gotten out all the boxes.

Down on all fours, in the dust and dirt of the basement floor, I crawled. I surveyed the area and, just as I was about to back out of the dank space, I spied something in the corner way behind the boiler. It looked like a piece of wood, or a small box. I reached in and touched the mysterious item but I could not reach far enough under the pipe to pull it out.

I pushed myself closer to the floor and stretched as far as my arm could reach and still I could only get my fingertips on the object. When I did touch it, I knew it was not wood nor a box, but a book. "Who would wedge a book in the basement behind a boiler?" I thought as I strained once more to reach my prize. Making myself one with the floor, I pulled my body closer under the plumbing of the boiler and just as I was about to give up the book came loose from the space in which it was wedged, and fell into my hands.

Slowly, so as not to hit my head or get myself wedged in under the boiler, I backed out with the book held tightly in my hand.

When I finally shimmied out, I sat on the floor and tried to wipe the dust off my head and clothes to no avail. Next I turned the book over and over in my hands. It was old, covered with soot but seemed to be intact.

I reached into my back pocket and pulled out a rag I was using to wipe my hands and slowly and carefully wiped the cover of the book. The soot fouled the creases on the cover of the book making a dark black mess, making it impossible to read the title on the cover. Slowly, carefully I worked the cover clean until I could read the title. When I saw the title, embossed in large gold letters on the cover, I knew I had to show this to the guys.

Chapter 21

I headed over to the house next door and found the guys in Roger's room talking about the strange board we found earlier. I heard Mark say something about a ghost when I burst into the room.

"I don't know about a ghost, but I have seen a book, and you guys need to see it right NOW."

"What is going on?" Mark sat upright on his brother's bed.

"Guys, seriously, I found something. I really don't know what it means but it has to do with the thing we found in the box. Let's go downstairs and I'll show you, but you have to swear, for now at least, we tell no one about the box or the book I am about to show you. Agreed?"

"Agreed," came the reply from the brothers.

So we headed downstairs to the basement. I pulled out the book from under my shirt and proceeded to tell the guys how and where I found it.

"So, wait a minute," chided Roger. "You found this book about gypsies in the basement and you want us to believe that the thing we found can let us talk to the dead? Really, how stupid do you think we are?"

"Look, I know how stupid you are, but this book is real," I said as I handed him the book. "Open to the chapter on Spirit Boards and see for yourself."

"Hey, I wanna see, too," exclaimed Mark as he pushed closer to his brother and they both began to read from the same section I had read earlier.

After a few minutes of reading, both boys looked at me with faces a little ashen and somewhat unsettled. Roger was the first to speak. "Oh my God. This can't be real! This book says that this board, or whatever it is, has some kind of magic and we can talk to the dead and tell the future. We are going to be rich," he trumpeted as he fell back laughing on the couch.

"Think of it. If we know what is going to happen and when, we can bet on some horse race like our father does and we will always win."

"Roger, you are truly an ass," I told him as I pulled the book from his hands. 'You are making fun of this, and this could be very serious. I have no idea what is real and what is not, but I do know that this spirit board, or whatever it is, has been around for a long time and some people say it has powers. This thing we found is old and someone went through a great deal of trouble to lock it up and hide it until we found it. So just shut up if you don't believe and I will take my book home."

Mark jumped in telling his brother, "Look, Robbie's right. We have no idea what we have in our hands. It could all be bullshit or it could be real. Why not read a little more and see what else we can discover?"

"Ok, Ok, "sighed Roger, a little beaten by what his younger brother and I had said. "I promise no more kidding about being rich. Let's get the board and see what we can learn from the book."

I looked at the clock and it was 11:30, so I told the guys, "Mom is making meatballs and she invited you two for lunch. Let's get the board and the book over to my house and we can spend the rest of the afternoon, after lunch, in the basement seeing if we can figure this out. Our basement has a small room that no one uses and we can hide the stuff there and bring it out as we need. Agreed?"

"Yeah, that makes sense. We need the book and the board hidden and there is no place to hide it here. Besides Mom will not be home till later and I love your mom's meatballs! Let's eat," called Mark as he headed to the door, racing the two of us to lunch.

Chapter 22

The next day Mama seemed to be in a very good mood. She was full of energy and smiling all morning. "Roberto, how would you and the boys like a lunch of fresh sausage sandwiches today?"

"Yeah, that's great." I was looking for an excuse to get the guys together to do some more work on the board. "I'll call over and tell them to be here for lunch."

I walked next door to get the guys. I told them of the lunch plans and Roger said, "Great, but how do we get rid of your mom so we can figure out about the board?"

"I don't know, but we will figure it out. Let's go."

After eating our fill of fresh sausage and homemade Italian bread dipped in tomato sauce, we were full and as excited as could be. We wanted to head down to the basement to work on the book and the board, but we had to figure out a way to get out of the kitchen without Mama being suspicious. Mom solved that problem when she said she felt a little tired and was going to take a nap before Papa came home. At first I was glad she was leaving us alone, but later I grew concerned that she might be getting sick again.

So, with mom in her room and the house to ourselves, we headed down to the basement. Now our basement was little used but was furnished as a family room with couches and armchairs and a coffee table. The perfect setup for three boys wanting to learn how to talk to the spirits. We opened the book to the chapter on spirit boards and read the following:

The first Ouija boards were made of coffin wood, and the planchette used a coffin nail as a pointer.

"Coffin wood and a coffin nail? You have got to be kidding." exclaimed Roger as he reached into the red box and pulled out our board. "I don't know what coffin wood looks like, but this pointer sure looks like a nail," he said, turning over the planchette revealing what indeed looked like a small nail.

'Gimme that," I ordered, reaching for the planchette as Mark came closer to help me examine the nail.

Sure enough it looked like a small nail, but way too small to use on a coffin. Mark agreed but Roger retorted, "Maybe they break the nail off so that it is small enough to fit in the planchette thing and that is why it looks too small."

Okay, maybe the nail was broken off to make it fit better, we agreed as we kept reading. Soon we came across the following admonition:

Don't use a spirit board alone or if you are ill--you're spiritually susceptible to possession.
Don't use a spirit board in places where death has occurred or risk possession (i.e. no graveyards).
Do not let the board go thru the whole alphabet or numbers in order--it's an attempt for the spirits to escape.

"Okay, now this is getting a little weird. There are rules to this thing. Don't do this and don't do that. What do you do?"

"Shut up Roger, and let us figure this out," returned Mark, pushing his brother to the other side of the couch. "If you can't shut up, leave us alone, or just sit there and be quiet."

"Okay, okay. . . Look, you guys, this is just a little strange. They tell us what not to do with the thing but do they tell us anywhere what we can do?"

"Hang on. Let me look a little more. There has to be some directions for this thing someplace." I thumbed through some pages to see if I could indeed find directions. Soon I came to a chapter entitled "Using the Spirit Board." I read the following:

The use of the spirit board requires proper preparation to prevent the seekers from contacting a negative spirit. Therefore, it is important that the seekers find a quiet room where they will not be disturbed. The room should be free of interferences and light should only be provided by white candles. The white candle will serve to protect the seekers from malevolent spirits and can be used to focus the energy of the seekers to attract the desired spirit.

Time of day is also important. The best results come in the early evening as there is a lesser interference from the living.

Never use the spirit board in an area of death. Never use a spirit board to contact a recently dead person as they may not know they are dead and refuse to leave once contacted.

Energy within the room is very important if the seekers hope to be successful. Never use a spirit board alone. Always have three of more people but no more than seven people. The energy of these people will help to contact the spirit and, if forced, can be combined to banish a negative spirit should one be contacted.

Once the room is ready and the candles are lit, place the spirit board upon the knees of two persons seated facing each other. It is preferable to have a man and a lady, but any two seekers can be accommodated. Place the planchette in the dead center of the board. The seekers should place their fingertips lightly upon the planchette with little pressure allowing the planchette freedom to move about the spirit board.

Only one person should be asking the questions. This allows a connection between the spirit and the seeker and will result in a more intimate session. Never let the spirit control the questions. Be sure the questions are clear and concise so as to avoid confusing answers. To obtain the best results, it is important that the seekers should concentrate their minds upon the questions being asked and avoid other discussions. Frivolous questions must be avoided and all persons in the room should conduct themselves in a serious manner throughout the session. Failure to be serious might allow a negative spirit to come into the session without warning.

At the end of each session it is important that "Goodbye" is stated to the spirit and the spirit replies in kind. This is done in the following manner. First the seekers clearly state the session is over and say "Good Bye". Then they ask the spirit to say "Goodbye" by moving the planchette over to the word "Good Bye" printed on the spirit board. This is of critical importance in that it may prevent a malevolent spirit remaining with the seekers after the session.

Once the spirit says "Good Bye" the board must be wiped with a clean silk cloth. Then the board should be wrapped in the same cloth and returned to a locked box made of wood to prevent the spirit from remaining behind. The planchette must also be placed in the proper location within the wooden box.

After reading, this we were exhausted. I looked at the clock on the wall and was startled to see it was almost suppertime. Where had the time gone? We got down here just after lunch and now nearly five hours had passed. It was as if time rushed past.

Mark and Roger quickly got up and headed out the door to go home to their supper. Roger turned back and said, "I'm not sure of what we just read, but I am sure we found something. Let's decide tomorrow what we should do. Until then, no one else can know what we have learned."

With that I put the red wood box containing the board and the book in the back of a cabinet in the store room and headed upstairs thinking, 'What do we have here?'

Needless to say, I had a hard time sleeping that night. Spirit board, ghost, communicating with the dead, danger that was all that ran through my mind. My stomach was nervous as I must have gotten up five times that night to go down the hall to the bathroom.

I tossed, I turned, and try as I might I was not able to fall asleep. What did we find and what do we do with it? All I know is this is either the most dangerous thing I have ever found or the biggest joke on us all. Which one it was we would soon find out.

Chapter 23

For the next couple of days I was kept busy doing chores. My father decided it was time to paint the porch steps. I had to sweep and wash the steps by hand to get all the grime off each step. Then he wanted me to scrape off the chipped paint and then help with the final painting. I didn't have any time alone that me and the guys could spend investigating the Ouija board. It wasn't until Thursday afternoon that we had a chance to return to our mystery box.

About two o'clock in the afternoon the guys knocked on the side door and I let them in. "Hey guys, mom and dad are out shopping and will be gone for a few hours so we have some time until then to see what else we can discover. Come on in and let's get started."

So we headed down into the basement, got the box with the board and the book. Mark unwrapped the board and planchette. He wiped it down and looked up "Now what?"

"I have no idea" I said. "Let's see what the book says." I carefully thumbed through the book to the book ark I placed there earlier to see what we were to do next.

"Here we go, look here it tells us how we use this thing"

I turned the book so we all could see and together we read the following:

It is very important to set the proper mood for a successful session. First clear the room of all distractions. Light a single white candle in the center of the room where one can fix their gaze on the light of the candle to calm the senses and open the mind to the spirit world.
Once the stage is set, Place the board on the knees of two persons, a lady and a gentleman are preferred but are not necessary. Next place the planchette gently in the dead center of the board. Place the fingers of your hands, lightly but firmly, on the planchette so as to allow it to move easily and freely about the board.
There should be a third person in the room whose function is to remain silent and to record the letters as spelled out by the planchette. Only ONE person should ask questions of the spirit board so as to avoid confusion. The person asking the questions should keep the questions clear and plainly put with no nonsense questions being asked.
To obtain the best results it is important that all persons present should keep their minds open and concentrate on the questions asked and not be distracted by other topics. Have no one at

the table that will not sit quietly and seriously as this is a dangerous business and could attract the presence of malevolent spirits if care is not taken. BE CAUTIOUS

"What is a malevolent spirit?" asked Mark

"I don't know. Let's look it up," I said as I went upstairs to get my dictionary from school.

I came back down and Mark and Roger were sitting there reading from the book. "Robbie, look at this" Roger called as he handed me the book.

Do not use the spirit board in your home as this is where you are most under the influence of a malevolent spirit.

"So here is that malevolent thing again, what does it mean?" asked Mark a little more concerned.

So I looked up the word malevolent and read the following:
Wishing evil or harm to another; showing ill will; evil or harmful to others

"That's not good is it?" a now frightened Mark sighed as he sat back down onto the couch. "That's not good at all."

"Don't be a baby," the older and wiser Roger chided. "Nothing is going to happen; it's just some dumb board and a bunch of spooky hokum. Nothing is going to happen. Is it?" Roger turned toward me looking a little unsure of himself.

I didn't say anything, just looked at the guys, the board and the book and sat down on the chair a little frightened and more than a little perplexed. After a minute of silence I broke the spell and quietly said "What now?"

Roger finally quietly spoke, "I guess we try it."

"Are you sure?" I asked.

"No, but if we don't try it, we will never know, will we?"

"I guess not," I said, while looking at a clearly frightened Mark. "Hey, Mark, you ok?"

"Yeah, sure," came the unconvincing reply. "How do we do it?"

"Well, we don't have a candle, but we have enough people, so Roger and I will sit with the board and you write down what it says, OK?"

"Sure, I guess."

Roger and I moved the chairs until we were facing each other with our knees touching. I could feel Roger's knees shaking a little. I am sure mine were too but neither one of us said anything. Mark carefully placed the board on our knees and gently placed the planchette in the dead center of the board.

"Now what?" Roger asked.

"I guess we put our fingers on the planchette and start asking questions."

Carefully, as if the planchette were on fire, we laid our fingers down one at a time until all our fingers were lightly resting on the sides of the carved piece of wood.

Nothing happened. We waited a minute or two and nothing happened.

"Maybe you are supposed to move it around so it gets the idea of what to do," whispered Mark.

We moved the planchette all around the board, careful not to make a figure eight or to follow all the letters or numbers in order as we were warned by the book earlier not to do that.

We stopped moving the planchette and waited a minute and still nothing. Then Roger remembered, "Aren't we supposed to ask a question?"

Of course, the board responds to questions and we didn't ask any. No wonder nothing was happening.

"Ok, you ask a question."

"Not me, you do it" Roger tossed back the challenge to me.

"Ok, ok."I proceeded to ask the following: "Is anyone here with us?"

At first, nothing happened, until suddenly, as if by some strange force, I could feel a pulling on the planchette. I looked at Roger and he looked at me. "Stop moving the planchette!" we both said in unison. "I'm not."

Soon the planchette stopped near the word YES etched onto the board. We both jumped. The board went flying, the planchette hit Mark in the face and three boys tore out of the room, up the basement stairs, and huddled in the sunlight of the kitchen.

We must have hid in the kitchen for a good five minutes breathing hard and staring at each other in wide-eyed fright. Then Roger laughed suddenly and said, "You scaredy cats. I moved the planchette. I was just trying to scare the hell out of you and I did!"

Mark took a swing at his brother shouting, "You're an ass. You scared the hell out of us and I got hit in the head." Mark wiped a small cut on his forehead. "That thing could have poked my eye out. You're such an ass."

Roger laughed again, but I sensed he was not quite as bold as he wanted us to think. He was a year older but I could see that maybe there was a little more going on than he wanted us to believe.

"Look you two. The directions warned us not to joke around. This is serious. What if something was there and what if Mark really lost an eye; we would all be in serious trouble. So come on, Roger, either take this seriously or I am out of this right now"

"Me, too," said Mark, punching Roger in the arm for good measure.

"All right, I am sorry. From now on I will be serious, promise. Let's go back down and clean up the mess. That was enough for today anyway. Next time we will do it right with a candle and everything."

So we marched bravely back down into the basement room, picked up the chairs and dragged them back to the kitchen, wiped down the board and cleaned the planchette and put everything back as it was. We packed away the board in the safekeeping of the box and the guys prepared to leave.

On the way upstairs to leave from the side door Roger turned to me and said, "We need to be really careful next time." He turned and the two brothers went out the side door and across the driveway to their house.

What did he mean by that? I wondered. He said he moved the planchette, so what was there to be "careful" about? I headed upstairs to wait for my parents to get home. I knew I was looking forward to another sleepless night.

Chapter 24

I spent most of that night tossing and turning, my mind playing out over and over again the session in the basement. What really happened? Was Roger being an ass and joking around? If so, why did he say we had to be careful the next time? If not, then what did we encounter? I was confused, tired, and more than a little scared. I awoke before the sun and could not get back to sleep, so I headed to the kitchen for something to eat.

I was startled to see my father at the kitchen table, just sitting there with his head in his hands looking down.

"Papa," I called out quietly, "what's wrong?"

It was obvious I had startled him because he nearly jumped out of the chair and spilling his cold cup of coffee all in one move. "Robbie, Jesus, you scared the hell out of me. What are you doing up so early?"

My father seemed agitated more than startled and that worried me even more, so I ignored his question pulled up the chair across from him and asked again. "Papa, what's wrong?"

After a moment and a deep sigh, my father whispered, "Mama, she had a very bad night."

'What do you mean?" I asked, leaning a little forward trying to hide the fright that was beginning to build in my mind. "What is wrong with Mama?"

"I don't know." he began. "She seemed alright when we went to sleep but soon she began to toss and turn and began to talk in her sleep about the witch. Then she had trouble breathing and she began to cough and cough. I was worried so I tried to wake her but she would not wake. I tried to shake her, I spoke with her and finally I slapped her. I never meant to slap her; I just didn't know what to do. She would not wake. I was scared. She would not wake."

My father was distraught to say the least. He was not a violent man and he would never hit Mama, but he did and he was scared. I didn't know what to do so I just sat there staring when he spoke again

"She just lay there and suddenly she turned over and opened her eyes as peaceful as if she was having a beautiful dream. I could see my hand print, red and spreading on the side of her face, and she just looked up and smiled at me and said, "Good morning, dear. What time is it?"

"Robbie, I was stunned. She had no memory of the nightmare nor did she feel the slap or the burning there must be on her face. I do not understand. I told her to go back to sleep, and I came in here. I looked in a few minutes later and she was fast asleep and smiling, really smiling. I did not know anyone could smile in their sleep. So I came back in here and then you came in and so here we are."

I was stunned silent. I just sat there; I didn't know how to respond. Papa also was quiet; I could tell he was thinking, rolling over the events in his mind. He hit mama, not in anger, but in fear. What could frighten a man so much that he would strike his wife?

After a little while, I could see Papa settling down, and he got up from the table and put his half full coffee cup in the sink and announced, "Robbie, I have to go to work, but I need you to look after your mother. Make sure she is Ok. Stay close today, please," he pleaded.

"Sure, Papa, of course I will. I promise." And with that, once again, he tousled my hair just like in the old days and off he went out the door to work. I sat there a few minutes. I had a rough night and now this. It was almost too much. But I swore that I would watch over Mama today and I did.

But nothing happened. Mama got up and came into the kitchen looking well rested and none the worse for wear. She looked at me a little surprised. "Well, young man, what are you doing awake this early?"

"I don't know," I lied. "I just couldn't sleep so I thought I would keep Papa company before he went to work."

"That's nice. Now what can I make my young man for breakfast? How about pancakes?"

And so it went the rest of the morning. Mama made pancakes; I did the dishes as if nothing happened last night. I could see she had no memory of anything happening, and for this I gave thanks. I could tell Papa tonight that all was well and perhaps I could make him feel better.

I stayed near Mama all morning and by lunchtime she began to sense that I was watching her. After lunch she smiled at me and said, "Ok, young man, you have been hanging on to my apron all morning. I turn and you are right there. What's going on?"

"Nothing," I lied again.

"Well, then go find your friends and have some fun. Summer is moving on and soon school will be back in session and its back to work for you three, so have some fun while you can and get out of my kitchen." She playfully tried to swat me with a dish towel. "Now scoot."

"Ok, I'll see what Roger and Mark are up to," I said. As I rose to leave the table, there came a knock at the side door.

"Speak of the devils," Mama said, laughing. "I'll bet that's them right now." Sure enough, the boys were at the door looking a little excited.

Before they could say a word, I ushered them downstairs to the basement, I didn't want my mother to overhear what they had to say.

Roger spoke first, "Did you have any dreams last night? Anything strange happen? Did you feel different somehow?"

I was stunned; I did not know what to say. "No, I tossed and turned all night but I did not have any dreams. Why?"

"Well, Mark and I had dreams all night and it seems we had the *same* dream"

"Impossible," I said. "There is no way you two could have the same dream."

"Well, we did." They told me this story:

Roger began, "Last night I was tossing and turning half the night. I felt strange like someone was in the room, but I knew no one was there. I

73

must have fallen asleep but it was as if I were still awake, I could see my room but it was different, colorless sort of. I don't know, just different."

Mark chimed in. "I saw the same thing. I swear, I was asleep or awake. I couldn't tell and the room was there but dull, like Roger said, colorless."

Roger spoke slowly, "Then, I thought I saw someone in the room, but not, fully, just a shadow or a shape of someone or something."

"Suddenly, I could hear someone speaking," Mark took over the story. "A female voice, not clear, sort of distant. I could not understand what it was saying. It seemed like words but not words, until I heard the word "Witch."

Roger jumped in. "Yeah, witch like in some movie, I could hear the word over and over like someone chanting witch, witch, witch over and over. Then suddenly I woke up and I was scared, real scared."

"Me too, I heard the chant and woke up scared as hell," Mark cut in.

"Witch, are you sure the word was witch?" I asked thinking of what my father said he heard Mama say in her sleep. "You heard the voice chanting witch?"

"Yes," they said in unison.

Now I was scared. How could the guys have the same dream and my mother say witch in her sleep enough to scare my father half to death? I was stunned and didn't know what to say. We sat there silently for a few minutes and Roger finally spoke up. "We have to use the Ouija board again. We made a big mistake last time. Remember the rules, about saying goodbye? Well, we didn't. We just put everything away and ran the hell out of here."

"What do you mean?" I asked, still reeling from what I was just told. "Goodbye. What are you talking about?"

"Look here," Roger said forcefully as he picked up the book, found the directions for ending a session and began to read. "It says right here *before you end your session make sure you close the session by making the spirit say Goodbye or it is possible the spirit may remain. If the spirit doesn't want to say Goodbye move the*

74

planchette to the words on the board Good Bye and close out the session "We didn't do that; we didn't say goodbye"

"Ok, Ok, I remember. We didn't say good bye. Do you really want to open this up again?" I asked a little tentatively. "Do you really want to chance it?"

"Yes, we have no choice," Mark replied. "And the sooner the better."

"Ok," I said, "let's get everything set up."

And so we did. Roger got the chairs from the kitchen, Mark got the white candle lit and sat down with a pad of paper and I retrieved the box with the spirit board and carefully unpacked the contents. When we had everything out and ready I said, 'Ok, same as last time. Roger and I will work the board and Mark will write down what the board points to and no fooling around PERIOD. Agreed?"

"Agreed!" came the short reply, and we began the session.

Roger and I were sitting knee to knee with the board resting on our laps. Mark was off to the side near the candle, ready to write the letters from the board. I took a deep breath and we began to slowly move the planchette slowly around the board while I asked, "Is there someone here with us?"

We were slowly moving planchette in small circles, when suddenly the planchette moved in a straight line and stopped over the word YES printed on the board.

We all gasped but held our place. I asked, "Are you a spirit?" as Roger and I once again moved the planchette in small circles. Again, as if by its own control, the planchette stopped on the word NO printed on the board.

I asked, "If not a spirit, then what are you?" This time the planchette moved as if by magic. I could feel my fingers on the wooden instrument, but I could not feel any movement in my muscles. It was as if I had lost control of my hands.

As Roger called out the letters and Mark wrote them down, I was astonished as slowly the planchette spelled out:

75

NOTTHESAMEASBEFORE

We looked at the letters and could not make heads or tails out of them until Mark started to break the string of letters into words.
"Not the same as before"

"What does that mean?" I asked in a whisper for fear of scaring the spirit, and myself. "Not the same as before what?"

Since I was the one designated to ask the questions, I asked again, "You must tell me the truth. If not a spirit, then what are you?"

Slowly the planchette spelled out:

ONCEAWITCHNOTASBEFORE

Again, Mark broke down the string to read:
Once a witch not as before

A witch, how can that be? The guys dreamed about a witch and my mother had a nightmare about a witch and now the board is telling us there is a witch among us. It could not be; it just could not be.

More than a little frightened I asked "Does the witch have a name?"

The planchette now moved quickly to the word YES.

"Will you tell us your name?" I whispered.

NOTTODAY

And suddenly the planchette moved to Goodbye on the board.

Not today and then goodbye. Who was in control? We sat there a little stunned so I asked a few more questions, but nothing happened. We could feel there was a change in the room; the energy was somehow different. The room felt...colder.

Roger spoke up first. "What the hell was that? Are you sure that you were not moving the planchette?" As he looked me in the eyes, I could tell he was hoping I would laugh and tell him I moved it just to scare him. But I didn't.

I looked back into his eyes. "No, I swear it wasn't me"

With the session ended by the spirit, or witch or whatever it was, we quietly wiped down the board, wrapped it up in the silk wrappings, and returned it to the box.

We did this in absolute silence, each lost in his own thoughts and fears. Mark looked at his older brother for assurance. "Now what?"

"I guess we try again tomorrow." Roger said as he blew out the candle.

Chapter 25

The next day while Mom was cleaning the house (we were expecting a big family meal on Sunday), the boys and I headed once again down to the basement to pick up where we had left off. Roger and I set up the chairs as before while Mark once again set out to prepare the white candle. We all worked in silence at our appointed task, keeping our thoughts (and fears?) to ourselves.

When the room was ready, Roger asked, "You ready?"

"Ready as I can be," I replied, not sure of what to expect. "Let's get started."

We all took our places as before. Roger and I knee to knee, the board settled on our lap. The room darkened, lit only by a candle, and a small table lamp in the far corner. Mark sat with his pad and pencil ready to transcribe the letters as they appeared under the pointer. And so we began.

We lightly settled our fingers on the planchette, and slowly moved the pointer around the board in large lazy circles, avoiding figure eights, while I asked, "Are you here?"

At first nothing; the planchette seemed to move completely under our control. I asked again a little more forcefully, "Are you here?"

Suddenly the room felt like a cool breeze came out of nowhere. I shook from the chill, my shoulders shuddering from the change in the temperature. The planchette at first hesitated under our control then suddenly but surely moved and stopped over the word YES.

"Are you the same person who was here yesterday?"

The planchette spelled out letters one at a time and Mark translated when they were done "NOT A PERSON."

"What does that mean?" Mark asked, a little unsure of what was happening.

"It's not a person. Look, there is no one here, so it's not a person. It must be a spirit or a witch right. Didn't the board say it was a "witch" yesterday?" Roger said, trying to make some sense out of the words.

"Yeah, that's right. The board spelled out "witch" yesterday. Let's try that," I said as I began to ask the next question.

"Are you the same witch that was here yesterday?"

The planchette moved slowly and Mark read out the letters one at a time until the board finished

A WITCH ONCE NOT AS BEFORE AWAKE

It seems the thing spelling out letters was very specific. The directions did caution us to ask specific questions, so maybe the spirit board also answered in specific ways. But what did it mean, *not as before and awake*.

So I asked, "Are you dead?"

The response came quickly: BETWEEN

"So you are not dead but not alive correct?"

Again the response came quickly as the planchette rushed over to the word YES

It looked like I was getting the hang of this. Ask a specific question and get a specific response. Ok that seemed easy enough.

"Do you have a name?"
MANY
"Will you tell us your name?"

ASK LATER

"No, I will ask now. What is your name?" I spoke forcefully.

ASK LATER

Roger spoke up and declared, "Look, whatever you are, we are in charge, not you, so tell us your name and do it now."

'Wait, Roger. Careful, we have no idea what we are dealing with here. Don't push," I cautioned.

"Look, remember the directions. Don't let the spirit take charge. Well, it is trying to take charge, so I am trying to get control back." At this Roger shouted, "Now, tell us your name!"

Nothing happened. We sat quietly for a few minutes but still nothing happened. Suddenly there was another breeze and the planchette moved quickly over to GOODBYE and then nothing.

We tried for another half hour but got nothing. It looked like we pissed the witch or whatever it was off and so it left.

"Nice move, dumb ass. Now what happens?" complained Mark.

"Look, we cannot let this thing take control, so I was just trying to tell it that we were the boss. OK. So maybe it took off, maybe there was nothing here, but either way there is nothing here now so let's get out of here and try again later."

I agreed with Roger, so once again we went through the ritual of wiping down the board, wrapping the planchette, and putting the room as we found it. Mark blew out the candle and we turned out the light and headed back upstairs.

The guys headed out the side door to go home and I headed the rest of the way upstairs to help Mama with the rest of the cleaning, anything to forget what was happening in the basement.

I called out to Mama to see where she was and asked what I could do to help. She didn't respond. I looked in the kitchen, then the living room, then the dining room and no sign of Mama. I figured she must be cleaning the bathroom. As every Italian knows, a clean bathroom is critical to a clean house, but the door was ajar and no one was there.

Now, I was a little concerned. Mama could have gone out for something, but it was not like her to leave the house without calling down to tell me she was going out. I called again and again and still no reply.

I headed down the short hall to the bedrooms and looked in my room and it was empty. Well, there was only one place left, and the door to my parent's room was closed. I knocked quietly and called out. Nothing. I knocked a little harder and called a little louder. Still nothing. Now, I was getting scared. Where was she?

I tried the door knob. It turned easily, so it was unlocked. I slowly opened the door, knocking as I did so and calling out, all at the same time. I was shocked at the sight before me.

Mama was in bed; her hair was disheveled across her face. She was sweating profusely. I could see the sheet was wringing wet, and her pillow case was covered in sweat. I rushed to her side, calling, "Mama, Mama what's wrong? Mama, it's me, wake up."

At first she didn't respond. She just lay there like a limp doll. I shook her slightly and tried to move her wet hair from across her face so I could look at her face and into her eyes. As I did so, I jumped back "You look like you have seen a ghost," she whispered smiling.

'Oh, Mama, I came in and you were, … were" My voice trailed off.

'What, Robbie, what is it?"

"Oh, Mama, I was so scared."

"It's okay, Robbie. Everything is fine. I was just a little tired from cleaning the entire house and I must have taken a nap. I'm fine."

I didn't understand. Fine? She was not fine. She looked like she was sick, or dead or something. Her eyes were rolled back and she was covered in sweat and she had no memory of anything except taking a nap. I was confused, lost and a little more than scared. I couldn't tell her what I saw as I knew she would not believe me. So I just gave her a hug, looked into her eyes to make sure all was well, and left the room.

I knew something had happened, but what it was I had no idea. Could it have been from what happened in the basement? If so, what did it mean? Can we be in some kind of danger or is there something else? I had no idea what to do, so I did nothing. Unfortunately, I would live to regret that inaction.

The next day, as soon as I could break away from my chores, I headed next door to tell the guys what happened yesterday. I ran across the shared driveway and knocked on the side door. "Mark, Roger, it's me." After a few minutes and no one came, I called out, "Come on, open the door." I shouted a little too loud as I pounded excitedly on the screen door. "Come on, guys, open the door. It's important!" I shouted again, still knocking.

No answer. Maybe they weren't home. 'Damn, they have to be home' I thought and started pounding the door again. Soon Roger came to the door and looked out the screen door right into my eyes.

I stepped back, what I saw could not have been. His eyes looked blank for a second. Blank, like he didn't know who I was. He just stood there staring. Then, as if someone slapped him up the side of the head, he shook from head to foot. His eyes brightened and he said, "Hey, Robbie, what's going on?" as if nothing happened.

I looked at him and said, "We have to talk. Something is going on, and I don't know what's happening."

"What do you mean?"

"Not here," I said. "Get Mark and head over. I'll tell you then."

A few minutes later I had shared my story about my mother and what happened to her yesterday. The guys just sat there staring at me as if I was going crazy, and I thought maybe I was.

"Look, this all started with that damn Ouija board. That stupid witch and all the mumbo jumbo. We have to quit using that thing before something happens."

"Don't be a baby, Robbie," chided Roger. "It's just a dumb board and you are making a big thing out of all this. Let's see what she has to say today and then we can decide. OK?"

"Yeah, come on. We can't stop now," Mark jumped in. "Besides it's just getting to be fun."

'Fun' was not exactly what I was thinking, but I relented, and we set up the room as before.

So we all took our places once again, Roger and I sitting knee to knee, the board balanced between us and Mark ready to transcribe what the board spelled out. I put the planchette into the dead center of the board but, before I could ask a question, the pointer began to move erratically in a large figure eight.

Soon the planchette began to move slower and spelled out:

NOTSTUPIDSTRONG

What the hell? We did not ask anything, but the board was sending a message. Mark translated:
"Not Stupid. Strong."

It was as if the board, or the spirit or something, heard us talking before we even sat down. Roger called the board 'dumb' and now the board is telling us it is 'strong'. What was going on?

As he read the words once again, the planchette started to move wildly, this time in large circles. Then it slowed again and spelled out:
LESSONLEARNED

We all stared at each other while Mark read the message. "What does that mean?" questioned Mark. "What lesson?"

"Could..., I mean is it possible that the witch is the cause of your mother's weird behavior?" whispered Roger, not really wanting to voice the concept.

I began to say something when once again the planchette moved over the word YES printed on the board.

Roger and I both jumped back and took our hands from the board, causing the planchette to fly across the room. "That just can't be. There is no way this is real," I thought out loud. "This is not happening."

As Mark went to get the planchette, Roger replied, "Yes, it is happening. Real or not, it is happening."

"Robbie, you are too close to this thing. Let me ask the questions from now on and let's see if this thing starts to affect me or my family. Ok?" Roger said.

"I would rather we just stop completely, but if you want to take over... fine." I settled in, and Roger took over.

So, once again, we sat knee to knee with the board balanced and the candle burning when Roger asked, 'Did you try to hurt Robbie's mom?"

Slowly, slowly the planchette spelled out:

L E S S O N L E A R N E D

"Ok, if you are trying to tell us something, we get it. You are strong, right?"

The pointer quickly moved over to the word YES on the board.

"Do you mean any of us harm?"

The planchette began to move in circles, then figure eights. It moved for two minutes spelling out nothing then slowly letters became clear
NO FREEDOM

"Freedom? Freedom from what?" asked Roger, a little confused.

The planchette just sat there as if the witch were gone.

"Are you trapped?"

Nothing.

"Are you lost?"

Nothing.

Frustrated, Roger finally asked, 'Tell us your name, and tell us NOW."

That did it. The planchette came alive and moved so fast and so erratically we almost lost contact with the device. Rapidly the pointer spelled out:

ANNEANNEANNEANNEANNEANNEANNEANNE

Over and over again. Then it stopped for a second and began to spell out another series of letters, over and over again.

JEFFERIESJEFFERIESJEFFERRIESJEFFERIES

Then just as quickly, the planchette moved over the word GOODBYE and stopped. No matter what we did, or what we asked, the planchette was dead.

Mark sat there staring at the paper with the letters written trying to make out the message, when suddenly it hit him. "It's a name," he shouted. "It's the name of the witch."

"Well, what's the name?" I asked, wondering if I really wanted to know or not.

"Well, I think its Anne Jefferies. At least, that is how the letters repeat."

"Do you really think that's a name?" Roger asked quietly.

Well, there is one way to find out. Let's head to the library and look it up and see what we can find.

"Yeah, we can head there tomorrow," Roger stated as he began the ritual of putting the board away.

Well, we had a name. What it meant, I had not a clue, but tomorrow, hopefully we would find out.

Chapter 27

The library at Sheepshead Bay High School was located on the second floor of the main building. The school was open all summer as there were summer school classes and adult education classes going on all the time, so access to the library was no problem.

The entrance opened up into a large room filled with dark rich wooden bookcases from floor to nearly seven feet high. In the center of the hall was a large round desk manned by Mrs. Holliday, the school librarian. Mrs. Holiday was a slightly rotund woman in her early sixties with nearly white hair piled in a tight bun on her head. She wore bright colors all the time and today was no exception. She was fêted out in a lime green blouse that accentuated her ample bosom. Below this she wore a simple light brown skirt, which went nearly to the floor, just in case a bit of ankle was to show. She was always friendly to the students as she felt that anytime a student came into the library of their own accord was a time to celebrate the richness of the education process.

"Good morning, boys," she called cheerily as she saw us walk into the room. "What brings you here? Surely you do not have summer school classes. You three are some of the best in the school so what can we do for you?"

"We have a project we are working on." I stammered out a reply, not exactly sure why we were there ourselves. "We need to look up a history on someone."

'Well, you came to the right place. Who are you looking to find?"

"Anne Jefferies" I replied.

"Well, let's go see what the card catalogue can show us, shall we!" came her cheery reply as she rose up from her chair and began the long walk to the back of the library.

Our school library, although modern for its day, was not like any library of today. There are no computers that you could punch in a search and instantly get 500 responses. No, this was the old way. A laborious search through the card catalogue, followed by a walk through the research stacks guided by the old Dewey decimal system locator number that you wrote in pencil on a small slip of scrap paper found in abundance on the card catalogue cabinet. Or you could spend your time in the dusty racks of the Encyclopedia Britannica found on the third floor where everything you could ever need to know was written in one of thirty-six volumes of heavy red tombs of information. The tricky thing was that to find something specific you had to know where to look and Mrs. Holiday knew every inch of the library better than anyone.

"So, what was that name again?" she asked as she put on her reading glasses that hung from a pearl encrusted chain around her thick neck. "Was it Anne something?"

"Jefferies," I replied, spelling out the letters as if I were a talking Ouija board.

"Well, let me see what we can find."

Mrs. Holiday began pulling out card filing draws one after another and writing things down on slips of paper. One after another, drawers opened and closed with the slam of wood hitting wood. I think we jumped at every slam. After what seemed to be forever, Mrs. Holiday turned to us and said, "Here you go, boys. This should get you started." As she handed us five slips of paper each with a different set of Dewey decimal system locator numbers, she advised, "Start here, and if you need anything else, just stop at the front desk." At this she smiled, turned, and vanished from the stacks as she headed back to her desk.

We looked at the information we had in our hands and were somewhat incredulous as to the amount of information on this Anne Jefferies. She must have been famous, somehow, but what really worried us was that she was real. Up until this time, we were hoping to find nothing on this Anne Jefferies and that would prove the Ouija board was a fake, but with this much information, it was hard to discern if the board was a fake or not.

'Look, maybe this name is just some famous lady and not the same person the board claims to be. It's just a coincidence," Roger tried to rationalize. "Let's see who this lady was and get out of here, Ok?"

"Sure," came our reply, and we headed off to the stacks to find our first book.

We headed to the stacks, guided by our locator number, and came across a book entitled <u>Popular Romances of the West of England</u> by Chatto and Windus published in 1903. The book was about two inches thick and covered in blood red leather like binding. It looked old and not often opened since the top of the book and the lower spine appeared to have some dust on it.

The next book was a very thin volume of only about forty pages called <u>Anne Jefferies and the Fairies: And Other Cornish Fairy Tales</u> by Kelvin Jones.

"Fairies? What the hell is going on?" called Mark a little too loudly.

"Shut up! You are going to get us thrown out before we find out what we came to find out. Come on, let's get the other books and see what we have," barked Roger as he turned with the next location in his hand.

We marched down the long aisles with books on either side housed in dark wooden bookcases. The books were stacked from the floor to two feet over our heads and the aisle seemed to go on forever... The smell of dust and book mold was all around us. We were heading into an area of older books and aisles that only the senior class members ventured into with their girlfriends to steal a kiss or cop a feel.

"I don't like this," whispered Mark. "We have enough books now. Do we really need more?"

Roger didn't even turn around; he just stopped short and looked to his right. He took the paper with the locator number and started to search the books one by one. He checked about ten books, stopped, and went back to the first book and checked again. "It's not here," he stated. "The book is not here. It should be right here and it's not. Where the hell is it and who would want it?"

'Look we have enough," Mark said again.

"Ok, fine. We will head over to the reading room downstairs and see what we have. Did you bring the note pad I told you to bring?"

"Yes, I have the pad and two pencils in case. Now let's get out of here."

Mark turned and so did Roger. I followed them down three flights of stairs and into the reading room. The reading room was a brightly lit room with several large tables with heavy wooden chairs. Around the periphery of the room were individual study carrels where you could sit and study in complete privacy. No one ever used them unless they were trying to hide a comic book from a nosey teacher. The room was empty; after all it was summer, and who would expect someone from the public school to spend any time in a library unless they were ordered by someone. A fate worse than death to some students. So, for this reason, we had the room to ourselves.

We settled on a large table, scarred from years of student abuse, far away from the door so that we could see if anyone came in and still had time to hide what we were doing. We put our books on the table and hesitated. What would we find and would be proof the board was real, or was this all a wild goose chase and Anne Jefferies was a nobody? We had no idea.

Since Roger was the oldest and Mark was our scribe, it fell to me to reach out and open the first book we found, and I began to read:

"Anne Jefferies was the daughter of a poor laboring man, who lived in the parish of St. Teath. She was born in December 1626, and said to have died in 1698."

"Oh my God, she was real!" exclaimed Mark.

"Hold on. Just because this Anne Jefferies was real, that does not mean this is the same Anne Jefferies from the board. This could just be some common name and she was just some common person. Let's read on first before we scare ourselves half to death. Keep reading, Robbie," Roger ordered, taking command of our group.

I continued:
"She was, by all accounts a bright and curious girl though, in common with the majority of the population at this time, she never learned to read. West Country tales of fairies and pixies held a strong fascination for the girl and she often ventured out after dusk searching the Valley for the Good People and singing a fairy song.

When she was 19, Anne went into service at the home of the wealthy Pitt family. One afternoon the girl was knitting in the arbor outside garden gate when something so alarming happened to her that she fell to the ground in a convulsive fit. Anne was later found by members of the family and taken up to her bedroom where she remained ill for some time. When she finally regained consciousness the girl related an incredible story.

Anne said that she had been in the arbor knitting when she heard a noise in the bushes, then six tiny men appeared, all dressed completely in green with unusually bright eyes. Their leader, who had a red feather in his cap, spoke to her lovingly and then jumped into her palm, which she placed on her lap. The little man climbed up her body and began kissing her neck, which he apparently enjoyed. He then called his five companions who swarmed all over her body kissing her until one of them put his hands over her eyes and she felt a sharp pricking sensation, and everything went dark.

Anne was then lifted up into the air and carried off. When she was set down again she heard someone say 'Tear, Tear' and her eyes were opened. The girl found herself in a paradise land of temples, palaces, gardens, lakes and brightly colored singing birds. The richly adorned people who lived in this magical land where human size and spent their time dancing and playing, and Anne herself was treated like royalty.
 She again met her fairy friend with the red feather in his cap, but whilst they were alone together his five companions arrived accompanied by an angry mob. In the ensuing struggle her fairy lover was wounded trying to protect her and the same individual who had blinded her before did so again and she was once again taken up into the air, this time with a great humming noise and finally found herself back in the arbor.

There seem to have been various side effects of Ann's apparent visit to fairyland. According to Moses Pitt, after the incident she ate no food at their house and she claimed to be nourished by the Good People themselves. Apparently Anne soon began to exhibit powers of clairvoyance and healing. Anne on one occasion healing her mistresses' injured leg by the placing of her hands on the injured body part. Before long hordes of people from all over the county were visiting her for her cures. It was said that Anne could also foretell the future and identities of the people who would visit her, where they came from and what time they would arrive.

But Anne's strange abilities soon came to the attention of the Justice of the Peace in Cornwall, John Tregeagle. In 1646 he accused her of communing with evil spirits and according to popular sources, charged her with witchcraft, had her imprisoned in Bodmin jail with very little food or drink. Amazingly Anne continued to enjoy good health, being fed, as she claimed by her fairy friends.

In the end, perhaps due to the public furor aroused by the case, after six months with minimal food and water, Anne was allowed to go free and found employment with a widowed aunt of Moses Pitt, near Padstow in Cornwall. She continued to work on her cures and subsequently married a man named William Warren. The family moved to Devon in 1693, but she refused to speak about her experiences, probably fearing further punishment. She told the brother-in-law of Moses Pitt, Mr. Humphrey Martyn, that she did not want her life made into books or Ballard's and that she would not discuss the matter' even for 500 pounds'. Incidentally Humphrey Martyn was married to Moses Pitt's sister, who as a four-year-old child had also seen Anne's fairies and apparently been given a silver cup by them

We were stunned silent. After I completed reading the section on Anne Jefferies, I closed the book and simply sat back in the chair. No one said a word for a full ten minutes, after which time Roger spoke up and said, "What do the other books say?"

I looked at him a little stunned and simply reached for the next book and opened it and began to read silently. After a few minutes of silent reading I said, "This book says essentially the same thing. Anne was taken by fairies, ate very little, was imprisoned, and she could heal people and tell the future. There was, however one more frightening aspect to the story. I read on.

Twenty five years after the death of Anne Jefferies, in 1723, the son of Constable John Tregeale, a Mr. Nathaniel Tregeale, was going through his father's things and came across an old family bible. While thumbing through the pages a sheaf of paper fell out.

Upon gazing at the precise lettering and elegant handwriting Nathaniel confirmed that the missive was penned by his father's hand. The final note of Constable Tregeale read as follows:

The witch Anne Jefferies died in the late fall of 1698 at which time she was buried in the cemetery behind the parish church, St. Teath. Myself and Mr. Johnathan Waggnor were entreated by Minister Pitt to join him in a *task most perilous, the removal of the witch Anne Jefferies, from the holy cemetery in which she was buried.*

Minister Pitt declared that the body of a witch cannot be allowed to rest on hallowed ground and thus he compelled me and Mr. Waggoner to help him to rid the cemetery of this unholy demon. So at ten o'clock on the evening of her burial, Minister Pitt, Mr. Waggoner and I proceeded, with much trepidation, to take to spade and dig up the demon body of the witch.

Since the grave was fresh, the work was easy so that we quickly reached the coffin. With the aid of a rope we were able to draw the coffin from its grave and place it safely on a wagon that Minister Pitt had provided for this purpose.

Carefully as we might, we covered the grave so as not to arouse suspicion of our presence and evil deed we had just completed. The grave returned to its original condition, Minister Pitt entreated us to move the wagon outside the holy cemetery grounds and into the nearby woods replete with unconsecrated ground. Here Minister Pitt performed a strange ritual.

From under his cloak he drew out a length of chain. He explained that this chain, blessed in the holy water of the baptismal font, we were to wrap around the coffin to prevent the unholy body within from ever being released. We followed his instruction and wrapped the chain once around the coffin.

Next he produced a lock, and thus he prayed "This lock, blessed by me in conjunction with the Holy Mother Church, will seal your fate to lie in this coffin for all eternity." We then dug a grave in the woods and dropped the coffin, wrapped in chain, into the depths.

Once again Minister Pitt prayed "Oh unholy evil I condemn you in the name of the Son, Jesus, to remain in the region between heaven and hell forever." At this he sprinkled holy water into the grave and continued. "Oh unholy evil I condemn you in the name of the Holy Ghost to remain in the region between heaven and hell forever." Once again he sprinkled holy water and said for the third time, "Oh unholy evil I condemn you in the name of God the Almighty to remain in the region between heaven and hell forever." As he was about to sprinkle holy water onto the grave, a lightning bolt appeared from a clear moonlit sky and struck the large oak tree not 10 feet from the grave site, splitting the tree fully in half and leaving a two foot scorch mark from the tree to the head of the grave.

We all jumped back in fright as this sign compelled us to complete our task as quickly as possible. Minister Pitt administered the last of his holy water into the grave which Mr. Waggoner and I quickly buried. We tried, as best we might, to hide the grave and the scorched earth in hopes that no one would find our dastardly deed and hold us as grave robbers.

When the last spade of earth fell upon the grave Minister Pitt declared, "Now she is held prisoner between heaven and hell unless released by a ghost talker, and they will never find her grave. Come, we must be off before we rouse suspicion of what evil we have done this day."

And so we three left the woods, returning to our homes and never speaking again of the deed we did that night.

"What the hell have we done?" I said, my voice barely above whisper

"Calm down, Robbie. You are acting like Mark. Look, we now know that this Anne Jefferies was real and some real strange things happened to her. So let's put these books back before anyone knows we read them and head home. From there we can decide what to do, but for now I think we need to get out of here. Agreed?

"Agreed," we said in unison. Mark headed out to put one book back while Roger and I returned the others. We met back at the front entrance near Mrs. Holiday's desk.

We tried to sneak past but she looked up a pleasantly asked, "Well, did you find out all you needed about Anne Jefferies?"

"Yes, we did," I replied. 'And more' I thought to myself.

"Well, you all come back anytime you like. I love to see my best and brightest in the library anytime," she said and waved us goodbye.

We walked down the front steps of the building and the rest of the way home in silence, each lost in our own thoughts of what we read and learned about the mysterious Anne Jefferies. When we got to my house, Roger turned to his brother and me and said, "Not a word of this to anyone. We have to decide what this means and what the witch or whatever she is wants. Promise, not a word."

"I swear," came the cautious reply.

"OK, then tomorrow we figure this out once and for all." With that, he put Mark in a headlock and rubbed the top of his head and pulled him toward their house. I headed into the house to get ready for supper and another sleepless night.

Chapter 28

The next day the guys came over right after lunch and we went directly down to the basement to discuss what we learned about Anne Jefferies. "I thought about this all night," Roger began. "What we know is this: Ann was real, she was a witch or something and she could tell the future. She also saw fairies and did not need food to survive. She was imprisoned in her grave and she wants freedom."

"Ok, so what good does that do us?" I questioned.

"Hang on. I am just going over what we know; what it means we need to figure out."

Mark chimed in, "I say we use the board again and find out what she wants and then decide. Maybe she wants to help us or tell us our future. So far she seems ok and in her story she healed people and told them the future. There was nothing bad or dangerous, right?"

After a moment of thought Roger said, "Well, he's right. So far, there has been nothing to indicate Anne was bad, or malevolent as the book warned. She did help people and she did not want fame or fortune so I agree. Let's give it one more try and see what she wants." So once again we went about setting the room for another session at the Ouija board. By now everyone knew their job in setting the room and, in less than ten minutes, Roger and I were once again knee to knee with the board on our lap while Mark was seated near the candle ready to transcribe that day's messages. And so we began.

Roger and I rested our fingers lightly on the planchette and slowly began to rotate the pointer in circles around the board. As I was getting ready to ask the first question, the planchette began once again to move rapidly on its own. It moved first in large circles, then in figure eights, and finally began to settle on individual letters.

NOWYOUKNOW

Mark translated, "Now you know."

"Know what?" I asked.

THETRUTH

Came the reply.

"So, you can tell the future?

The planchette glided over to the printed work YES on the board.

"Will you tell ours?"

YESFORAPRICE

"What price?"

WEWILLSEEASKNOW

"Ok, then start with Roger. What is his future?"

At this Roger perked up. "Why me? I'm not sure I want this thing to tell my future. What will she want in return?" It was too late to complain the planchette had already started moving rapidly and spelled out the reply

HERBDOCTOR

Translating the message, Mark said quizzically "Herb doctor. What is that?"

"I don't know, maybe it was some kind of job back when Anne was alive. You're next." I then asked, "What is Mark's future?"

MANOFLAWS

"Man of flaws. Great, I am going to be a jerk."

"Let me see that," I said reaching for the notebook. "Not flaws, laws. You are going to be a man of laws, like a lawyer maybe."

"That's much better." Mark laughed, much happier with his future.

"Your turn," Roger said matter-of-factly.

At first I hesitated. I didn't know why but I was a little scared. I took a deep breath and let it out slowly to build up my courage. Hesitatingly I asked, "What is my future?" Nothing happened. I asked again and still nothing.

Roger chided, "Well, looks like you have no future," which caused Mark to chuckle and me to worry. "Ask again."

And so I did. "What is my future?" I asked more demandingly. This time the planchette began to move
without any preamble it spelled out:

APRICEMUSTBEPAID

"What does that mean? A price must be paid," said Mark after translating the message. 'What price?"
The planchette began to move again.

FREEDOM

Freedom. Freedom from what? I thought to myself. As we sat there the planchette began once again to move rapidly spelling out word after word.

FUTURESCANCHANGEPAYMENOWORPAYTHEPRICELATER

It took a few minutes for Mark to translate. Futures can change; pay me now or pay the price later.
We sat there for a minute or two trying to figure out the message when once again the planchette started another message:

THEREAREMANYFUTURESIWILLTELLYOUONE
AMOTHERDIESATTWENTYONE
FOURYEARSLATERFOLLOWSASON

This was the longest message and it took all three of us to figure out what it said. After a few tries we came up with:

'There are many futures, I will tell you one. A mother dies at twenty one, four years later follows a son.'

We all sat there stunned. We had no mothers who were twenty one, so we were safe there. So who was the son who would die four years later? We had no idea. Roger was the first to voice an opinion "This thing is

96

messing with us now. It makes no sense. A future is a future. It doesn't change, right?"

"I have no idea," I mumbled, "but she is talking about me."

So once again, we turned back to the board and, moving the planchette in small circles, I asked, "You want freedom. How can we give you freedom?"

YOUARETHEKEY

"Key? What key? I don't have a key."

"No, not have a key. You are a key." Mark said excitedly. Pointing at the letters he wrote in the notebook. "You are the key."

Now I was stunned, scared, and a little pissed off all at once. I looked up at the ceiling and shouted, "Look, Anne, or whoever you are, I am no key and you will never be free from whatever holds you so bug out."

"Hey, be careful. We have no idea what this Anne can do," cautioned Roger.

"What the hell can she do?" I shouted back to hide my growing fear. "She is dead, not real, gone whatever. She can't hurt us and I'm getting a little tired of wasting my time with this stupid board."

Without warning, and with no question asked, the planchette moved for the last time that day:

IAMHERE

At this instant several things happened all at once. The light bulb in the lamp in the corner exploded. The candle we had in the middle of the room blew out. Mark jumped and tossed his notebook into the air hitting Roger in the head, causing him to jump in the darkness knocking over the Ouija board. The planchette hit me in the chest causing me to jump, knocking over the chair I was sitting on which caused me to fall backwards. I then crashed to the floor and hit my head on the hard cement floor. Everyone was shocked silent. Then, all at once, we jumped up and ran out of the basement. We shoved each other out of the way as we clawed our way up the side stairs leading to the driveway and freedom from that damn board.

So there we stood, in the driveway, bent over as if we were going to puke. The three of us were breathing so hard it was like we just ran five miles. I was huffing, Roger was coughing, and Mark looked like he was crying and trying not to show it. Slowly, things calmed down. Our breathing slowed and our heads cleared. Mark wiped his nose on his sleeve. I finally took a deep breath and said, "We have to go back down there and clean this up before anyone finds the Ouija Board. If they do we will have some explaining to do and I do not want to go there."

"There is no way I am going back down there," Mark whined.

"Robbie's right. We all have to go down and put the board away and clean up before we are in trouble with the living!" Roger tried to joke as he put Mark in a headlock and started to drag him to the door.

Mark fought hard against his brother. He was really scared. Roger let him go and I could see, for the first time, compassion in Roger's eyes. "OK, fine, OK. Robbie and I will clean up. You head home and not a word to anyone, promise?"

With relief in his eyes, Mark said, "Promise," and he headed off across the driveway and into their house.

"Come on, let's get this over with." So we headed cautiously down the stairs, expecting to see I don't know what. The only light to guide our way came through the basement window. Of course there was nothing to see but some chairs knocked over and a broken light bulb. So Roger and I silently went about the chore of cleaning up from the session. Roger put the chairs back into the kitchen while I swept up the broken glass. Roger went through the ritual of putting the Ouija Board away as I went into the workshop store room to get a fresh bulb. Soon the room was as before with no signs that anything happened.

There we stood in the kitchen when Roger broke the silence, "I think we have to destroy that thing."

"You took the words right out of my mouth. But how do we do that?"

"Tomorrow we get that book of yours and find out. But we do it someplace else in case Anne somehow finds out and then we are in more trouble."

"How is a dead person going to find out?"

"Look, I have no idea about any of this anymore," Roger said forcefully. "All I know is this is wrong and we need to stop it. We may have gone too far or it's all bullshit. Either way, we end it now before something really happens. OK?"

"You're right. Tomorrow we get the book and find out what we need to do to end this once and for all."

Roger slapped me on the back, said, "bye," and headed home. I took one last look around to make sure everything was in its place and headed upstairs. Tomorrow this will all be a bad memory, I told myself. Boy was I ever wrong!

Chapter 29

That night we sat down to supper of homemade baked ziti with a side of meatballs. I just loved my mom's meatballs. I could eat them every day. It was a tradition in our family for all of us to sit at the dinner table and enjoy the company of family. My dad always said that "family was the most important thing. Money is nice but family is everything." So though we did not have much money, we did have a strong family and always great food!

That night everyone seemed happy and relaxed. We chatted about how our day went. I had to lie a little as I certainly couldn't reveal what happened in the basement earlier in the day. Papa told us about his job in the city and how he hoped to get a promotion soon so he would be able to make a little more money and buy us some nice things for Christmas later that year. It was an idyllic evening until we heard a sound in the kitchen. It sounded like a scream mixed with a cry. The cry was like something in pain or very angry. Papa and I turned toward the sound but we were shielded from the kitchen by a small closed door. Papa threw his napkin onto the table and both of us were on our feet.

"Vincenza, are you Ok?" Papa called as he opened the swinging door. I was right behind him, so close that when he stopped in mid stride I walked right into him. I was shielded from seeing what he saw, but I soon spun to his side and stood there in shock.

Mama was on the floor, passed out. She was not moving and barely breathing. Quickly Papa dropped to one knee and caressed her head and called to me to go and get Uncle Rosario. I stood there for another second when he shouted, "Now, go now!"

I ran out the side door into the driveway. I hit the sidewalk at a full gallop and turned right. I ran as hard and fast as I could down the block past five houses to the house at 2220 East Fifth Street, where my aunt and uncle lived.

Fortunately, in the close knit Italian section of Brooklyn, people rarely locked their front door. I climbed the stoop steps in two jumps. I hit the screen door and pulled open the inner door in one swift motion and screamed, "Uncle Rosario, come quickly. Something happened to Mama. Help, Mama is hurt."

Uncle Rosario must have been at his own dinner table because when he came into the parlor where I was shouting he still had his napkin tucked under his chin. "Robbie, slow down, son. What happened?"

I was out of breath and my heart was pounding. I almost couldn't get any words out I was breathing so hard. I finally stuttered, "Mama passed out in the kitchen and Papa told me to get you right away. Please come with me. Mama needs you."

My Aunt Emanuela came into the parlor wringing her hand with the dish towel. She must have been working in the kitchen when all the commotion happened. "Robbie, what's wrong? You're a mess."

"Mama passed out in the kitchen. Papa is with her and he asked me to get Uncle Rosario to help. We are wasting time. Come with me please, Uncle. Hurry," I pleaded.

"Ok, let's go and see what is wrong." At that, Uncle Rosario and I rushed out the door. Aunt Emanuela followed close behind. I tugged my uncle along to help hurry him up. We arrived at the house and headed right to the kitchen.

Before we got to the kitchen, we were shocked at the sight of Mama and Papa sitting quietly at the dinner table. Papa was holding Mama's hand and lovingly stroking her cheek and speaking soothingly to her in Italian. Uncle Rosario looked at the scene in front of him and then looked at me sternly. Before he could say a word to me, I said, "Uncle, she really was laying on the floor in the kitchen. She was not moving. Papa, tell him."

My father looked up at us and he said, "Roberto is right. She was on the floor. She slipped and fell and was not moving when we found her. I sent Roberto to get help and, when he left, she opened her eyes and asked me, 'Why am I on the floor?' She had no idea what happened. I can only thank the good Lord that she is all right."

At that, Uncle Rosario walked the few steps to the table and stroked my mother's hair and asked, "Vincenza, are you sure you are all right?"

"Why the big fuss? "she replied as if nothing happened. "I am fine. I don't even remember falling. I have no bumps or scratches anywhere. I am fine, really I am."

Breathing a sigh of relief Papa got up, kissed Mama on the cheek, gave her a pat on her head, and walked Uncle Rosario to the door. I could hear him apologizing for disturbing my uncle's supper. As their voices faded, I turned to Mama and looked into her eyes to see if she was really all right.

For one split second I did not recognize my mother's face. She seemed different. She had a smile on her face, not a happy smile but more like a sneer. Her eyes, her eyes were wrong. Mama had beautiful brown eyes and, as I looked into her gaze, I could swear her eyes were a deep blue.

Before I could catch my breath, her face changed back to her own and she said, "Roberto, I am fine. I don't remember what happened. I was on the floor with your papa next to me and I had no idea why. I am fine now so don't worry. Promise?"

I promised, but I didn't know how I was going to be able to keep such a promise, because I was worried down to the bone.

Chapter 30

When the guys came over the next day before lunch, I chose not to say anything about the events of the night before. If this Anne Jefferies had anything to do with this, I didn't know. All I knew was today was the day we would figure out how to end all this and get back on with the rest of our lives. I dug out the book we had found and put it in a shopping bag. I called to mama to tell her we were going to the library and we headed out the door. Mama called, "You boys be careful and don't get into any trouble at the library. Be home by supper."

I called back, "Ok," and we were off.

Once again, as we entered at the front of the library, there was Mrs. Holiday firmly entrenched at her desk. Today she was decked out in a bright red blouse, white slacks and a cardigan sweater neatly arranged at the back of her chair. When she looked up and saw us come in, her countenance brightened and, smiling, she half whispered, "Twice in the same summer you are in my library? If I did not know better I would say you have evil on your minds." Then she laughed and continued "How can I help you today?"

Roger built up his courage and replied, "Nothing today, Mrs. Holiday. We have some work to do to get ready for school in three weeks and we felt it best to come here."

'Well, isn't that just great. Our best students getting a head start on the rest of the children. Good for you. Let me know if you need help," she said cheerily as she settled her reading glasses back on her nose and looked back down into the books she was checking back into the stacks.

"Yes, Mrs. Holiday," I called as we quietly and quickly rushed past before she noticed the bag in my hand and asked to see what we had in it. It was against the rules to bring a bag into the library. Often some of the public school kids would bring in glue or scissors and go into the back of the stacks and damage the books. There was no way we wanted Mrs. Holiday see the book we were carrying for fear of the questions she would ask.

Once we were safely past the front desk we quietly headed down to the reading room. Once again we had the room completely to ourselves. We found a table near the back of the room, turned on the table light and took out the book and laid it on the table.

"Ok, now what?" asked Mark.

'You get out the notebook and pencils, Robbie you look in the book to see if there are instructions as to how we destroy a Ouija board, and I will make sure no one comes in," Roger said, setting out our tasks

I opened the book and looked through the table of contents. Nothing about how to get rid of a Ouija board. There were chapters on history, a section on instructions for use, but nothing on how to get rid of the thing.

I turned to the back of the book to see if the index was any help and nothing there either on destruction. I looked at Roger and said, "I can't find any instructions on how to destroy this thing. What do we do now?"

"Let me give it a try," Roger whispered as he reached for the book. He opened the book and randomly looked at several pages. He stopped to read one paragraph aloud,

Since there is no way of truly knowing if a spirit is good or evil, it is important to keep in mind that the spirits will often use false flattery and lies to gain your confidence.

"Great, so that's a big help," Mark whined. "That doesn't help us at all."

"Shut up. I am trying to find something," Roger snapped.

"Hey, here is something." Roger read again,

Sometimes an evil spirit will permanently inhabit a board. When this happens no other spirits will be able to communicate through that particular board. When this happens the board must be *destroyed to prevent the malevolent spirit from hurting anyone.*

"Nice to know, now how do we do it?" Mark said, his frustration and some fear beginning to show. "If the book says we have to destroy the board, it has to tell us how, right?"

"I don't know, let's keep looking." As he turned the page he began to read again

BEWARE if the planchette begins to count down through the numbers or makes a figure eight before replying to a question or moves to all four corners of the board and refuses to respond. An evil spirit has been contacted.

Roger looked at me and said, "I definitely remember the figure eights before the planchette moved, right?"

Not saying a word, I nodded my agreement.

"I don't remember the four corners thing, do you?"

I shook my head no, still unable to find a voice.

Roger continued to read.

Ouija boards that are not properly disposed of will allow the spirit to go free and haunt the owner. NEVER burn a Ouija board, it will scream. If you hear the scream you will be dead in three days.

"Ok, so what's next, what do we do?" Mark nervously asked, a little more fear coming through.

"Nothing. That is the end of the chapter and there is nothing else on the subject," a frustrated Roger said, flipping through the pages to find something else we needed to do.

After a few more minutes, we put the book down feeling defeated. There were no instructions on how to destroy the board. We were convinced we had an evil spirit and we were doomed somehow. Here we were in a library, filled with references and books; surely there must be something we could find.

"Look, let's head upstairs and to the card catalogue. There just has to be something here we could use to find what we need."

"Good idea," the boys said in one voice.

"Let's avoid Mrs. Holiday," cautioned Roger. "If she finds out what we are looking for, we're dead."

So we headed up the back stairs to the second floor. The back stairs let us out right near the card catalogue so we didn't have to go near Mrs. Holiday. "Mark you stay a little back and keep an eye on Holiday. If she heads this way whistle and Robbie and I will hide what we are doing," Roger ordered as he and I headed to the card catalogue.

As Mark stood watch, I asked Roger, "What do we look under?"

"I don't know. Just start looking."

And so we did. After about half an hour of opening and closing drawers, Roger excitedly called to me. "Robbie, come here quick. I think I have it."

I came over from my section of the card catalogue and looked at the drawer marked "O". The card in Roger's hand was entitled "A True History of Ouija – A Trip to the Paranormal."

"Why that one?" I asked. I didn't see the connection.

Roger read the rest of the card, "A scientific study of the Ouija board, how to use and be protected from it."

"Bingo. That has to be it."

Mark saw the commotion and came over. "Guys, you are making too much noise. Holiday will be here any minute if you two don't quiet down." Looking at the card in Roger's hand, Mark continued, "What's that?"

"Hopefully, the answer we need. Come on. The book is on the third floor according to the locator. Let's get the book and get out of here."

So we trotted up the back stairs to the third floor and the dusty older stacks. Roger had the card in his hands, a definite no no. You are never to remove a card from the drawer. You are supposed to write the number down on the slips of paper next to the card catalogue, but we were so excited we took the card and ran off. Up one stack and down the other until we got to the right section and there it was, exactly where the locator said it would be. Roger reached up and slowly pulled the book down from the rack. The book was only about an inch thick and about eight inches tall. Roger flipped it to the last page and saw there were only 117 pages.

"There is not much book here," Roger said, a little disappointed. "It better have what we need or we could be in bigger trouble. It's getting late and we have to get home soon or we will be in more trouble.

Look we are never going to get through this here. And besides Mrs. Holiday is going to get suspicious soon and ask what we are doing so what's say we "borrow" the book and read it at home and return it later?"

"Steal a book from the library. Are you crazy? We'll be caught," Mark said.

"Look, we have the shopping bag. Holiday did not say anything when we came in, why would she say anything on the way out?"

"No way."

Roger stepped in, "Robbie's right. We have to get out of here and the only way is to take the book. Robbie, you carry the bag. Mark, you get on my side and, when we get to Mrs. Holiday, you stay between me and her so she can't see me and I will put the book under my shirt. It's real thin and no one will notice."

"I don't know," Mark stammered.

Roger reached out and slapped Mark on the back of the head and looked hard into his face and said, "That's what we are doing, so buck up. Now everyone, ready we're out of here."

We made the necessary preparations. Roger stuffed the book in his shirt, I held the shopping bag with our other book and we headed down the stairs to the first floor. At the bottom of the stairs, we took our positions. Mark and Roger side by side, me close behind with the bag on my left, shielding it from view. When we turned the corner, we all breathed a collective sigh of relief when we saw Mrs. Holiday's station abandoned.

"She must be in the bathroom or making the rounds,' assumed Roger. "Quick, get out, but don't run."

Walking together, as if we were one body, we were out the door and down the steps. We did not break rank until a block from the school when we stopped to catch our breath. We walked the rest of the way home virtually in silence each to his own thoughts. We stole a book from the library, but we had no options. We needed the book and could not have someone ask us why. It would just be too hard to explain. So along with everything else, we were now thieves as well.

Chapter 31

The next day was Saturday. My parents went shopping, as was their usual tradition. Roger and Mark came to my house in the early afternoon with the book. I met them at the side door. Roger tried to come in but I stopped him, saying, "Look, maybe we should not do this here. The Ouija board is in the basement and what if Anne Jefferies is still here and she finds out we are trying to destroy the board? Maybe we should go to your basement to be safe."

Roger thought for a minute and replied, "Sure, why not." He spun on his heels and headed back across the driveway. I followed Roger to their house. Soon Mark joined us, and we were all in the basement looking at the book.

Mark, once again, was designated as our scribe as Roger and I sat on the threadbare couch, the book between us. Once again we started with the table of contents to see if there was a chapter on destruction. Nothing. We turned back to the index. No help there either. Frustrated we started to read, there were only 117 pages so there had to be an answer there somewhere. We skipped to the middle of the book and Roger began to read

Ouija boards can be dangerous. They can bring in all types of spirits, good and evil. Sometimes they can open a portal to allow evil to come through. To prevent further harm to the owner the portal must be closed and a ritual must be followed exactly in order to assure the destruction of the portal followed by the destruction of the board itself

"Yes, we got it. Finally here are the directions to destroy this damn thing. Mark, write this down." Roger continued to read and Mark wrote down every word:

When you destroy a Ouija board you must take great care to do it correctly or there can be dire consequences to the users
Prepare the following:
Sea Salt
Incense or other burning fragrance
Lighter fluid
Matches
5 small stones 2 or 3 inches in size
A very sharp scissor or sharp knife

"Where are we going to get that stuff!" exclaimed Mark. "We don't have sea salt."

Thinking for a minute, I said, 'Yes, we do. Mom has some in the kitchen. She uses it for cooking sometimes. I have some incense that I got for my birthday so we can use that. Matches are not a problem and there are stones everywhere. Look we got it all." I tried to assure Mark and Roger continued to read:

Holy water
A small spade or shovel

"I suppose you have holy water in your sink," Mark whined.

Now, that I don't have.
Roger piped up, "Tomorrow is Sunday; we can get some from church."

"And what are we going to say we need it for, if we get caught? Should we add "liar" to our growing list of offenses?" I said. "Remember, Sister Angelina said it was a sin for a kid to play with holy water. So we can't just walk up and take some, we have to be real careful."

"So, we start with books from the library and now we are stealing holy water. What next, we rob a bank?"

Mark was getting on our nerves with his whining. Roger turned to him and said, "Look, we're all in this now up to our neck. If you don't want to help, fine. Get out. Robbie and I will do it ourselves and leave Anne Jefferies all to you. Do you want that?"

"NO!" Mark shouted. "No, I'll help", and he didn't say another word while we studied the instructions for destroying the board.

"So, now what?" I asked.

"Let me see. Ok, here we go" and he continued reading:

Until you can properly seal the portal, pack the Ouija board upside down in the original box. You need to go to a quiet area where you will not be disturbed. Remove any mirrors from the area

110

or the spirit may try to flee into the mirror. Do not discuss what you are going to do out loud as the spirit that came through the portal may hear

"Oh no. That's a problem. We have been reading this out loud all this time."

"Too late now." Roger continued to read:

Make sure your last session with the Ouija board was ended properly. You must make the spirit end the session by moving the planchette over the words Good Bye printed on the board. If not you will need to open another session and properly close the session before you can proceed.

"I don't think we did that. Remember? We all jumped up when the light bulb broke and Mark headed home and you and I cleaned up," I recalled.

'You're right. Ok, so we have a real quick session and close the board. If we don't do this right, I have no idea what could happen." Roger continued reading:

When everything is ready light the incense or fragrance sticks and let the smoke fan over all present and begin with a prayer
Dear God of light please protect us all from the evil we have encountered.
When the prayer is finished take the board out of the box and put it face up on the floor being careful not to let the planchette come in direct contact with the board.
Place the planchette upside down on the floor next to the board at the cardinal point (North).
Next sprinkle the sea salt in a circle around the board and planchette saying
No spirit can cross this line.
Place the 5 stones around the board in a 5 pointed star pattern beginning with the cardinal point (North)
As you form the star with the next 4 stones say:
I call for Raphael, Guardian of the East
I call for Michael, Guardian of the South
I call for Gabriel, Guardian of the West
I call for Urel, Guardian of the North
Please hear my prayer.
Please assist me in the destruction of this board.
Send back any spirits that have crossed over using this portal of darkness.
I ask that this portal of darkness be forever closed by the Hands of Light.
Now cut the board into 7 pieces of different size using the scissor or knife.

Break the planchette into 7 pieces.
Cover the pieces of the planchette with silk and spray on the lighter fluid.
Light the silk and continue to let it burn until there is no trace of the planchette or the silk.
Take the 7 pieces of the broken board and dig 7 holes at least a foot deep.
Place a piece of the board into each hole sprinkling holy water on the pieces of the buried board saying the following prayer:
I ask that the portal of darkness be forever closed by the Hands of Light.
Bury each piece of the board and stamp down the soil to hide the hole.
The purpose of this is to make sure the board and the planchette can never be used again.
Once the ritual is complete the portal of darkness should be closed.

Exhausted, Roger looked up and closed the book. "That's all it says." We sat there in silence stunned by what we read and what we had to go through to close the portal. We had one more session ahead of us, even if only to close the session properly so we could destroy the board.

Chapter 32

The next day was Sunday, and I got up way earlier than normal. I had work to do. The first problem was getting holy water. Since we normally went to church on Sundays, I would have access to holy water, but how do we "borrow" some? I thought for a while and came up with a plan I hoped would work. In the center of the church was a short aisle that led to the bathroom and the baptistery where there was a font filled with holy water used for baptism. It seemed simple enough; I could sneak away for a few minutes, telling my parents I was going to use the bathroom. I could dip a small empty bottle into the font and get enough holy water for the job ahead. Perfect, or so I thought.

As is tradition in our family, we did not eat before church. We never ate on Sunday morning before receiving the body of Christ at Holy Communion. As a reward for having endured another fast, we would come home to a traditional Italian Sunday meal. So, skipping breakfast, we headed off as a family for a leisurely stroll to church.

As is another tradition, we met Uncle Rosario, Aunt Emanuela, and, of course, my cousin Linda. Linda complained all the way to church. She was much too old and modern to be going to church with her family. She wanted to go with her friends, aka the boys. Even at a tender age of sixteen, her only thought was of boys, ever the concern of her father.

So we walked, Linda leading the way, and me bringing up the rear with hopes of finding Roger and Mark so I could share with them the plan to get the holy water. When we got to the steps of Our Lady of Grace Church, I saw the boys on the steps with their parents looking around for me. I headed over and, pulling them away from their parents, I quickly explained the plan.

Mark, ever the worrier, said, "Are you really going to steal holy water from the baptismal font? If you get caught you're in big trouble."

"If I don't, then I am sure we are all in bigger trouble with the witch."

After a second of contemplation, all he could say was, "True."

The question was 'when do I make my move?' If I did it now, my parents would be less suspicious. They would figure it was better to go to the bathroom now than in the middle of mass. But, if I did it now with all the people going to their seats, I had a higher probability of getting caught. Weighing the risks for a moment, I decided to go now. So I made my move.

"Mom, I need to go to the bathroom. I will meet you and Papa in church. OK?"

"Oh, Roberto, must you go now? The church is filling up and Father will start mass in a few minutes. How will you find us?"

"I will find you. I really have to use the bathroom." And, before she could object, I took off at a trot up the stairs and up to the hall directly to the baptistery.

There was no one in the hall since everyone was heading through the center doors into the main church. Perfect, I thought. As I walked the last ten feet through the hall I heard someone call, "Roberto!"

I turned to the right and standing directly in front of the baptismal font was Father Murphy. I was stunned silent.

"What is the matter, Roberto? The devil has your tongue?" chided Father.

"No sir, I mean Father. I was heading to the bathroom before Mass." I recovered quickly.

"Good, I am glad you are here. I need an altar boy and the Good Lord sent me you. Hurry now and go to the sacristy and get ready."

"But, Father, my parents, they will worry where I went."

"It will be hard for them to miss you, Roberto. You will be on the altar with me. Now go," he commanded. "I do not want to delay Mass."

"Yes, Father" I said, disappointed that I could not stop and get the holy water. I headed to the sacristy as I was told and donned the black and white vestments of an altar boy. As we assembled at the entrance to the church and the organ began to play, I could see my mother looking around for me. I knew she would be mad if I missed the beginning of mass, but as the processional began, the entire church assembly turned to face the procession. I could see her countenance change until she was beaming to

114

see me leading the procession holding the crucifix high in the air for all to see. She went from disappointment to pride in a second. I wonder what she would have thought if Father Murphy had caught me stealing holy water instead. Anyway, I was still in a fix. There was no way I would be able to get back to the font and get the holy water now. I needed a second plan.

Father Murphy, as always, performed a solemn ceremony. He spoke the words clearly and with a deep sense of emotion. He spoke from the heart. Today's homily was all about "the evil among us." I froze. I felt like he was talking directly at me. Father began, "The world is filled with evil. Evil is everywhere. The devil and his minions are among us. They walk among us. They speak to us. They lie to us. And we believe them." I was astonished. It was as if he knew what we were doing.

"The devil wants to control us. He offers us our hearts' desire, predictions of the future. All lies," he shouted, slamming his hand on the pulpit. I almost jumped out of my seat and barely missed knocking over the tray with the wine of Communion sitting at my right. "The devil and his demons are all liars. Do not listen to them. Resist temptation. Turn to our lord Jesus Christ for he is the light and the Son of the one true God. Jesus is the truth and the way."

The sermon continued, but I must have stopped listening. I sat there thinking. Did we conjure the devil or maybe a demon? This can't be good. We have got to find a way to stop this thing and destroy that damn board, but how? We still needed holy water.

I performed the rest of my duties as altar boy from rote. I assisted in the trans-substantiation rite; changing bread and wine into the Body and Blood of Christ. I assisted in the process of Communion, holding the gold platen below the chin of the communicant. I washed the gold cups and cleared the table of the Lord. All the while I was thinking, "Am I in league with the devil or a demon?"

When Mass was ended and the congregation rose to leave, I departed the altar and headed back to the sacristy to put away my gown and the rest of the linens from the altar. I was still thinking about how to get some holy water when Father Murphy suddenly appeared at the entrance to the sacristy, as if by magic.

"Roberto," he called and I jumped at the sound.

"My, you are distracted today, young man. I scared you twice in one day. Too bad I could not do that more often." He laughed.

"Yes, Father" I stammered, not knowing what to say.

He looked at me quizzically for a moment, then smiling he said, "I wanted to thank you for the help today," reaching out as if to shake my hand.

I reached out with my right hand to meet his and, instead of shaking my hand, he grabbed it with his left hand and placed a small vial in my palm.

"What is this, Father?" I asked, looking at the vial in my hand.

"It is holy water from the sacred spring at Lourdes. You know the place where the Virgin Mary appeared. I wanted you to have this as a way of saying thank you for all you have done for me today."

I was stunned again. Holy water from a sacred spring. This was much better than holy water 'stolen' from the baptismal font.

"Thank you, Father. Thank you very much," I said, shaking his hand a little too long.

"That's all right, Roberto. Now run along and find your parents," he said, pealing me off his hand and turning me toward the door.

"Thank you again, Father," I called excitedly as I left the sacristy. Now I would not have to commit another sin by stealing holy water. I hurried out of the sacristy, down the main aisle and out the front door to find my parents chatting with my uncle and aunt. Linda had already disappeared.

"Well, there you are my little altar boy," beamed Mama. "I was so proud of you today."

"I was corralled by Father Murphy at the last minute," I protested. "Can we go now?" I asked, hoping to get home before anyone asked any questions about the vial of holy water from Lourdes still in my hand.

"Yes, let's go home, get out of these clothes and sit down to another of Mama's Sunday meals," said Papa. "I am starving." And we all turned to walk home.

Chapter 33

The next day we began the task of collecting the rest of the items we needed we could complete the ritual and destroy the Ouija Board once and for all. I met the guys at their house and shared with them my good fortune of having holy water.

"Holy water from Lourdes!" exclaimed Mark as he viewed the vial from several different angles. "This has got to be better than water we might have stolen from the church."

"Yeah," I agreed much relieved I did not have to steal the water. "Now we don't have to worry if stolen water won't work," I tried to joke.

"Great, now what about the rest of the stuff we need?" asked Roger. We headed down to their basement for fear that if we met in my basement, where we kept the board, the witch Anne Jefferies might find out. We all had arms full of the required items. We carefully placed our cache on the floor and took inventory.

"Holy water, matches, candles, sharp scissors," I began when Roger cut in.

"I also brought a small hand saw; I figured the board may be a little hard to cut with scissors"

"Good idea." I continued, "Hand saw, spade, incense and matches. We still need something to light the fire."

"Well, lighting the fire is not a problem. There is some fuel in the garage we can borrow, but how and where are we going to burn it?" asked Roger.

"Good point," I said.

We thought for a while and Mark came up with an idea. "We have a small barbeque in the garage that we used to use for hot dogs. Maybe we could use that?"

"Great idea. No one is using it anymore so no one will know we borrowed it either," offered Roger, slapping Mark good heartedly on his back.

"Ok, we are still missing sea salt," added Mark.

"No, we are not," I said, reaching into my pocket. "I took this from Mom's kitchen supply." I proudly showed the guys a small box labeled Fresh Sea Salt.

"Good, so are we missing anything? "asked Roger as I went over the list again.

"One thing, five small stones to complete the ritual."

"Now, that could be a problem. Where are we going to get five small stones?" questioned Mark.

Thinking for a minute, I said, "We can head over to Coney Island Pier and pull some small stones from under the pier. They will be smooth and we can easily find five stones small enough for our purposes."

Mark lite up and said, "Wait here. I have a better idea." And before we could say anything, he jumped up and dashed off and ran up the stairs and out of the basement.

'What got into him?" I asked Roger.

"No idea."

Seconds later we heard Mark jumping down the steps. Breathless, he ran into the basement. He was holding a brown paper bag. Excitedly he thrust out his hand and said, "Look in here. I have been collecting smooth stones from the beach at Coney. Maybe there is enough here for what we need." He turned the bag over and spilled out about a dozen rocks.

"These are perfect," said Roger, searching the collection and picking through the stones looking for five that would suit our purpose. "Here we go. These five will do. Robbie, go over the list one more time and make sure we have everything."

Doing as I was bidden, I went over the list once again and recited, "Matches, fuel, candles, incense, spade, scissors, saw, sea salt, five stones and holy water. Check and double check, we have it all."

After a moment of silence, we gathered the items into one paper bag I brought for this purpose.

"Now what?" asked Mark cautiously.

"Good question. I guess we get the board, do one final session and close the board properly, then destroy it," said Roger matter-of-factly.

"There is no way we can do this in my basement. My folks would kill me if I set a fire in the house," I said.

"Ok, then, we do this in the garage," replied Roger, giving this some obvious consideration. "We pick a Saturday when all our parents are shopping. We get the board, get the stuff and get it done. Agreed?"

"Agreed" we replied in unison.

Chapter 34

It was two passing Saturdays before both sets of parents were gone at the same time. Mine were out on their usual Saturday shopping errands and the Donato's were out visiting family. Finally we were alone and we were ready. At least we thought we were ready.

First we set up everything in the garage. There was an old card table with wobbly legs that we set up in the center of the garage. On this we prepared the candles and the incense. We put the stones in the center of the table and the bag of sea salt and holy water were placed where the wobble would not accidently spill them. Outside of the garage there was a small space between the garage and the neighbor's house where we had a small garden with a fig tree. We set up the old barbeque near the back, hidden by a fence and the tree. The fuel and the matches were on the ground nearby. We were set at last.

Looking over everything and finally satisfied with the results, quietly as if led by an unspoken voice, we turned and headed to my basement to get the board and finish this ritual. Silently we headed down the stairs only to be met by a blast of cold air. "What was that?" Mark asked as he led the way.

"Nothing," said Roger, giving his brother a slight shove. "Keep going" And so we did.

We retrieved the red wood box containing the Ouija board from its hiding place. As I lifted the box I thought I noticed that the box felt heavy. I mean heavier than usual. I quickly dismissed the idea as excitement playing a trick on me and hurried up the stairs and out into the driveway. Still in almost complete silence, we headed toward the garage. I could swear that with every step I took toward the garage the box, containing the Ouija Board, got heavier and heavier.

While Roger and I prepared to unpack the board for the final time, Mark took out his notes on the steps of the ritual. It was his job as our scribe to make sure we did everything exactly as the ritual required.

As we unpacked the board, I told Roger, "Now, we are going to do this quickly. We have to open a session and then, as quickly as we can, we force the board to say goodbye and get on with the you know what," careful not to mention our real purpose, in case the witch would hear.

"Got it. In and out, fast as we can."

"Everyone ready?' I asked sitting across from Roger with the board on our laps and the planchette carefully placed in the dead center of the board.

"Ready," came the reply, and so we began.

"Anne, Anne Jefferies are you here?" I asked beginning our session.

The planchette went wild. Moving first in circles and then in large figure eights. Finally it began to spell out words.
IKNOWWHATYOUAREDOING

Mark translated, 'I know what you are doing.' Before we could say anything the planchette moved again

STOP

"Ok, we will stop, goodbye," I said, trying to trick Anne into saying goodbye. The planchette moved in figure eights again
YOUWILLREGRETTHIS

"You will regret this," Mark translated. He continued, "She knows what we are doing."

"Shut up, stupid," Roger screamed, admonishing his brother. "We are not doing anything but saying goodbye." Again the planchette moved this time almost right out from under our hands, as if it no longer needed our contact.
IWILLBEFREE

We did not have to wait for a translation as now we were following the letters and speaking them out loud out of fear. I looked at Roger and tried to signal him to help me move the planchette directly over the printed word GOODBYE on the board. Roger somehow got my unspoken message as he nodded his head and slowly we moved the planchette toward GOODBYE.

The planchette took on a life of its own. First, it would not move at all, as if the planchette had been glued in place. Then, once again it moved wildly. This time both our hands did slip off, but that did not stop the movement. It spelled out once again

STOPIWILLBEFREE

I had an idea. What if we could distract Anne and somehow move the planchette over to GOODBYE? I didn't want to say this out loud so I said, "If you are here, Anne, prove it." I stared directly at Roger and caught his eye. He raised his eyebrow as if asking, 'what are you doing?' I looked at him and then moved my eyes deliberately over to GOODBYE printed on the board. I did this several times before Roger nodded his understanding.

"Yes, Anne, if you are truly here, prove it," called Roger following my lead.

Suddenly, the candle on the table lit up on its own. Mark shrieked, and Roger and I jumped. The table wobbled but nothing spilled. We felt the planchette lighten up and, in unison, Roger and I called out "goodbye" and quickly moved the planchette over the board to GOODBYE. Soon as we did that, we took our hands off the planchette. Out of nowhere we heard a shriek and then a scream and the entire garage shook. We knew we tricked Anne and closed the board. Now we had to finish the job.

Mark took out his notes on the destruction ritual, and we began. We moved over to the table and set the board face down in the center of the table. Since the candle was now already lit, Mark lit the incense. After a few minutes, the incense began to give off a fragrant smoke. We let this waft over us and we all said in unison "Dear God of Light, please protect us all from the evil we have encountered." Roger then carefully picked up the board and placed it face up on the garage floor, making sure that the board did not come in contact with the planchette as instructed. Mark then asked, "Which way is North? We need to place the planchette north of the board."

Roger pointed to the rear of the garage, and Mark carefully placed the planchette near the north corner of the board. I prepared the sea salt and sprinkled a circle around the board and planchette saying, "No spirit can cross this line."

As soon as I said these words, we heard another shriek and suddenly the candle flame flashed up as if it were sprayed with gas. Mark jumped and nearly knocked over the table.

"Careful. If you spill anything, no telling what will happen. We can't stop now, no matter what. Mark, what comes next?" Roger asked, trying to be calm, but failing as his voice cracked.
"The stones, the stones come next."

As Mark read the directions I placed the stones around the board in a five-pointed star pattern beginning with the cardinal point (North). As I did this Mark read out loud the following prayer,

> *I call for Raphael, Guardian of the East.*
> *I call for Michael, Guardian of the South.*
> *I call for Gabriel, Guardian of the West.*
> *I call for Urel, Guardian of the North.*
> *Please hear my prayer:*
> *Please assist me in the destruction of this board.*
> *Send back any spirits that have crossed over using this portal of darkness.*
> *I ask that this portal of darkness be forever closed by the Hands of Light.*

Again came a shriek and a rattle as if the entire garage was shifting off its foundation. "What's next?" yelled Roger over the shriek. "Quickly, what's the next step?"

"Cut the board into seven pieces," directed Mark. "Just start cutting the damn thing up."

I pulled out the scissors and soon found these to be useless. The board was made of hard wood and the scissors could do nothing. Roger picked up the board and started to saw through it with the small hand saw, but this was taking too long. With every stroke of the saw the shriek got louder and it seemed a wind began to circle inside the garage. I knew I had to do something, so I grabbed the board and slammed it over by knee breaking it in half. Roger grabbed one of the pieces as I slammed the other again over my knee. Now we had four pieces.

The shriek grew louder until it seemed to burn in our ears. We knew we needed to do something before everyone in the neighborhood heard the noise and came running to find out what we were doing.

We all three grabbed a piece and tried to break them over a knee, but they were too small and all I succeeded in doing was hurting my knee. "Now what?" I called over the shrieking noise.

"Hang on," called Roger over the maddening sound. "I have an idea. At this he ran to the back of the garage and came back half dragging and half carrying a large cinder block. "Use this," he shouted.

I saw what he had in mind. I took one piece of the board and, leaning it on the edge of the block; I pushed with all my might. I was rewarded with a sharp crack as the board broke. We had five pieces and we needed seven.

Mark grabbed another larger piece and flipped it over to me. I caught it with one hand and, bending down, I placed this piece on the block and pushed again. Nothing. Pushing harder and praying out loud for the strength, I heard another crack and now we had six pieces.

Looking at the remaining pieces, I knew that there was no way we were going to break another piece this way. Looking around I spied a small red brick. I had an idea. I leaned the largest piece I could find at an angle on the cinder block and hit the board with the brick. At first nothing happened. As I got ready to swing the brick again, Mark called out "STOP! Look, there on the floor is a small piece. That makes seven."

Sure enough, my attempt with the brick had caused a small piece to break off at the corner. The ritual did not say the pieces had to be large just that there had to be seven of them. Suddenly, as I bent down to pick up the piece, the shriek was silenced. There was not a sound anywhere. The wind inside the garage died down and it seemed calm.

I called out to Mark, "What is the next step?"

Mark fumbled with his notes. He almost dropped them, but he recovered and said, "We have to burn the planchette and the silk wrapping, and bury the seven pieces of the board and sprinkle them with salt."

"Ok, grab the planchette. I will take the pieces of the board and let's head outside to the barbeque."

So we headed out. Quickly, we went out of the garage, turned right, and hurried into the far reaches of the garden where we had set up the place to burn the planchette. Mark carried the planchette to the barbeque and dropped in the silk-wrapped planchette. Roger covered it with lighter fluid.

"Not so much!" I called. "We don't want to burn the garage down. Easy."

Roger stopped and, putting the fuel can down away from the fire, he grabbed a match. Striking it, he said, "Burn, Witch," and he threw the match onto the soaked silk. There was a flash of flame, followed by a whoosh and another wailing cry. Roger had really soaked the planchette and so it was only about a minute or two for the entire thing to be destroyed. As the planchette burned, the wailing first got louder, then softer and softer as the planchette finally burned to ashes. As the final lick of flame burned out, the shriek also died away.

"One final step," Mark said, almost at a whisper, "we bury the seven pieces of the board." For the burial we crawled out from the garden to a small space behind the garage. There was about a two- foot space behind our garage and the garage behind ours. There was no way anyone would be able to use this tiny spot of land so it was the perfect place to bury something that needed to stay buried. We had already prepared seven holes at least a foot deep. As Mark dropped a piece of the board into each hole, I sprinkled each piece with holy water and Roger added the sea salt. As we buried each piece, we recited the following prayer in unison, "I ask that the portal of darkness be forever closed by the Hands of Light."

As we buried the last piece and stomped down the soil over each hole, we breathed a collective sigh of relief. It was over. We picked up our tools, emptied out the barbecue, and cleaned up in the garage being careful to put everything back where it came from. When we were done, we stood at the garage door and surveyed the area to make sure we left no sign of anything having happened there. At that moment, we made a pact never to speak of this again to anyone, ever. We agreed and swore an oath.

Exhausted, we headed each to our own homes to clean up.

It was just about suppertime when my parents came home. Papa rubbed my head and said, "Roberto, what did you do all day?"

"Nothing, Papa. Really nothing," I lied. If they only knew the truth, I thought to myself. I remember I went to bed early that night and fell asleep. It was a deep dreamless sleep. It was the first good rest I had all summer.

Chapter 35

I woke up late the next morning. I felt as if a great weight was lifted from my shoulders. I opened my eyes to see bright sunlight streaming through the window. A million dust particles danced in the light, swirling on the air currents. I finally felt at peace. I just didn't want to leave the bed and break the mood. Or was I just afraid that the ordeal was not over? I didn't know, but I did know that I had to get up. So, carefully, so as not to break the mood, I eased out of bed and prepared to meet whatever was going to happen now.

As I left my room and headed down the short hall to the dining room I heard, "Well, finally he gets out of bed." The greeting came from my father, who was chuckling in my general direction. "Not many more days left of summer. School starts in two weeks."

I was stunned. School started in two weeks? That couldn't be! Where had the summer gone? Had we really spent the entire summer with the Ouija board? My mind was flooded with a myriad of thoughts. I stuttered a response, "I'm really hungry. Is there anything for breakfast?"

Mom chimed in, "Breakfast? It's nearly noon!"

Again I was stunned. I had never slept that long. What happened? I was a little confused and all I could say was, "I'm sorry, I must have been really tired."

My parents just looked at me then at each other. Papa shrugged his shoulders and said, "Boys need their sleep."

Mama made me an eggplant sandwich on fresh made Italian bread smothered in a sweet basil sauce, with a side of sliced apples. I sat at my place at the table and just stared at the food. My head swam with thoughts. I felt relieved just a few minutes ago and now I was confused. I took a bite of the sandwich and considered my next move.

As soon as I finished lunch, I got dressed and headed next door to see what was happening to Mark and Roger. As I was leaving the side door to cross the shared driveway, I saw the door to the house next door open and the guys come charging out.

"Hey, we were just coming to see you. Did you sleep through the whole morning?" called Roger as he pulled me toward the front yard.

"Yeah, you?"

"Yeah, both of us did. What the hell is going on?" answered Mark.

We kept walking as I was trying to understand what was happening. I listed in my mind the events of the previous afternoon. We did everything right. We followed the ritual the best we could. The board was destroyed and the planchette burned. It had to be over, right? I asked myself.

When we got to the end of the driveway, we turned left toward my front porch and stopped dead in front of the sycamore tree. There, lying on the ground was a dead bird. Next to it was another dead bird. As we looked behind the tree we saw another dead bird. Three dead birds were just lying on the ground.

Roger bent down to examine the birds. He picked up a stick and moved the birds around and flipped them over. He looked up and said, "Their necks are broken. How the hell do three birds break their neck at the same time?"

Before anyone could say another word I heard a sharp sound coming from the front porch of the house. The window was open in front of the house and I could hear what sounded like a commotion.

I bounded up the stairs, opened the screen door, and headed into the front parlor. My parents were in the next room, the room that Grandma Lily used as her bedroom. They were standing over the bed looking down at Grandma.

Chapter 36

Once again I was to see Mr. Dimitri. This time I saw him solemnly climbing the front porch steps and watched as he rang the doorbell to our home. He had come to claim the body of my grandmother. Things progressed rapidly from there.

Mr. Dimitri and his assistants greeted my parents and offered their sympathy for the recently departed. We all gathered around the bed and were led in prayer by Mr. Dimitri, after which we were ushered out of the room so the body could be removed.

My parents and I retired to the dining room where my mother offered espresso to my father and milk to me. We munched on freshly baked cookies, chocolate chip and oatmeal raisin, and sat quietly, each absorbed in their own thoughts.

My father was the first to break the silence. "We have much work to do," he sighed. "There are calls to make and decisions for the arrangements. We have so much to do. Where do I begin?" He was clearly overburdened by the passing of his mother.

My mother tried to comfort him by giving him a hug and stroking his hair. She whispered, "She had a long life. She was very happy and she did not suffer. She is with the rest of the family, and I am sure she will watch over us." Planting a kiss on his cheek, she continued, "Come let us tell Emanuela and Conrad. They must be the first to hear; they can help with the arrangements."

Once again my father sighed and, gathering all his strength, he picked up the phone to call his brother and sister to tell them the news. Within thirty minutes, the family was all gathered in our dining room where plans were being made for the final arrangements.

Our dining room soon became the center of operations. Since there was no need for me to be there, I left to sit alone in the front parlor. I thought about my grandmother and how much I would miss her. As with all Italian matriarchs, she was the energy that kept the family close. She would be sorely missed.

The next day we all got dressed in our finest Sunday clothes and headed down to the funeral parlor to meet the rest of the family and complete the ritual that is an Italian funeral.

The first viewing was for the immediate family only. We all assembled in the waiting room before we were allowed to enter the room where my grandmother lay in her bronze casket. There were my parents, aunts and uncles and associated cousins. All were dressed in various shades of black. After we greeted each other, it was time to go into the room. Mr. Dimitri came to the assembly and, before opening the door, he led us in prayer. When we were finished, he slowly opened the two doors and led my parents by the arm to the center of the aisle and then helped them walk to the casket. My aunts and uncles came next and the cousins completed the parade.

Each of us was allowed to quietly come to the coffin where we knelt on the padded kneeler. We each were allowed a private minute with my grandmother. When it was my turn, I slowly knelt and said a quick prayer. I then turned toward the coffin to look into the face of my dead grandmother for the first time, but not the last.

All Italian families seem to say the same thing at a funeral. "She looks so good." "Her color is better now than when she was alive." "She is at peace." "I just love the way they fixed her hair." "That was her favorite dress" (even if it was just bought yesterday for the purpose of the burial). On and on the platitudes would go.

My grandmother's funeral was no different. As soon as we all had our moment alone at the casket, we were to take our seats and await the rest of the mourners. My father and Aunt Emanuela and Uncle Conrad and their respective spouses occupied the positions of honor in the front row.

The cousins were allowed to sit or mill around as they wished, as long as we were quiet and did not make any disturbance. Well, that never lasts too long.

As soon as the rest of the mourners started to come into the room, the room took on the atmosphere of a party. Soon each mourner followed our path up the center aisle and slowly walked to the coffin to say their prayer. They then went to the immediate family seated in the front row, kissing them on the cheeks, offering their condolences. Once this ritual was complete, they were free to walk about and catch up with old friends or other members of the family. Within the first hour, it was hard to believe there was a dead body in the room.

People were milling around, chatting, telling jokes, or otherwise catching up on family business re: gossip. There is no better time to catch up on family gossip than at a funeral. Everyone is there in one place, and one can easily start a rumor, as well as determine the veracity of the latest gossip. Yes, it was a typical Italian funeral.

As all this was going on, I was quietly observing the scene from the back of the room. My cousin Linda and I were chatting; I confess I really wasn't listening as she was once again talking about boys, a subject that I couldn't care less about. As I pretended to listen, I happened to catch a glimpse of something out of the corner of my eye. A movement or perhaps a figure passing through the room.

I couldn't quite make out what it was. It was like a flash of movement in the opposite corner of the room and then it was gone. "Linda, did you see that?" I asked.

"See what? Robbie, are you even listening to me?"

"No, not really," I absently replied.

"Jerk," she replied punching me in the shoulder as she stormed off.

For the rest of the evening I tried to keep a sharp eye out for something to happen, but nothing did. I spoke with those who came to pay their respects. My parents introduced me to dozens of people, telling me this is so and so, who is related to so and so. I wasn't listening. I was looking at the shadows hoping to see what I saw earlier, but nothing.

Soon Mr. Dimitri announced it was time to pay our respects for the evening and the visiting hours would be closing in fifteen minutes. As such, the procession started once again. The mourners came up the center aisle, paid their respects to the deceased, said goodbye to the family, and quickly departed. We were the last to pay our respects and thus the last to leave.

The next day was a repeat of the day before. Once again we all met in the hallway, Mr. Dimitri repeated the solemn prayer and opened the doors allowing the mourners to file past the coffin and take up their prescribed place in the front row. On this second night the room was more crowded than the first as now all of our neighbors, friends and others came to pay their respects to my grandmother.

Once again I found myself in the back of the room. This time I was alone and thus more able to concentrate on anything out of the ordinary. For the first hour, nothing seemed out of place. I spoke with my relatives, met more folks I never heard of before, and was generally bored when suddenly, just like before, I saw a quick movement. This time I was ready.

I followed the movement out of the corner of my eye and there, hidden by a large display of flowers, I could see a figure. Not a complete figure but more like an outline of a figure. I concentrated hard trying not to move, afraid I would lose sight of the figure, but it stayed in my field of vision. I started to move closer to get a better look and, for an instant, the figure became clearer. The figure seemed to get more solid and seemed to turn in my direction. Then, suddenly, the form was as clear as anyone else in the room. I stared at the face of the figure, and it stared back at me with a smile. It was my grandmother. She looked right at me and smiled. I was just about to shout when Linda came up behind me and hit me hard on the back of my head.

"You are still a jerk," she called, still angry from the previous night.

As I turned back to the flower display, the figure was gone. I knew, however that, just a moment ago, my grandmother had made an appearance at her own funeral. I was sure of it. I can't explain it, but I knew she was satisfied with how the arrangements turned out, the display of flowers, and the number of people who came to see her off. She smiled right at me and was gone.

I didn't know what to do, so I did nothing. It seemed no one else had seen the same figure. Or if they did, they, like me, said nothing. Soon it was time to close for the evening and Mr. Dimitri came and led us in prayer. The mourners soon filed out, and we were once again last to leave. Tomorrow would be the time for final good bye and the burial in the family plot.

The next morning, instead of Mr. Dimitri, we were met at the door by Father Murphy, our parish priest from Our Lady of Grace. This time Father led us in prayer and, once the doors were opened, he led us in solemn procession to the front of the room and stopped us at the coffin.

There he stood next to the coffin as each of us in turn knelt down, said a short prayer, and then turned to the deceased to say our final goodbye. My parents planted a kiss on Grandma's forehead. My father held his mother's hand for the last time and slowly moved to his seat. The rest of the family followed suit each saying their own private goodbye.

When it was my turn, I knelt and said a prayer and, turning to face my grandmother for the last time, I could swear that I saw her smile. The same smile I saw last night as the figure pretending to be my grandmother looked at me from the shadows. I shook off the feeling and proceeded to sit down next to my father as I awaited the final prayer and the closing of the casket.

Once everyone said goodbye in their private moment, Father Murphy began the final prayers. He seemed to say the prayers as if he were speed reading them, saying ten prayers in the space of what seemed to be less than a minute.

Soon it was time for all of us, except my father, and his brother and sister to leave. Only her children would be allowed to witness the final closing of the casket, another Italian tradition. This was more practical than spiritual for, when a loved one dies, they are often laid out with all their best jewelry. The final closing allows the immediate family to remove this jewelry in a fashion that no one sees and thus is able to preserve the jewelry for gifts to the family.

Soon the casket was closed, and we all headed to the cemetery where my grandmother would be laid to rest. Father Murphy presided at the ceremony and, within ten minutes, he sped through a Mass for the dead. Shortly thereafter, Mr. Dimitri handed everyone in attendance a lily, both as a symbol of eternal peace and to honor my grandmother whose name was Lily. As the casket was lowered, we said our final goodbyes and headed to our cars. As I stood before the grave and gazed into the depths of the hole that would soon contain my grandmother's mortal remains, I tossed in my lily and wondered how long my grandmother would remain at peace.

Chapter 37

Italian men are historically close to their mothers, and my father was no exception. I know he loved my mother and loved and respected me, but when his mother died it was like a little of him died as well. He was not as happy as before, not as likely to laugh so quickly. He did not mope as some might have, but he lost a bit of himself. We all noticed that things were not quite the same as before.

There was, however, good fortune for the Mauro family. With the passing of my grandmother, my father and mother inherited the house in Brooklyn as their reward for caring for Grandma for so long. Her estate also included some cash and property in Piazza Armerina, her hometown in Italy. The cash was split up among the rest of the family, but the property was held as any Italian knows. Land is the only thing that endures.

So our family was more secure now than ever. My father owned his home for the first time in his life, we had some savings, and I was rid of Anne Jefferies (or so I thought).

After a few weeks, life got back to normal, at least relatively normal for us. School started and Mark and I headed back to our second year of high school while the older Roger headed to his third year. We were still considered the cream of the crop, liked by the teachers, and envied by the student body.

Something else interesting happened that summer. The girls in school, once a tribe of oddballs and losers, changed to a more mature and sophisticated offering. Either we were growing up or they were, but the results were most pleasing.

Most of the girls were into the hip athletes. The football players got the cheerleaders, the baseball players got the drum majors, and the wrestlers had the pick of the rest. Unfortunately, neither Mark nor I were athletes and so we could only stand idly by and watch the courtship dance.

One part of the return ritual to high school was a little daunting for the three of us. It seemed a rite of passage that every English teacher in all the grades assigned the same first assignment, "What I did over the summer."

Well, there was no way we were prepared to go into our summer journey, so we had to make up everything which made the assignment much

136

harder. I wrote about the family trip we never took, and Mark came up with a story about a summer job as a delivery boy for the local drug store. Big mistake.

It seemed we were to write about our actual events and not made up events. It seems our teacher, Mrs. Falony knew Mr. Drackett the druggist that Mark supposedly worked for. Since Mark wrote a great story, Mrs. Falony just had to make comment to Mr. Drackett and the rest is history. Mark got a D on the paper. Fortunately, my subterfuge was not discovered, and I was allowed to slide by.

Chapter 38

Life was generally good. A few months after Grandma's passing, things began to look up a little. My father was a little less depressed and even allowed me to take some furniture from Grandma's room to put into my room.

I always cherished her antique Bentwood rocker. Grandma told me it was her mother's chair and, when she was a baby, her mother held her in her arms and rocked her to sleep in that very chair. When my father was born, Grandma rocked him in the same chair too. I too had a memory of being rocked in that chair by my own mother.

The chair was a beautiful light honey oak, hand hewn wood with a high back made of hand braided cane with a seat to match. The arms were well worn and polished by the oils from decades of hands rubbing the soft wood. One could almost feel energy in the wood. The rockers swept up from the floor in a single bend of wood. The seat, repaired by hand several times over the years, was covered by a handmade needlepoint with the words: "*Amor de madre, amore senza limiti,*" which translates to "a mother's love knows no limits." I had always loved this chair and now it was all mine.

I had placed the chair under a window, the only window in my long but narrow room, in such a way that I could enjoy the sunlight that streamed in from the evening setting sum. The warmth and energy from the afternoon sun filled the chair with light and made it even more inviting. I also situated a floor lamp over the right shoulder so I could read by the soft light of the yellowed shade. The chair was the centerpiece of my belongings and the last thing I saw from my bed at night and the first thing I would see in the morning.

Having that chair in my room reminded me of my grandmother. It was like having her spirit, her energy, right there with me or at least I had hoped so. You see in our family, like most Italian families, the dead were always with us in spirit or in fact. Having this chair brought me close to my grandmother; I had no idea, however, how close.

Chapter 39

The first time I felt something strange was about three weeks before the Christmas break from school. The teachers were loading us up on work as they had a schedule to keep and we were two days behind due to snow days. So the students, once elated to have a day off from school, now had to pay the supreme penalty of doing more work in less days. I was feeling the pressure to get things done but seemed to have some problems knowing where to start. `

One night sitting in my favorite chair by the light of the lamp, I was reading my science book. I loved the sciences as I seemed to have an aptitude in this area. I was nearly exhausted. I decided that reading would do me no more good since whatever I read fell right out of my memory. Slowly I closed the book, but instead of getting up and going to bed I just sat in the chair and rocked. The rocking motion was soothing, so soothing in fact that I must have fallen asleep. Much to my amazement, however, I could feel the chair still rocking.

The air in the room also changed. It seemed charged somehow. There was the feeling that there was raw energy in the room. I could only liken it to being outside in a storm, when the hair on your arms stands up on end in response to the energy charging the air just before a lightning strike. I was at that point between sleep and awake, near dreaming and near awakening, when the shroud of reality is weakest. I knew the chair was rocking and I also knew I was not rocking it. I stayed in this quasi conscious state for a few more minutes just enjoying the rocking and the soothing feeling of peace when suddenly I heard my name being called out. Not loud, but just a whisper.

"Roberto, rest now. There is much work to do, but now it is time to rest. Roberto rest."

I knew the voice. It was the pleasant, loving sound of my grandmother. I heard her voice deep in my head and knew she was there. I rested but soon my conscious mind startled. "The voice of my grandmother? It couldn't be," the voice of sanity that we all have in our head shouted.

At this I jumped fully awake and felt the chair rock gently one more time before my startled body lurched and nearly knocked the lamp over. The air was cold and charged with an energy that I could feel and almost see. All around me were tiny specks of light. It was as if the air was filled with dust motes, floating in the beams of sunlight that stream through a window on a bright summer day; only it was dark and the only light came from a shaded lamp. Still the room sparkled.

I rubbed my eyes and tried to convince myself that I was dreaming. I rose from the chair and watched it rock, once, twice and come to a stop. "See stupid," said the voice of sanity, "no one is there. Time for bed."

I changed into my night clothes, turned off the lamp, and headed to bed. Exhausted, however, I struggled between sleep and watching the rocker to see if it would move again. It didn't. The energy in the room also dissipated and once again all was quiet. I finally fell asleep, but could not get the sound of my grandmother's soothing voice out of my head. It felt like she was right there with me.

Chapter 40

The strangest part of this whole experience was the next morning. Instead of being exhausted from lack of sleep, I felt unusually refreshed, like I slept deep and sound for many hours. I could not imagine why I felt so good but I thanked my grandmother with a quick prayer and headed off to school.

A few months later, nearing spring, I was once again out of sorts with school. I had a big project due in English and a project for the science fair due in the same week. I was, once again, twisted in my head and just could not focus on getting either one done effectively.

One night I was alone in my room. It was well after midnight and everyone was asleep. My window was a little open to let in the fresh, near spring, air. I lay there in bed tossing and turning, knowing I was getting nothing done on the two projects, but not able to focus on either. I was working myself up into a state when I happened to look over in the dark at my rocking chair.

The air surrounding the chair was once again filled with floating sparks of light. I could feel the hairs on my arms begin to rise. I stared at the scene, wondering what was happening. Suddenly, I could have sworn the chair moved. Just a little, but just enough to show something was not right. Then I felt it, the breeze from the window. A soft light spring breeze moved the curtains. The moon was full, streaming a white light in the window. I sighed. I knew it was the breeze that moved the rocker, and the moon was lighting my room.

I started to settle back down, hoping to fall asleep when, out of the corner of my eye, I saw movement near the rocker. It must have been a trick of light, the clouds moving across the moon or something passing the window. Something easily explained. Then the rocker moved again, and this time it was no breeze. The sparkling lights seemed brighter and were moving in a spiral. The spiral was getting tighter and tighter, as the light sparkled brighter and brighter.

Slowly, the rocker first moved forward and then back. The entire room seemed to pick up some energy. The chair moved again, this time a little further. Back and front. Back and front, over and over. The spiraling light seemed now to be in a tight ball and was wavering high over the chair. I was paralyzed in my bed. I wanted to jump up and stop the chair, but I was frozen in place.

The room went dark. Suddenly there was a shining near the dead center of the chair. It was as if a ball of energy had formed in the chair and was the source of the movement. It looked like someone had just sat down in the middle of the chair. I knew I must be dreaming, so I shook myself awake but nothing happened. I was already awake and the chair was moving, slowly as if the energy ball could not both form light and move the chair at the same time.

I was scared, real scared. The first thought that came into my head was Anne Jefferies. Somehow, she had survived the ritual last summer and now was here to claim her retribution. I almost got up the nerve to shout but, as I was about to shout, I heard a soft calming voice.

"Roberto, it will be fine. Tomorrow will be better." Suddenly the light in the chair faded and the rocking stopped. I felt strangely at peace. The voice I heard was deeply familiar. Not the threats from Anne Jefferies at all, but the voice of my grandmother. I laid back down in my bed and once again fell fast asleep only to awaken in the morning, before the alarm, well rested and at peace.

Once again, I said a short prayer of thanks to my grandmother and headed off to school. That day I was able to focus my efforts on the English paper and finished it before supper. I was amazed and thankful to be done, but the dreaded science project loomed ahead. I had two weeks to get the entire project researched and completed.

Focusing my efforts, I made significant progress completing the research portion of the project and collected the necessary data to write the report. It was nearly complete but I only had three days to turn it in before the final due date. Once again I was stressed out.

The next few days were spent locked in the library collecting and collating the data and trying to write the final report. I was told by my science teacher that he was "expecting good things from his best student," pressure I did not need at all.

With two days to go, I locked myself in my room and focused all of my energy on the science project. I was so tired I could not concentrate so I decided to take a nap. As I lay fully clothed on the bed, my head swam with data from the project. I couldn't rest. I lay there in the dark trying to clear my mind when I saw something that frightened me. It was neither the rocking chair nor a ball of light. It was, however, someone or something in my room.

There in the center of the room was a hazy form. All I could see was what looked like a fog, or a cloud with a shining light around it and suddenly it was gone. I lay there a minute and tried to figure out what I just saw when the rocking chair was once again starting to rock. Slowly at first, then faster, as if someone had just sat down.

Then I heard the voice once again. This time I was not scared but welcomed the soothing sound. "Roberto, what are we to do with you? I am here for you and always will be with you. It will be fine. Now rest and tomorrow all will be good."

This time I grew bold and said, "Grandma, is that you?"

Silence.

"Please, please, Grandma, is that really you?" I pleaded.

First silence then, "Yes, I am here, but soon I must go. Now rest and tomorrow will be better."

"No, don't go, stay. I want to talk with you; show yourself to me, please." Then, nothing.

Soon I fell asleep and once again awoke well rested, but a little unnerved. Was that a dream, or a nightmare? I wasn't sure. All I knew was that there were no ghosts and my grandmother was not in my room. I must have been more exhausted than I thought.

Strangely, however, when I got to school and began to work on the rest of the science project, the pieces I was struggling with last night seemed to fall right into place. The words came quickly and, in just a short time, I finished the paper and felt good, real good.

I knew it was crazy, and there was no way any of this was real. I was just tired and imagining everything, right? Real or imagined, I got an "A" on the project.

Chapter 41

I was developing a strong affinity in school for the sciences, especially biology. My teacher, Mr. Adams, said I was his best student. He and I often had esoteric discussions on the origin of the universe and how the body works. I soon became very interested in learning how the body worked and how energy somehow is involved in everything we do. If you think about it, we exist only because we have some form of energy coursing through our system. Our mind is "awake" because chemicals in the brain react with certain cells and cause an electrical impulse which sends a signal throughout the body. Our heart beats because there is electrical energy sent to the heart muscle causing it to beat. We move because our muscles contract due to electrical stimulation. When there is no energy in the system, we are said to be "dead." We can measure this energy through EEG's and EKG's and actually graph the energy that represents life. This information was fascinating, and would soon pay a very important role in my future.

Mr. Adams often said that we are "all part of the same universe." In fact, he believed that we are all made up from the same matter as the stars and planets and other forms of solid matter that floated in the universe. He would tell me that we, and all matter, living or inert, were all made up of star dust. Energy is what makes us "alive." Scientific theory states that energy cannot be created or destroyed, only changed; he felt that when we die the "energy " that make us "alive" would return to the universe where it came from in the first place.

Essentially, we as living beings were made up of matter and energy from the universe and when we die our energy goes back into the universe from whence it came. He felt that the "afterlife or heaven" was our energy returning to the center of the universe where our conscious mind would travel forever. Our energy would be free and unfettered by a corporeal body; we were free to travel throughout the universe. His theory was truly heretical for a practicing Catholic, let alone a school teacher; so this became our little secret. One day, when we died, we all would find out if his theory was true or not. Until then we shared this only between ourselves.

Sophomore year soon came to an end, and summer was fast approaching as was my sixteenth birthday. I really was not expecting anything special to happen, except this year I would be allowed to go places on my own. Let me explain.

Italian parents are very protective of their children, especially Italian mothers. Since I was her "baby" and only child to boot, I was kept especially close to home. I was not really allowed to go very far from home except to school, the library and, on rare occasions, to the soda shop, all relatively close to home. But, at sixteen, I became a MAN, or at least that was the argument my father was having with my mother! My father did not want me to be a "Mamoni" aka "Mama's Boy." He wanted me to grow up and be self-reliant and not be tied to my mother's apron strings as many young Italian men are. It seems that, in some Italian households, young men, and not so young men, will stay with their mama until their thirties or even later.

As my father's son, I was to be like him, self-reliant. Let us not forget, however, that my father and his mother lived in the same house from the time he was born until the time she died. But let's not confuse the facts. I was to have my freedom at sixteen and that was that.

My mother argued that sixteen was too young to be allowed to be on my own and she was not going to budge on this. Nothing could change her mind once she made a decision. And just like every Italian woman she would eventually get her way, and a compromise was struck.

On June 18th, the morning of my birthday, my mother prepared a special breakfast of all my favorite morning foods. There was fresh baked Italian bread, lightly toasted, a hot plate of pancakes covered in fresh strawberries and whipped cream swimming in maple syrup, and fresh squeezed orange juice, red, of course, as she had gone out and bought blood oranges, a special Italian delicacy. Finally there was hot espresso and fresh biscotti to finish the meal. We all sat down and enjoyed this special occasion.

We dined like royalty that morning. There would be no presents to open, as we did not have the extra money to buy foolish things such as birthday cards or gifts. We celebrated, however, as a family, which I appreciated more than any gift money could buy.

As we got close to finishing breakfast, my father said to me, "Robbie, your mother and I have reached a decision." At this he rose from the table and started walking to the side door of the house. He beckoned me to follow him. I was confused, but I rose from my chair and, without saying a word, I followed him out the door and down the stairs to the door that led to the driveway.

He opened the outside door, but did not go through it. Instead he held it open and motioned me to precede him out the door. I was still confused, but silently I followed his lead.

I took one step outside and stopped, stunned. I turned around to look at my father; he was still holding the door open and smiling broadly. He said "I know it is not much, but we wanted you to have it."

I turned around again is disbelief, and stared at a nearly new 26" Italian racing bike. The frame was a deep red with a seat made of black leather. The handle bars were chrome and pushed way low so that you could cut the wind as you rode. On each side of the hand grips were hand brakes, one for the front and one for the back wheel. There were no fenders, which only added extra weight. But the most amazing thing was a controller, fixed on the handlebar and operated by the press of your thumb, which changed gears so that you could adjust how much work you had to do depending on the terrain. This was the best gift I ever received and it was completely unexpected.

I turned to look back to see that my mother had joined my father in the doorway. I rushed back and gave her a big hug and thanked her. I turned to my father, shook his hand, and thanked him. I was about to jump on the bike and try it out when my father said, "Not so fast. I know you are sixteen now, but your mother is still concerned that you are too young to be off on your own. You must tell her where you are planning to go and when she should expect you home. If you do this and keep to your word, there will be no problem. If, however, you do not keep her informed, the bike can leave as quickly as it came. Agreed?"

"Yes, of course," and I jumped on the bike and road off, forgetting to tell them where I was going.

Chapter 42

With my new set of "wheels," Mark, Roger, and I had a new-found freedom that summer. The guys already had bikes from last year; Roger, a used one from the bike shop, and Mark got his hand me down from Roger. We discovered that our bikes opened a whole new world to us and allowed us not only to get some exercise, but learn some new things.

A short, 1.18 miles from home was an open space known as Gravesend Park. I know that this is an odd name for a park, but it was named in honor of the site's proximity to Gravesend Cemetery. Because of this location, the name could literally imply that the park was located at the end of the graves. The park boasted open space, a baseball diamond, basketball courts, and, most importantly, handball courts.

Handball is a very simple but extremely competitive sport which pits individuals against each other in a game of skill and speed. Handball is like tennis except there is no net and both players are on the same side of the court.

A handball court has a wall at one end that is twenty feet wide and sixteen feet high. The floor is twenty feet wide and thirty-four feet deep. The object, using only your hand, is to hit a small hard rubber ball against a wall in such a fashion that your opponent cannot return the ball against the wall before the ball bounces twice. The game requires great skill, speed, and stamina. It could also be very dangerous as I would soon learn.

That summer, the three of us perfected our abilities by playing almost every day. We actually were really good by the end of the summer. Despite several sprained fingers, two wrenched ankles, and many days with swollen hands, we developed into truly competitive players. Our goal was to return to school in September and join the handball team and become "athletes" and, therefore, "attractive to the ladies!" A noble goal. Learning to play handball, however, was also the first step I took in the journey to the event that would soon change my life forever.

Summer ended all too quickly and soon it was time to return to school, Mark and I would be juniors and Roger, a senior. Sadly, this was the last year that the three of us would ever spend together.

Chapter 43

We returned to school and, as soon as we were able, we tried out for the handball team and were selected to the first team. Our first goal was accomplished. Unfortunately, the girls did not really see the handball team members as athletes; in fact, they avoided us even more.

This year in school for me was focused on learning as much biology and chemistry as I could. I was good in this area and wanted to learn more. Mark spent more time focusing on history and Roger had decided that pharmacy was his road to success. He applied to and was accepted into the pharmacy program at Brooklyn College. Our last year in high school together soon came to a close, and summer was once again upon us.

Now, anyone who has ever spent any time in the company of teenaged boys knows that boys of this age will do some really stupid and dangerous things. In fact, they will do some things without regard to life and limb or property and have no fear doing it. Since teenage boys all felt they were immortal, they had nothing to fear in the first place. If the Ouija board fiasco was any indication, we were no different.

I remember the day very well. It was the morning of June 18, my birthday, and the guys and I decided to have a marathon day at the handball court. The day was just perfect, sunny but not too hot and humid, just a perfect day for a bike ride and handball competition.

The ride to the park was a short two miles on open pathways, but if one cut through the cemetery, you could cut off a good piece of the trip. With its rickety old fence, nearly demolished headstones, and large crooked trees, the place looked like the set of a horror movie.

The Gravesend Cemetery was first opened in 1643, when private land was donated by the Governor of New Amsterdam to the Quakers who decided to build a final resting place for the dearly departed. Later, at the behest of Thomas Spicer in 1658, the graveyard was enclosed by a fence, when he donated twenty guilders in his will. It is believed that Lady Deborah Moody, founder of the Gravesend community, rests within these hallowed grounds. In addition, many old names are recorded as resting here, such as Cowenhoven, Ryder, Van Nuyse, Jefferies, Wycoff and Van Sicklen. The Van Sicklen family also left land to the cemetery in 1675, but this donation was to be used solely for the Van Sicklen Family and so it was kept as a separate burial area. There was a cobblestone and brick pathway winding through the graves to allow one to walk through the cemetery at peace and contemplate the dearly departed.

On that bright June morning we decided to race to the handball courts. The first two to arrive would play the first match. We headed down the street from the house, across the avenue, and off to the park. I was well in the lead with Mark close behind and Roger a distant third. As we came around the road I could see, off in the distance, the gated entrance to the cemetery; the gate had long since fallen open and no one had bothered to repair it. I switched gears and headed through the gate, a little too fast, however, for the transition from roadbed to cobblestone. I hit the front brakes to slow me down and skidded for a few feet before I was able to gain control once again. Mark had made up for lost time and was about ten feet behind me with Roger closing fast. I came off the bike seat to gain more speed and pressed the pedals as hard and fast as I dared. I jumped forward and was about to make a hard turn to the right when I saw her.

As I came around the curve of the cobblestone path, I could see, standing in the dead center of the path, what looked like an older woman dressed in old clothes. Not old as in rags but old as in old fashioned. I could not make out any features. I was pumping the pedals too hard to have the time to get a closer look. I could see, however, that if I did not do something, and do it quick, I was going to slam right into her.

Now I know what happened next happened in a split second, just a blink of an eye, but for me time changed. Things slowed down. I could feel the bike slow down. The wheels were still spinning hard and fast, but the sense of time slowed so that I could see everything as it unfolded.

First, I hit the brakes, hard. The bike immediately began to skid in an uncontrolled slide to the right of the cobblestone path. As the bike jumped off the path and onto the dirt, I could clearly see that the old woman had raised her right arm and was clearly pointing in my direction. I could still not see her face but I had the distinct impression that she was saying something to me and she was laughing. Yes, she was laughing, not afraid that she would be run over, but pointing at me and laughing.

As soon as my bike's front wheel hit the dirt, all control was lost, and I flipped off the bike and was airborne over the front of the handle bars. I could feel myself flying, and could distinctly hear the sound of a cackling laugh as I headed forward and toward the ground. The next thing I heard was the sound of a thick branch breaking as I slammed my shoulder, and not my head, into a grave marker. For a moment I was confused. The sound of the breaking branch was followed by an immediate and excruciating pain in my right arm. It took me a second to realize that the sound I just heard was my arm breaking and not a branch. I sat there dazed; Mark and Roger jumped off their bikes and came running over to see if I was OK.

Still dazed and in a great deal of pain, I asked, "Did I hit her?"

I heard Mark say, "Hit who, "then, "oh shit," before I passed out.

I don't know what happened next, but I soon came to on a hospital gurney with my father staring down at me with the combined look of concern and anger and my mother sobbing. I felt a great weight on my right arm and soon learned that I was in a plaster cast from nearly my shoulder to my wrist.

My father was the first to speak. "I am glad you are okay, but the bike is destroyed. You have caused your mother no end to worry. What do you have to say for yourself?"

All I could come up with was, "I am sorry."

"Yes, I am sure you are. No bike and the rest of the summer in a cast." My father chuckled feeling relieved I was okay. "Let's get out of here," he said helping me down from the gurney and into the waiting arms of my mother.

The doctor came in and told me that I could take aspirin for the pain and to come back in eight weeks to remove the cast. No other instructions were offered as he headed off to see the next emergency. Relieved that I had only broken my arm, I headed out the door between my parents and headed home.

Chapter 44

My arm throbbed and ached all night. I took some aspirin, and then took some more. If one is good, four must be better. Now my stomach was upset, and my arm still throbbed. I tossed and turned, not easy to do with a cast. I couldn't sleep. I don't know if it was the pain or the aspirin but, sometime in the middle of the night, I began to hallucinate. Or at least I hoped I was hallucinating.

I was asleep or awake, I don't know which, when I could have sworn I saw something in my room. My room was dark, lit only partially by moonlight. I could make out most of the furniture, my desk, the desk lamp, a book case and my grandmother's chair at the end of my bed. Off in the corner, opposite from my desk I could see a dark shadow. It was one of those shadows that is not caused by backlighting but seemed to be a dark solid mass, hovering and shimmering about five feet off the floor. I stared directly into the mass and heard something that sounded like "soon".

Again, I don't know if I was dreaming or awake but, after a minute or two, the shadow seemed to actually get darker and I heard a voice laugh "soon" and, without a sound, the mass disappeared and everything was quiet. I tossed in my bed, still in pain and far from comfortable, and tried to figure out what happened. I must have fallen asleep for the next thing I knew the sunlight was streaming in my open window and the room was bright and warm. What a night.

I headed out to breakfast to find out I had slept till almost ten o'clock. My mother greeted me with concern, "How are you feeling? Is there much pain?" Before I could respond she continued, "Here sit down and I will get you something to eat. Mark and Roger stopped by early this morning to see how you are doing. I told them to come back later."

All I could muster was, "Thanks, Mom. I feel tired and my arm hurts a little."

Eating with my left hand was not easy. My mother had to cut up my food into bite-sized pieces so I could stab them with my fork and try to get some into my mouth before it dropped off. So much for being an independent MAN with my own wheels. Now I had to rely on my mother just to feed me. I was able to eat about half of what she prepared before exhaustion and frustration made me give up.

I slowly got up off the chair and, feeling a little light-headed, immediately sat back down. I thought I heard a woman laugh. It had to be my imagination again, when suddenly my mother looked out the kitchen window and said, "Looks like the boys are worried about you. They are in the driveway coming across to the side door. I will let them in." She wiped her hands on the ever present dish towel and headed to the side door to let the boys in.

Once again I got up from my chair and this time I was much better, so I followed her to the door and greeted the guys with a wave of my cast and said, "You should see the other guy." Mark and Roger just looked at each other and didn't say a word. Roger motioned to me and signaled we should go downstairs. My mother was already back in the kitchen so the three of us headed down to the basement.

As soon as we got there, Mark excitedly said, "Did you see it?"

I shook my head. "What do you mean *it?* *It* was some old lady jumped out on the path."

"What old lady?" came a chorus from the boys? "The headstone, did you see the head stone?"

"Of course I saw the headstone, right before and right after I slammed into it."

'Wait a minute," said Roger. "Let's back up here a minute. Robbie, you go first and tell us exactly what you saw."

I went over the accident as best I could. I told them I hit the brakes to slow down as I came around the corner. There was an old woman on the path in front of me. I tried to stop the bike and avoid hitting her, but I lost control and flew off the bike and broke my arm when I hit the headstone.

Mark and Roger looked at me for a second and then at each other. Roger continued, "What old woman? There was nobody there. Did you see the name on the headstone?"

What did he mean "nobody was there?" I was aghast, "I saw her plain as day. There was an old woman dressed in old fashioned clothes, right there

153

in the middle of the path." I then remembered, "She was pointing at me and laughing." As I said this I began to have some concerns as to what I saw.

"Look, we swear there was no one there, but did you see the name on the head stone? It was MAURO," Roger exclaimed. 'It was Mauro; how the hell could that be? What the hell is happening?"

"Slow down," I said. "You mean to tell me that the gravestone that I hit, the one I broke my arm on, had my name on it"

"Yes," was all Roger could whisper.

"That's impossible."

"Sure, impossible maybe, but I swear that is what it said."

I was more than a little concerned. My name on a grave marker! That just could not be. "OK." I said after giving the situation some thought. "Let's go over there and find the marker and read what it says once and for all."

"There is no way I am going back there. Not after what Robbie said about an old woman. Remember the summer with the damn spirit board? I am not going through that again," argued Mark.

"Don't be an ass," Roger said, giving his brother a punch in the arm. "We all go together."

"Look, I agree we need to go, but I can't go right now. My arm is throbbing and I am exhausted. I slept like crap last night and I am just not up to the challenge. What do you say we go tomorrow, if I feel better?" Mark looked relieved that we would not go today and Roger sighed, but he felt sorry for me so we all agreed to go tomorrow.
The next day I was feeling much better. I slept well and the throbbing was still there but I could live with the pain. After lunch, I headed next door to get the guys and check out the sinister headstone.

We walked to the park, since my bike was broken and I could not hope to borrow one and ride with a broken arm. We arrived in silence to the open gate of Gravesend Cemetery. The area seemed spookier somehow. I am sure it was my imagination, but I felt the air get thicker as soon as we entered the cemetery grounds. Slowly and silently we followed the cobblestone path, looking for, but hoping not to find anything out of the ordinary. We came around the bend in the path, the point where I first tried to slow down. We could actually see skid marks left by my tires, so we knew this was the exact spot.

We followed the path and saw where the front tire left the cobblestone and found a tire track in some mud showing exactly where I lost control. We stopped for a minute and looked around. There was nothing to indicate anyone was there. How could there be? What struck us as a little off was that the whole area was silent. Not a sound. No birds, no wind in the trees, no sound at all. I could almost hear my heartbeat.

We stepped off the path and followed the supposed flight of my body before hitting the gravestone. It was evident from the trajectory that I landed on the backside of the stone so there was no way I could have seen any name on the front side. We also noticed that the stone was broken; the upper corner of the stone was missing.

Slowly we walked around to the front of the stone; we were actually holding our breath. There, carved into the stone in large block letters was the name MAURO. The name, however, was incomplete because the name would have continued had the stone not been broken. It was strange; however, that the remaining letters did spell out my name, but what was even stranger was the epitaph carved below the name.

We had to move some brush and leaves to read the last line but the following words were deeply etched into the stone face:
> *Death is a debt*
> *Due Nature*
> *I have paid my due*
> *And so must you*

Chapter 45

The rest of the summer, like all summers, was over way too quickly. The cast came off in mid-August to reveal a pasty white, somewhat shriveled example of my former arm. I knew that handball was out for my senior year since I had eight weeks of physical therapy ahead of me. The only good news was this was my last year in school. Once I graduated I was on my own, or so I thought.

Mark and I headed back to our final year of high school while Roger headed off to Brooklyn College where he was preparing to pursue a career as a pharmacist. Since I was really good in the sciences, especially biology, I soon came under the mentorship of my biology teacher, Mr. Adams.

Mr. Ron Adams would soon become an instrumental force in my life, guiding me along a path that I had not considered. Ron was a graduate of Rutgers University, a school located in New Brunswick, NJ with an illustrious history going back as far as 1766.

During our first month back in school Mr. Adams cornered me and asked "Well, Robbie, you're now a senior. Have you given any thought to which college you would like to attend?"

I really didn't think I had any real choices in the decision. My family was not poor but neither were we rich enough to pay for a college education so I replied, "I guess I will go to Brooklyn College like everyone else."

"Robbie, BC is an OK school but is well below your ability. You can do much better."

"Like what, we can't afford much else and even BC may be a little out of the running," I replied a little concerned about where this was going.

"Robbie, you are one of the best students I have this year. In fact, you are among the top ten students I have ever had. Don't sell yourself short," Mr. Adams lectured. "I believe with a little help and the right guidance you could go to a much better school."

"Sure, I guess so, but I really have not thought much about next year."

"I am not talking about next year, Robbie. I am talking about the rest of your life. Where you go to college will have a role in determining what becomes of you for the rest of your life. I know this is sudden, but, I think with a little help, you could get into a much better school, say Rutgers University in New Jersey."

Now, anyone who knows anyone born and raised in New York would know that there is no reason to leave New York or one of the five boroughs. New York has everything anyone needs. Many New Yorkers spend their entire life in the city or one of the boroughs, never needing or wanting to leave. New Jersey is a place that most New Yorkers have heard of but have no desire to visit.

"Sure, Mr. Adams, I appreciate the suggestion. Let me think about it and we can talk later. I'm late for class." Mr. Adams just smiled, knowing he now had an open door to guide me through on my college decision.

For the next few months Mr. Adams sought me out and told me all about the university, its rich history and how beautiful the campus is. Unlike the City College in Brooklyn, Rutgers was in a country-like setting, with rolling fields, a small lake and a beautiful view of the Raritan River. The buildings are of deep red brick, and each campus is unique.

OK, I admitted that this sounded interesting but, "New Jersey, Mr. Adams, really? How am I going to get there and home again? I won't know anyone and, well, where is New Jersey anyway?"

Mr. Adams looked at me and laughed, "It is less than two hours away by train. You can catch the train right near your home, ride into New York on the subway, then take the NJ transit directly to New Brunswick Station and in ten minutes you are right in the middle of campus. Nothing to it."

Well, this sounded plausible but I still had so many questions. Would I like it there? What will my parents say? Could we afford it? "I don't know, Mr. Adams. I need to talk with my father."

Mr. Adams was on a roll and he said, "Great idea Robbie, we can talk to him together."

The next thing I knew Mr. Adams and I were on a train going from Brooklyn to New York City and then off to New Brunswick on a guided tour of the campus and a meeting with some of Mr. Adams' professors. I was excited, frightened and concerned if I was making the right move.

Well, things sure changed when we arrived. The campus was just like Mr. Adams described it. Beautiful historic red brick buildings built along the crisp flowing Raritan River. Rolling hills throughout the campus yet surrounded by the small city of New Brunswick. Here there were shops, restaurants, bookstores and entertainment, all catering to the large population of students.

Rutgers College was founded as Queens College in 1776 along the banks of the Raritan River in New Brunswick, New Jersey. It was renamed as Rutgers College in 1825 in honor of Colonel Henry Rutgers. The school was an all-male bastion until 1918 when the New Jersey College for Women (later renamed Douglass College) opened. In 1864, Rutgers was chosen, over the more prestigious Princeton College, to be the sight of the first Land Grant College in the state and was tasked with offering educational access to a wider range of students boasted the university brochure handed out to all prospective students.

For me, the allure of Rutgers had to do with the area known as Cook College, named after George H Cook professor of Chemistry and Natural Sciences back in 1853. Dr. Cook was born on a small farm in New Jersey and spent a few years after high school as an itinerant worker before studying chemistry at Rensselaer Institute. Cook was a proponent of the concept that everyone could benefit from an education in science and he spent the better part of his energy making his dream of a science education available for all. In 1864 he helped found the Rutgers Scientific School, which later was named after him.

I knew I was good at the sciences, especially biology and chemistry. I really wanted to know how things worked and I was interested in learning more. Since this school was devoted to the sciences, I knew this was the perfect place for me to continue my education.

Not only was Cook College devoted to the sciences, it was also heavily invested in the agricultural industry with courses in animal husbandry, plant biology and food sciences. This was a real hands-on institution and I was a hands-on guy.

I met several professors in the biology department and even enjoyed a lunch at the dining hall, giving me a true "taste" of college life. I was hooked. Rutgers University beat the old campus at Brooklyn College any day. But what would my family say about it being so far away?

I was really excited about the day's events, but by the time we got home it was after dinner and mom was not feeling too well. She was having some more of her headaches and, although she wanted to hear all about my visit to Rutgers, she was not up to the strain. So we agreed to talk at breakfast the next day.

Since the next day was Saturday I had all the time I needed to go over the day minute by minute. Mom asked me questions about what I liked and what I didn't, but my father listened intently only saying few passing words. I really didn't notice my father's silence since I was too excited relating my replay of the events of the day. When I was done, my father didn't say a word but rubbed the top of my head, giving my hair a slight tousle, smiled at me, kissed Mom on the forehead and headed out of the room. My mom stood up too, and started clearing the table. I had no idea what that meant, but I assumed that Brooklyn City College was my next port of call.

I tried avoiding Mr. Adams when I got back to school because I knew he would ask what my father thought of my visit to Rutgers and I really had no idea what to tell him. Unfortunately, Mr. Adams was a man on a mission and I soon was waylaid in the hall.

"There you are. I have some paperwork for you to complete," Mr. Adams announced as I rounded a corner of the hall.

"Paperwork?"

"Yes, paperwork. I have your application for admission and several scholarship applications. We have a lot of work to do, young man, so why don't we get started?"

I met with Mr. Adams every day after school for two weeks, working on the application, writing and rewriting my admission essay, and completing a myriad of scholarship forms. I was more concerned that I still had not told my family that I was even applying to Rutgers. What would they think about me going out to New Jersey? Well, maybe I wouldn't get in anyway.

Not only did I get in, but with several scholarships based on academics and need, I had a full ride. Well, money would not be an issue. Now, I needed to break the news to my father who would probably think New Jersey is on another continent.

Wrong again. It seems that Mr. Adams had been speaking in private with my father and had convinced him that Rutgers was the best place for me and assured him that there would be no issues with paying for school as Mr. Adams had some pull with the admissions committee and with the scholarship committee. When I came home from school with my acceptance letter in hand, I proudly presented the letter and the offer of full scholarship to my father. He took the letter carefully from my hand, so as not to crease it and read each word aloud as proudly as he could muster. My mother shed a tear or two by the end.

When he was finished my father announced "This is a proud moment for our family. Robbie will be the first Mauro ever to go to college. This calls for a celebration. Vincenza, please bring out the wine that my mother brought back from Italy. You know the one we were saving for a special occasion." He turned toward me and continued, "What can be more special than our little boy growing up and going to college?"

We drank a toast to me and my good fortune. We drank another to my parents for all they did for me. Then, we drank a final toast to all the Mauros who could not be with us to celebrate. The bottle was empty and I had my first experience with being drunk. Even the hangover the next day was worth the cost.

Chapter 46

I wanted to share the news with Mark as soon as I could. He was also applying to several schools and I wanted to beat him to the punch. I headed next door, but half way across the driveway I saw Mark burst out the side door heading to my house and waving a sheet of paper.

"Hey, Robbie, I got in, I got in," Mark shouted.

I guess the excitement was contagious and I shouted back, "Me too!"

Mark looked at me sideways. "I didn't know you applied to Fordham, that's great."

"I didn't. I got into Rutgers and on a full ride."

"Rutgers, where's that?"

I laughed and explained to Mark the story about Mr. Adams and how he helped me get into Rutgers, where it was, and that I was getting a free education. He listened to my explanation, but I could tell he was disappointed. I asked him what was wrong and he replied, "I thought we would be together for another four years. With Roger at Brooklyn College, I just hoped we would both go to Fordham. Now, I won't know anyone."

"Hey, look, it is just a train ride away. We can do some weekends. I am sure we will see each other on summer break and holidays right?"

As I said this it occurred to me, my life was about to change again. My friends and family, so very important to my life so far, would no longer be directly and daily involved in it. Things were inevitably going to change. No matter what I did, things would be a little different from here on.

Mark sighed and, after a moment, he said, "Yeah I guess so." He, too, could see that things would never be the same, and they weren't.

Chapter 47

The rest of senior year went quickly. As is often the case once a high school senior gets into college, they have mentally left high school. We were not that different. My grades slipped a little, I missed a homework assignment for the first time ever, and I actually failed a math test. But, it was all chalked up to senioritis. I still graduated at the top of the class with Mark right behind.

Graduation itself was amazing. Since I was to graduate number one in my class and Mark number two, the day was all about us.

The June day was hot. It had to be eighty-five degrees at ten am with a forecast high of over ninety. To try to make everyone a little more comfortable, the ceremony was held outside. A huge canvass tent was erected on the football field to try to keep the sun off our heads. Unfortunately, there was no breeze at all so, even though we were out from under the sun, the air was so still that it remained sweltering under the tent. To make matters worse the crowd started to arrive two hours before the event to get the best seats. With a graduation class of nearly 500 students, the crowd grew huge and fast. With all those people under the tent the temperature continued to rise. I was sure it was over 110 degrees by the time the ceremony started. People were sitting there fanning themselves with the ceremony schedule. Someone at the school had the bright idea of putting out iced water at some stands around the tent, which caused a rush to get a drink. Unfortunately, the mass exodus to get some water, also resulted in long lines at the bathroom and delayed the start of the ceremony by thirty minutes, adding more time in the hot tent.

Well, we eventually got things going. My parents looked as proud as parents could be. Since I was the Valedictorian and Mark the Salutatorian, our parents were escorted to seats of honor right in the front row. As Mark and I sat next to each other on the stage, we had the perfect view of our parents, also sitting next to each other.

As with all graduations, there was the usual complement of speeches and admonishments to the new graduates to do more, do better, and make us all proud. All I heard was blah, blah, blah as I looked at the mostly blank eyes of my fellow graduates. We wanted to get our diplomas, get out of the heat, and get on with the parties at home.

After what seemed like an eternity, I finally heard the principal announce my name as he introduced me to the assemblage. It was time to give my speech to the class.

I really was not nervous, but I was hot. In fact, I was sweating profusely. I know it was out of decorum, but I was sweating so badly that the beads of sweat were falling into my eyes, so I took out my handkerchief and wiped my brow. Well, this brought a huge round of applause from the class and laughs from the parents. I guess they thought I was making a statement of, "Finally, we get to the good stuff."

As I made my way slowly to the center podium, I reached under my gown to get my speech. It wasn't there! I stopped in my tracks. I reached inside the gown again only to be hit by the realization that the speech was inside my jacket pocket, which I left in the gym because it was too hot to wear under the gown. Panic set in. The blood rushed out of my head and I thought I was going to throw up.

My parents were staring at me, wondering what was wrong. They heard me rehearse the speech a dozen times over the past three days. They knew I was not afraid of crowds, but there I was, dead stopped three steps short of the podium. Before anyone could make a move to see what was wrong I spied something out of the corner of my eye. It must have been a vision, or a hallucination, or a trick of the heat, but there at the end of the stage, standing off to the right was my grandmother. At least it looked like my grandmother. She was standing there in a dress that I have seen her wear many times for special occasions. She looked deep into my eyes and smiled. I thought I heard her say something, but I am sure I could not have possibly heard her because she was a good twenty feet away and the crowd was now making restless noises. But I am sure I heard her say, "Robbie, it will be all right. Just step up and make the speech."

Suddenly, I was bathed in a cool breeze. I calmed right down and made the short walk to the podium and delivered the speech I wrote, word for word, from memory. It was impossible, but I did it. As I came to the last line of my speech, where I was thanking the special people in my life I looked over toward the side of the stage to acknowledge my grandmother, but she was gone. There was no one standing anywhere near the area. It had to be my imagination, but I knew without her support, I would not have been able to pull it off.

Mark's speech followed, and soon we were getting our diplomas. The ceremony ended with the usual throwing of the caps, something we were all expressly forbidden to do, and a huge cheer from the new graduates. We processed out and came quickly back to the crowd for the usual congratulations followed by photos and much patting on the back. Roger had taken the time off from his studies to attend the ceremony. He handed out cigars to Mark and me. Laughing, we lit up, and someone snapped a picture of the three of us smoking a cigar and laughing. That was the last time all three of us were together ever again.

Chapter 48

Roger headed back to school at Brooklyn College right after graduation. He was enrolled in the pre –pharmacy program that ran through the summer so he could be out in five years instead of the usual six. He really never came home again after our graduation. He lived on campus and spent most of his free time studying. He did get home from time to time to visit family, but neither Mark nor I were at the old homestead when he did visit so we never could quite manage to get together as a group.

The summer of my eighteenth year was great. My family was exceptionally proud of my getting into college, even though it was in Jersey. Uncle Rosario would always tease me chiding, "Where was this Jersey, anyway? They probably never heard of good Italian cooking" and everyone would laugh.

I guess I was a little apprehensive about leaving home, but I knew that Rutgers was where I wanted to be. I couldn't wait to go there, but I still had the summer to go.

Mark and I spent the better part of that summer inseparable. We knew, deep down, that things would never be the same again once we left for college. Mark was heading off to Fordham for pre-law and I was heading off to "some other country" (as Mark called New Jersey) to Rutgers. So, we knew that summer was our last as boys. Next time we got together we would be different, so we wanted to hold on to what we had for as long as we could.

We did everything we could together. We played handball at the park until our hands were so swollen we had to soak them in warm water when we got home. We rode our bikes (I picked up a used one at the corner store for ten dollars) until our legs were exhausted.

To make a few dollars that year we hired ourselves out to the neighbors and did odd jobs. Mostly we cleaned out garages and swept junk out of basements. The work was not hard, the money was good, and it gave us a chance to be together to talk.

We talked about school and how glad we were to be out of high school. We talked about girls a lot. Neither one of us had any experience with the fairer sex, but we sure wanted to! Eventually we talked about the summer of the incident with the spirit board.

"Remember back when we had that 'problem' with the spirit board?" Mark said one day as we were cleaning out a garage.

"Remember? Hell, are you kidding? How could I forget? I thought we had opened a gate to hell or something. Remember? Jeez, wish I could forget." I pulled some old rubber tires out of the back of the garage.

"Well, remember what 'she' said about Roger? Something about 'herbs.' And now he is going to pharmacy school," he said, helping move some old boxes to the curb.

"Yeah, so."

"And me. Heading off to pre-law. Isn't that the same as 'Man of laws?' I mean, was she right in predicting the future?" I could see worry in his eyes as we lifted another heavy box to the curb.

"Look, I have no idea if she knew the future or not. All I know is we killed her and destroyed the damn board and that is the end of it," I said, not knowing if I was trying to convince Mark or myself. "It is done. The board is burned and buried. We followed the ritual to the letter."

"Did we?" Mark looked at me, and I saw the blood leave his face.

"Yes, damn it, we did. Now forget about that mess and help me haul this old table to the curb."

He didn't say another word about that summer, but I could see something was gnawing at him. He got too quiet and pensive as if he wanted to say something but thought better of it.

Finally I couldn't stand it anymore. Dropping the box of books I was carrying at his feet, I stood in front of him toe to toe and said, "Ok, out with it. What are you not saying?"

"You remember the ritual?"

"Sure," I said, incredulous he would even have to ask.

"Well, when we completed the ritual and had made the seven pieces and burned the planchette and buried everything behind the garage."

"Yeah, I remember. So?" I was starting to get worried.

"Well, a couple of days later, I went in the garage to get something for my dad."

"So?" I jumped in now getting really worried.

"I found another piece of the board."

"What?" I screamed. "You found another piece? Where? When? How? And why in the fuck did you not tell us?" I was scared, angry, and wanted to punch Mark's lights out.

"I didn't know what to do. So, I ah…

"So you what? Go on, so you what?" I demanded.

"I buried it." Mark said unconvincingly.

"You buried it. You sure? You damn sure better have buried it."

"I did, I did .I swear. I buried it alongside the other seven pieces. I didn't have any holy water so I said a prayer and buried it, I swear." Mark replied more pleading than convincing.

"Good. Then that's the end of it."

Mark stammered out. "I didn't want to say anything. Damn things were so weird and we finally felt we had this thing behind us. Hell, I was scared. I just wanted to forget I ever saw the piece so I did."

"So, why bring it up now?" I asked flopping down on another box I should have been taking to the curb. "Jesus, Mark. Why now?" I hung my head and ran my fingers through my hair.

"Well, I was thinking about what Anne said."

'Goddammit, Mark. We agreed never to say her name again." I punched him in the arm. He knew I was really mad now as I rarely ever swore.

"Ok, Ok. I remember the predictions about Roger and me. I was thinking the predictions were too close. Then, what the board said about you."

"The damn thing never said anything about me remember? It said there was a price for my future predictions and that price was freedom," I hurled back at him. "And we destroyed the board and took her freedom so there was no prediction for me, so DROP IT," I shouted.

Mark took a step back, obviously out of my reach. He knew I was liable to take another swing at him if he chose to continue. " Ok, subject dropped. Now let's get this place cleaned out and head home. I'm hungry."

We worked the next hour in complete silence. We took another look around and, satisfied we were done, we headed home. Mark knew I was still pissed. I could see he wanted to say something, but he didn't want to argue, so he kept his word and stayed silent.

When we got to our shared driveway, Mark turned toward his door. I called out, "Hey, man, I'm sorry. It's just, I've tried for so long to forget about that day that it pissed me off that you brought it up. Sorry."

"Hey I understand. I'm sorry for bringing it up." And he turned and opened the door and went in.

I stood there for a minute or two thinking. Eight pieces not seven. The ritual was not complete. Eight is the number of infinity and infinity meant freedom. What have we done? Or, rather, what have we left undone?

Chapter 49

The summer was over. Labor Day was approaching and freshman orientation was a week away. I was ready.

Labor Day weekend was going to be special this year at our house. This was the last weekend I would be home with my family before school started and Mom was going to make this perfect for me. She spent all day Friday in the kitchen preparing and fussing over all the dishes I loved. There would be lasagna, sausage and peppers, lemon chicken, freshly baked breads, and, of course, a cake. She seemed happy and healthy. The headaches were gone and all seemed well. It wasn't

Saturday was going to be the big celebration day, the family was going to get together and celebrate the holiday and say goodbye to me at the same time. By noon everyone was there. My Uncle Rosario and Aunt Emanuella came early to help Mom set the table. My cousin Linda came later. She wanted to be with her latest boyfriend. It seemed she had a new one every week. Uncle Carmine and Aunt Sandra came with my other two cousins Lillian (named after our grandmother) and Annette. The entire family was together laughing, teasing, and celebrating. It was just perfect.

As the meal was served, we all sat around the table in our traditional places, Dad, at one end, Uncle Conrad at the other. On one side of the long dining room table sat the Pinello clan and on the other the Mauro's. We laughed and drank and ate as one.

When the meal was over and the dishes were cleared my Uncle Conrad stood up from the table and lifted his glass. Everyone became quiet. Uncle Rosario and my father also stood, each with a glass in their hand, and turned toward me. I was a little surprised and frightened as to what was going to happen next. Uncle Conrad spoke, "I raise my glass to Roberto Dante Mauro. May he continue his education and make this family proud, even if he has to go to New Jersey to do it. Salute." Everyone laughed and raised their glasses and followed with, "Salute."

When the laughter settled down, my father stood up and again the room fell silent. He raised his glass and said, "Roberto, we could not be more proud of you. You worked hard to get to where you are, further than anyone in the family. You are our future. May you have a long and happy life, while you continue to make the family proud." The family followed again by raising their glasses and shouting, "Salute."

My father continued, " We know you will have some needs when you head off to the wilds of New Jersey so the family got together and we wanted to give you a parting gift." He reached into his breast pocket and pulled out a white envelope and ceremoniously handed it to me."

I was more than surprised. "Thank you," I stammered. "Thank you all."

I started to sit down and my father admonished "Roberto, open it."

I stood back up and, with shaky hands, carefully tore open the envelope. I slowly pulled out the contents. First out came ten crisp brand new twenty dollar bills. "Wow! Thank you, thank you all." I knew how much of a sacrifice this was for the family. "Thank you," I stammered again and began to sit down.

"Roberto, is that all that's in in the envelope?" my father said chuckling. "Look again."

More, there is more I thought. The money was more than I could imagine, but sure enough there was something else in the envelope. I opened the envelope further and drew out what seemed to be a ticket. I turned it over and read from the ticket.

"From New Brunswick, New Jersey to New York City, New York," I read. I looked at my father a little quizzically.

"Now you can never say you can't come to visit your mamma." He laughed raising his glass once again.

The family followed suit and shouted, 'Salute." They all burst into laughter and the celebration continued.

There was so much activity that day that I didn't notice that my mother did not seem to be celebrating. She served the meal, cleared the dishes, and served dessert pleasantly. When I did notice that she was unusually quiet, I chalked it up to her being proud and a little sad that tomorrow I would be heading off to New Jersey to start freshman orientation. There was more to it, however.

That night, when the table was cleared and everyone had said their goodbye and departed for home, we were finally alone. Exhausted, we retired to the parlor. My father and I shared a cup of espresso, but my mother was nowhere to be seen.

'Vincenza, where are you? Come sit with us. It is the last time Roberto will be here for a while. Come sit," he called.

No answer. He waited a moment and called a little louder. "Vincenza, come, where are you?" Still no answer..

Slowly, but deliberately he got up from his favorite chair and headed to the kitchen, expecting to see my mother washing the last of the dishes. I followed close behind. The kitchen was empty, the dishes washed and stacked. He called again "Vincenza?" Still no reply. His face changed as he began to look concerned. He headed down the hall toward the bedrooms and the bathroom.

The bathroom door was closed. He knocked and called, "Vincenza, honey are you all right? " When there was no reply, he knocked again. He tried the door, which was unlocked. He looked in and the bathroom was neat as a pin but empty. "Where is she?" he muttered more to himself than to me.

In unison we turned and walked the five steps toward their bedroom. The door was ajar, but from where we stood, we could not see into the room. We were thinking that Mama must have been so tired after the day's activities that she must have gone to bed early, not telling us so as not to end the celebration too early.

My father reached out and gingerly took hold of the door knob, almost as if he expected to burn his hand in doing so. Slowly putting pressure on the door, it moved open. He simultaneously knocked and called, "Vincenza, honey, are you asleep?" Still no response.

Slowly, he opened the door, until it was fully opened and we had a clear view of the room. It was dark, the shades drawn, and no lights on. When our eyes adjusted to the darkness, my father looked at the bed to see if mama was asleep. The bed was empty. I could feel my father tense as he looked around the room for his wife. She was nowhere to be seen.

My father slowly and deliberately turned in a circle looking at every square inch of the room, searching for something he missed, some clue as to my mother's whereabouts. Nothing was out of place and there was no sign of my mother.

Suddenly, my father laughed and turned and said, "Mama must be in the basement. With all the guests today, she must be putting the extra chairs and leftover food away in the basement kitchen. Come Robbie, let's give her a hand."

As we turned to leave the room, I caught my father's eye and saw that he still looked worried as if the idea of Mama in the basement was more for my benefit that for his. Slowly, we continued out of the bedroom and, as we made our way to the hallway, I stopped for just a second and looked into my bedroom.

I froze and my father walked right into me. "Robbie, Jeez, I'm sorry I didn't see you stop," he exclaimed apologetically. I didn't move.

"Robbie, what's wrong?" he asked as he followed my line of sight into the entrance of my bedroom. He saw it, too.

My bedroom was almost pitch black except for a single beam of pure white moonlight streaming in the bedroom window. The light was bright for moonlight and seemed to be focused onto something in the center of the room.

As our eyes adjusted to the darkness, we could just barely make out what the moon beam illuminated and I let out a gasp as my father pushed me aside to see what was wrong. He entered the bedroom and stopped. He stood ramrod straight as he stared at the vision of my mother. She was in my grandmother's rocking chair, slumped to one side and completely illuminated by the single beam of moonlight. It was as if the moon were pointing to her, keeping the rest of the room in shadow and casting a single white light on her visage.

My father regained his senses and rushed into the room. Dropping to one knee, he reached out and, taking my mother's hand in his, he put his other hand on her forehead, as I had seen my mother do a thousand times when I felt sick. "She is cold," he called to me. "She's so cold."

Suddenly he pulled his hand from her forehead as if burned. At the same time, Mama moved her head and looked directly into my father's eyes. I saw her face screwed up in a sardonic smile looking directly at my father. I couldn't be sure, but all I could see were the whites of her eyes. By the look on my father's face, I could tell he saw it, too.

Before we could react, from somewhere in the back of her throat, my mother croaked, "Soon, not now. But soon."

My father dropped Mama's hand, and seemed to jump back at this. Before he could recover, my mother opened her eyes and smiled saying, "I must have fallen asleep." She looked first at me, then at my father, and said, "What's wrong with you two. You look like you have seen a ghost!" At this, she snapped at my father with the dish towel still in her hands.

Laughing, she rose from the chair, kissed my father, came over and gave me a hug, then heading toward the bathroom, she said, "I guess I better get ready for bed" and left the room.

My father and I just stood there; staring at each other in disbelief. What just happened? Neither of us said a word; we were lost in our own thoughts. Maybe too much celebration, too much drink, and too much imagination were the cause. In any case Papa said, "Perhaps we all should get some sleep. We have a big day tomorrow."

I said, "Yes we do" and, turning to leave the room, I looked back and saw my father still standing there looking at the empty chair shaking his head. "Good night," I called. There was no reply.

Chapter 50

The big day finally came; I was off to college. I rose early from a deep, dreamless sleep to find my room lit by a strange white light which seemed to emanate from my grandmother's chair. Before I could gather my senses, the light was gone. I assumed my excited eyes were playing tricks on me and dismissed what I thought I saw and prepared for the day--what would turn out to be a very long day.

I had packed my meager belongings into a rather small suitcase. I had some clothes, an extra pair of shoes, some towels and, of course, books all stuffed into the one suitcase. My father also gave me another surprise gift that morning.

Many years ago, my grandfather served in the Italian army. It seemed he was a rather high ranking officer and, as such, he was given some privileges that others were not. One of these was a rather large leather pouch, one like those often carried by couriers charged with the delivery of important or perhaps secret messages. The leather was soft and still supple even after several decades of hard use.

My father called me into the dining room. "I know your grandfather would want you to have his bag. He was the most important man in our family, having been the only person with some education to rise above the others and achieve some fame for our family. Now you will carry on the tradition by being the first person in our family to graduate from college." Handing me the bag, he continued, "Make us proud and honor the family name." He hugged me for the first time since I was a child.

Quickly he straightened up and smoothing out the front of his shirt, he said, "Well, we better get moving, if you hope to get to school before dark. It is a long ride to New Brunswick."

I went back into my room, looked around to see if there was anything else I should take, and noticed my grandmother's pillow sitting on the chair. I thought, "I have something from Grandpa, why not something from Grandma, as well?" I quickly added the pillow and two more books, essentially to hide the pillow, into my new bag, picked up my suitcase, took one final turn, and left the room.

My mother and father decided they would accompany me to the train station. We walked almost silently the thirteen blocks from our home to the elevated IND line, which would take me to the New York City Penn Central Station where I would catch the train to New Brunswick. I was carrying my suitcase in one hand and had my grandfather's bag slung over my shoulder. Although the combined weight would normally have weighed heavily, it felt light as a feather. It must have been the excitement of beginning a new chapter of my life. I knew I would miss home, my family, and friends, but I also knew that this was the chance of a lifetime, and I was going to make the best of it.

All too soon we arrived at the foot of the train station. My mother began to cry. She reached out and hugged me as only an Italian mother could. She enveloped me in her arms and slowly rocked me from side to side, all the time kissing me on my cheeks and forehead. She never wanted to let me go, but soon my father said, "Vincenza, my dear, you have to let him go before he misses the train." He stepped forward and very gently touched her shoulder and then grasped her arm, again saying, "Come now. It's time to go home."

She soon released me from her loving grasp and my father stepped forward and took my hand firmly and pulled me close. With the other hand, he reached around and slapped me heartily on the back in the traditional Italian way. He never said a word as he stepped back, nodded his approval, and let go of my hand.

Turning to my mother, he said, "Come. Today, we too will celebrate. I will take you out to dinner on this fine happy occasion." He chuckled, grabbed my mother in a big hug, and guided her away from the station stairs.

I stood there for an instant and watched them leave. I could hear the train coming from far away as the station stairs and the steel girders began to rattle. No time to lose, I picked up my bags, dropped my token in the gate and entered the platform just as the train came to a stop.

The doors opened and disgorged the arriving passengers only to be immediately followed by the departing passengers pushing through the quickly closing doors. There was no time to hesitate. I was now on my own and heading to the future.

I was in New York's Penn Central Station by noon and decided to get a bite to eat. I walked around the various food vendors and decided on a famous NY hotdog with mustard, loaded with kraut on a hot bun. As I started walking toward the stand, I reached into my leather bag to get my money and felt something strange. There nestled between the two books and the folded pillow was a brown paper bag.

I don't remember putting the bag in the pouch and can't recall leaving the pouch alone long enough for anyone else to put something inside. I stopped and pulled out the paper bag carefully as if it would explode.

On the side in my mother's loving hand was written, "Roberto no need to starve on your way to school. I made your favorite meatball sandwich for the trip. We love you always Mamma."

I reached inside and there was the thickest meatball sandwich I ever saw. I changed course and headed over to the bench reserved for pushcart diners, sat down and unwrapped the sandwich, and took a huge bite.

I sat there for about an hour, eating and looking at the people scurrying about the terminal, waiting to board my train to New Brunswick. The train was scheduled to leave at two pm, so I headed to platform 25 at 1:45 to join the line of passengers. The train arrived on time, and we were shuttled through the platform doors to the tunnel leading to the track to board the train. Since I had a coach ticket, I boarded and grabbed the first window seat I could so I could look out the window during the ninety-minute journey from the big city to the distant suburbs of New Jersey.

Soon the train left the station, and we left the tall confining buildings of the city and entered the train tunnel under the Hudson River. The tunnel was dark with lights that flashed by as we passed through at high speed and emerged to a totally different environment.

Tall buildings gave way to grasslands and swamp. The train hurled south through lush grasslands replete with water fowl and seagulls circling overhead. I could only remember seeing such open land from the beach at Coney Island, but here on the other side of the Hudson was open land everywhere.

Soon, we left the open spaces and began to travel through cities of Newark, Elizabeth, Linden, Rahway, Edison, Metuchen, and finally New Brunswick. As the conductor announced the station, "New Brunswick, next stop New Brunswick," I rose from my seat and joined a line of what appeared to be fellow students all carrying bags, suitcases, and every contrivance to carry their belongings. They all seemed to have the same lost look in their eyes. Alone for the first time in an unknown place, they looked scared in a way. I only could hope I looked more confident as I felt the train lurch to a stop and heard the hiss of the air brakes as the doors swooped open. I was pushed from behind and followed the student in front of me. Before I could put my bags down, the doors began to close and the conductor shouted, "All aboard," as the train brakes hissed again, releasing the wheels, so the engine could tug the train cars out of the station.

I was standing there for a few seconds when I heard something strange. Someone was calling my name. It couldn't be. No one here knew me, yet there it was again.

"Mauro. Mauro. There you are." I hesitated and looked around. I heard my name again. "Robbie, this way," and, turning toward my right, I couldn't believe my eyes. There walking straight at me was Mr. Adams, my high school teacher. I looked at him in disbelief and said, "Mr. Adams, what are you doing here?"

First, he laughed and said, "Well, I am here to pick you up, of course!"

I shook my head and said, " Really? I don't understand."

'Well, let me help you there. I was given an offer I couldn't refuse. You see my old biology professor was getting up in years and he recommended me to the faculty and, well, here I am, the newest professor at Rutgers University."

"I thought all professors were doctors or something."

"Well, they are. I received my doctor of philosophy, or PhD, five years ago but could not find a position at University so I chose to teach at the high school while I waited for the right position. Well, the right position became available and here I am."

"Wow!" was all I could say.

"Wow is right. Now come along. I have another surprise for you," he said, reaching for my suitcase and heading toward the stairs.

I had no idea what was going to happen next so I grabbed my satchel and, slinging it over my shoulder, I ran after him.

Soon, we were heading through New Brunswick south on George Street toward the campus of the New Jersey College for Women. We made a right turn on Nicholl Ave and headed a few blocks west to Seaman Street. We continued along until we arrived at a very large stately home at 22 Seaman Street when Mr. Adams, I mean Dr. Adams, stopped, put his arm around my shoulder and said, "Welcome home."

Chapter 51

I stood frozen for a moment not knowing what to do or say. Dr. Adams laughed and said, "Another surprise. You see I lived in this very house when I was a student at Rutgers. The owners rent rooms to students and it seems a senior just left the residence. There was an opening and I pulled some strings and here you are."

Too much too soon was all I could think. I was assuming I would be in the dorms as part of a crowd not living in a stately home on the outskirts of campus with my own room. I was still trying to take it all in when Dr. Adams continued, "Come on, your room is on the top floor, and the view is stupendous." He bounded up the stairs and I had no option but to grab my bags and follow.

The front steps led to a large open front porch. The porch was guarded on three sides by a white post fence. The hand hewn floor boards were painted a deep gray which contrasted beautifully with the white paint on the house. The wooden shutters were painted to match the floorboards. Although well over 200 years old the home was in pristine shape. The owners obviously loved the house. There were several chairs on the porch, well worn, but comfortable looking. There was even a two person porch swing, perfect to curl up in and read on a summer evening. The front door was a large oak door, painted red with a center glass. Dr. Adams grabbed the handle and opened it, and we entered into a huge beautiful grand entrance way with dark rich walnut wide floor boards, polished to a mirror luster. There was a sun porch off to the left and a living room off to the right. Not giving me time to look around, there was plenty of time for that later; Dr. Adams led me toward the kitchen in the back of the house. "There are some secrets in this house," he said. "Come let me show you.

Before we actually entered the kitchen we came to a parlor with a grand fireplace offset on a large wall. The fireplace was made of gray fieldstone with a single seven foot granite mantle about six inches wide. There were some bric a brac on the mantle. To the right of the fireplace was a wall that was paneled with what looked like oak planks laid horizontally from floor to ceiling. The rich blonde color of the wall panel contrasted beautifully with the fireplace gray stone.

Conspiratorially, Dr. Adams drew me closer and said "Here is the first surprise." Reaching to the far right side of the granite mantel, he seemed to push something and I heard a slight pop as if a spring was released and a door opened in the paneled wall. I couldn't believe what I was seeing. A secret door? This door was actually part of the wall, cut perfectly to be hidden unless you knew where it was.

"Where does this lead?"

"Well to your room of course!" came the reply. Ushering me forward and through the door, I entered a narrow hallway. Directly in front of me was a wall of rich red brick. The same brick that made up the outside of the house. I could tell from the feel of the brick and the odor of fresh air that this was the outside wall of the house itself.

To my right was a steep, narrow stairway. The steps were made from roughhewn planks and carried no paint or color other than the natural dark from two centuries of wear. Even the stairs were odd. They were built into the wall and first went straight for three steps, and then ten steps up to an open space in what appeared to be the attic. I looked over my shoulder and Dr. Adams bid me go on, so I took the stairs one at a time until I came into a wide open loft. The space was large and very well-lit from a center set of windows in the roof.

"Come on, this is the best part," shouted Dr. Adams excitedly as he went to the center of the room and up a spiral staircase into what appeared to be another room in the roof.

I dropped my bags on the floor and followed up the spiral metal staircase and into a small room that was made almost entirely of windows. "What's this?" I asked, looking around at the incredible view.

"This is what was once called a widow's walk. It was said to be used by the wife of a sailor that was lost at sea. She would go to the widow's walk to look out to the sea and wait for her husband. Actually, this room was used as an observation room. Back in the time of the Revolutionary War this room played a role in observing traffic on the Raritan River. New Brunswick was an integral part of the war in the New Jersey campaigns and so many of the homes built these rooms to watch the comings and goings of the British."

"This house is that old?"

'Older, this house was built in 1745 and has seen a great deal of history. With that he told me this story. It was the horrible winter of 1776. The Revolutionary War was in full swing. The patriots were not doing too well. General Washington was encamped in the bitter cold at Valley Forge. His troops were dying from lack of food and supplies. All seemed lost.

General Washington earlier had recruited some noble patriots for a task most dangerous, spying on the British. These spies soon came to be known as the Culper Spy Ring. One of these brave men lived in this very house.

"Amazing," was all I could muster. "What happened?"

"Well, it was December 20, 1776. Washington needed desperately something good to happen or all was lost. His spies told him that the British regulars were camped outside New Brunswick and were supposed to be heading south to meet up with a group of mercenaries called the Hessians garrisoned in Trenton. If this happened the combined forces of the regulars with the mercenaries could have dealt a death blow to the nascent America."

Dr. Adams continued, "Washington needed confirmation of the British intentions so he called upon the services of his spies. From this very loft, a member of the Culper Spy team was able to see the British encampment along the Raritan River and was able to confirm the British were solidly encamped and were not preparing to move toward Trenton. With this information, General Washington crossed the Delaware River on December 25, Christmas Day, and attacked the Hessians the morning of December 26 dealing them a crushing blow and thus began to turn the tide for the patriots. You could say that from this very widow's walk, the revolution was saved."

I shook my head in amazement at being in this place in history when Dr. Adams dealt a final chapter to his story. "It is said that the spy never left his post and to this very day he can be heard on clear nights pacing the widow's walk making sure the British are not on the move."

Great, I thought to myself, all I need is another ghost.

We headed back down the spiral stairs into my room. Well, room was a misnomer; it was more like rooms. The space was open and divided into separate use areas. There was a sleeping area with a single bed and a study area with a desk and chair.

My eyes fell directly on the chair sitting on a small rug in the center of the study space. It was an old bentwood rocker, exactly the size, shape and color of the one my grandmother had and was in my old bedroom at home. I must have stared for longer than I thought because Dr. Adams shook my shoulder and asked, "Are you all right?"

Shaking my head to clear my brain, I stammered, "Yeah, I'm fine. Just too much all at once."

He laughed and said, "I'll let you settle in. Perhaps you will join me for dinner?"

Again I stammered, "Yeah, sure," my eyes still fixated on the chair.

He laughed once, slapped me on the back, and left me alone. I could hear his steps as he went down stairs, then silence after I heard the front door close. I was alone, but I did not feel alone.

I stood for a few minutes in the center of the room taking in my surroundings. I could feel the energy as if there were others with me, yet I knew I was alone. I shook off the feeling and began to unpack.

As I reached for my bag to pull out my clothes to hang in the closet, my hands were drawn to my other satchel that held my grandmother's pillow. I forgot I even had the pillow, but somehow I suddenly felt that this was the first thing I needed to unpack.

I opened the satchel, pulled out the pillow, and hugged it to my chest, as I slowly turned around the room. I could feel its energy slowly calming me. When I completed my turn around the room, I placed the pillow in the bentwood rocker and set it down exactly the way it was at home. I could feel the room sigh. I was home.

Chapter 52

The next three years at University was a dream come true. I spent a great deal of time attending classes and studying. I excelled in the sciences, especially chemistry and biology. I also did well in math but was a little wanting in the social sciences, such as English and History. I passed these courses with a B, but it took all I had and then some.

I also made some friends, but none compared to the relationship I once had with Mark and Roger. Mark was enrolled in Fordham and was heading to law school when he graduated. Roger was still pursuing a career in pharmacy. I decided biology was my calling, so I took as many classes in biology as possible.

My academic advisor, Dr. John Grun, was also the head of the biology department. He recognized in me an aptitude in biology, and soon he invited me into his lab to do some extra research.

His area of expertise was genetics, especially as it pertains to the development of viruses and the diseases they cause. Most of his research involved the study of Avian Infectious Bronchitis Virus, a disease that was especially critical in New Jersey as it had recently decimated the chicken population, causing millions of dollars in damage to the industry. He was developing a technique to define the genetics of the virus so this information could be used to develop a vaccine.

As a junior, I soon found myself working as his lab assistant, a position usually reserved for grad students, but it seemed I had a knack for lab work and could produce more research results than more senior students. I was happy to seclude myself in the basement lab for hours. It may have negatively impacted my social life, but I was content in my solitude.

Yes, things were going very well: good grades, a few dollars in my pocket, and a promising future. How quickly things can change.

Chapter 53

It was June of my junior year and things continued looking up for me. School was out for the summer and I was offered a summer job by Dr. Grun, beginning June 20, to continue my research in his lab. I decided to head home for a few days to visit my family and celebrate another milestone, turning twenty-one.

I headed downtown to catch the train to the city and then take the local to Brooklyn. The day was beautiful, bright and sunny, and I was anxious to see my father and mother.

What was a bright and sunny day seemed to be clouding over. By the time I got to the front porch, I looked up and could see the clouds actually swirling around as if there were going to be a storm. I didn't think anything of it and climbed the stairs to the front door.

My father must have been waiting for me in the parlor because I never got the chance to open the door. When it flew open, my father was standing there with open arms and a huge grin on his slightly older face.

"Roberto, come in," he said as he pulled me close, and greeted me with the traditional bear hug, three slaps on the back and a kiss on the cheek. I was home.

"Come, come inside. Mama is waiting in the kitchen. She has been working all day preparing all of your favorite foods." Then, he drew close and in a conspiratorial whisper said, "I hope you have a huge appetite! I am afraid she went overboard." Slapping me once again on the back, he put his arm around my shoulder and led me through the living room and into the kitchen.

As we entered the dining area my father called out, "Vincenza, look what the cat dragged in."

Swiping at my father with the ever present dish rag in her hands, my mother turned to look at me, declaring, "You are not eating. We will take care of that right now." It was always the same. No matter how often I came home my mother would always try to fatten me up. She stepped forward, threw her arms around me, and kissed me again and again.

"Come, sit down. You are all skin and bones. Don't they have good food in New Jersey?"

"Mama, really, I'm fine."

She turned around and grabbed a plate of her famous meatballs and, turning back to me, declared "Well, if you are so fine, perhaps I should give these to your father instead."

Just the sight and the smell of those delicious little handmade meatballs got my stomach churning. I sat down at the table. "Well, if you insist, I will try to eat!"

My father laughed and, sitting down next to me, called out, "Well, me too."

We all laughed and Mama sat down to join us while we ate. I filled them in on all that I was doing since I had seen them last. It was a perfect afternoon together.

Chapter 54

The following morning, after a hearty breakfast of homemade breads and eggs, my mother was really trying to fatten me up; I headed across the driveway to see if the guys were home from school. I looked up and saw that the clouds from yesterday had not dissipated, but seemed to get darker. The wind was moving them rapidly across the sky. The temperature was quite warm, and there seemed to be no breeze, yet the clouds were still swirling around. I could only assume one hell of a spring storm was on the way.

I knocked on the door, and was greeted by a familiar voice, "Coming."

Mrs. Donato opened the door and exclaimed, "Whoa, look who's here!" She pushed out the door and grabbed me in a bear hug. We rocked back and forth as she kissed me on both cheeks several times. A true Italian greeting. She then pushed back and said, "Let me look at you."

Examining me from head to toe she exclaimed. "Roberto, you are too thin. Don't they have food in New Jersey?"

I had to laugh as this was almost word for word what my mother said when she greeted me. I guess Italian mothers are all the same.

I followed her into the kitchen for another inspection. Mrs. Donato gave me another big hug and exclaimed, "My, my you are so tall, but you are all skin and bones. I hope your mama will fatten you up before you go back to school."

"Well, she is sure going to give it her best shot."

I then asked her if Mark and Roger were home. She shook her head and sighed as only a mother could, and said "No, they are not coming home for the summer. Mark has a job at school and Roger is doing some additional study. So, I will not see them until the end of the summer and then for only a few days. I miss them so."

We chatted for a few more minutes and then I gave her one more hug and headed toward the door.

She called to me, "Tell your mama to fatten you up a little!"

We both gave a laugh and I said, "I will be sure to tell her."

I left the Donato house and looked once again up at the sky as I crossed the driveway. The sky was almost green. I could see dark clouds swirling in a counterclockwise motion as if blown by high winds, but there was no wind. There was also the smell of ozone as if there were going to be a lightning storm, yet no storm was in the forecast. I stood there for a few minutes and then walked to the front of the driveway to get a better look at the unusual weather.

I got to the sidewalk and was shocked at what I saw. The clouds were swirling over my house and nowhere else! I know weather can be strange, raining with the sun shining or raining on one side of the street and not on the other, but to see clouds swirling in a somewhat tight circle right over my house was more than strange.

I stood on the sidewalk staring at the clouds when suddenly the temperature drew a chill. I actually shuddered as the drop in temperature hit me all at once. The wind picked up and I could feel a breeze on the back of my neck as if someone was standing close and breathing on me, yet I knew no one was there. I was frozen to the spot when I heard a sound in the wind. It was an eerie almost human sound as if a voice were riding the light breeze. I listened to the wind and heard what appeared to be a single word, "Soon."

I was shocked and quickly turned full circle on the sidewalk to see if there was someone nearby who could have said something, but no one was there. I looked up again and the clouds seemed to disperse. After a moment they were gone, and the sky was clear and bright as if nothing but bright sunlight was there all the time. I headed into the house, confused. I chalked it up to strange weather. A mistake.

Chapter 55

The next couple of days were spent as a family. We ate breakfast together and my mother made everything I liked each morning. Lunch was again all my favorites and dinner included my aunts and uncles. Even Linda deigned to spend a dinner with us, however, complaining all evening that she would rather be with her latest boyfriend. Yes, we were a very close family that second week in June.

My twenty-first birthday was coming up soon. My father and mother wanted to plan a celebration. I told them I really didn't want to make a big deal of the event. I was actually a little embarrassed at the prospect of turning twenty-one with no friends to help celebrate, so I told my father, "How about we just have dinner at home with the family to celebrate?"

"Of course, if that is what you want, we will invite everyone."

And so it began. My parents contacted all my aunts, uncles, and cousins and invited them to a big celebration on Thursday. My mother prepared a menu of all my favorite dishes. She sent my father and me out to shop for all the delicacies she needed. My father added some wines and a special bottle of scotch. It was a happy time as we joked and laughed together as we often did.

Things changed as the day approached. On Friday the clouds came back. This time they were dark and menacing. They swirled over the entire neighborhood but the darkest part of the vortex seemed to hover directly over our house. There was no wind, but the clouds churned in ever faster circles. Day and night, they were there getting darker and darker.

There was another strange change in the house. My mother, who was so excited about the upcoming celebration, seemed subdued. My father said it was because she was concentrating on all the food she needed to prepare, but I thought it was something else. Something deeper. She just didn't seem right.

Saturday morning my father and I woke at the usual 7:30. My mother usually was up earlier preparing the morning feast, but she was still in bed. My father turned to her and gently shook her but there was no response. He waited a moment and shook a little harder but still no response.

Now he sat up in bed and called her name as he shook just a little harder, and this time she turned and, with a very tired voice, replied, "Dante, I am so tired. Please, may I sleep a little longer? My head is heavy and I just do not have the energy to get up. I am so sorry."

Before my father could reply, she was fast asleep again.

Turning out of the bed he put on his slippers and headed out into the hallway. I was at this same time returning from the bathroom having completed my morning routine, and we met in the hallway.

"Good morning, "I called.

"Shhh," came the reply. "Your mother is not feeling well, and we are on our own this morning. Let's get dressed and let her sleep. We can have a father and son breakfast at the diner on Coney Island Avenue, just us men."

So we dressed and headed for the diner. Once again, as we left the house, I looked up at the sky to see if the clouds were still there. I could hardly believe what I saw. Again the sky seemed almost green with clouds, swirling this time in a clockwise direction. I pointed this out to my father who replied, "Looks like we will have a storm soon." Thinking nothing more, he put on his fedora and called to me, "Ready?"

We had a very enjoyable breakfast. My father asked about school and I told him all about my classes and some of the work I was doing in genetics. I knew he really didn't understand what I was saying, but he tried his best to look interested and asked several questions. We were having a great time but it was soon time to go.

"Come, Roberto, let's head home and check on Mama."

We got our things and walked home. As we entered the front door we could hear my mother in the living room. She was cleaning and dusting and putting everything just so, preparing for the company to come later in the week. She looked just fine.

My father walked up to her and gave her a big hug, whispering, "I am so glad to see you are better. I was worried something was wrong."

"I don't know what it was, but I was just so tired. I needed a little extra sleep after all this excitement. But I am just fine now."

We spent the rest of the day talking and cleaning the house in preparation for our guests. My mother wanted everything just perfect for my birthday. By the time dinner was over, I was exhausted and turned in a little early to get some reading done, so I was more prepared for the lab work I was going to do when I got back to school. It was a perfect day, the last perfect day for a very long time.

Sunday dawned and normally we prepared to go to ten a.m. Mass. I was up early and was dressed and ready by eight. As I was getting some breakfast, I could hear my father in the bedroom beginning to stir. I assumed he would get dressed and then wake my mother, who still seemed a little tired the night before.

As I was sitting down to some fresh bread slathered with butter, I heard a deep scream from my parents' bedroom. It was my father and he was shouting my mother's name. I raced to their room and threw open the door.
My father was standing over my mother. He had her by the shoulders and was shouting at her. "Vincenza, Vincenza, wake up!" he called over and over.

I raced to his side and looked squarely in my mother's face and saw immediately that there was no life there. Her eyes were as two dark marbles, fixed and shiny. Her skin was white and dry as if made of stone. Her hair hung limp covering her shoulders. She was dead. It couldn't be. I stood by my father's side and reached out to touch my mother's face. It was cold. Stone cold. She was gone.

My father knew it too, but he would not give up. For a full five minutes, he continued to call her name and shake her, but to no avail. Eventually, he lay her gently back in the bed, pulled up the covers, buried his face on her chest, and sobbed. The tears streamed down my cheeks as well.

I never saw my father cry before, so I had no idea what to do. I just lay my hands on his back to let him know I was there and let him get it all out. I choked back my own sobs to help give him strength. After about half an hour, my father calmed down and sat up. He wiped his tears on the handkerchief he always carried and said to me, "We had better call someone."

I looked at my father and, for the first time, I saw in his eyes a pain so deep I knew it may never heal. He lost the love of his life in a single instant. No warning and no reason. She was there and then she was not. I didn't know what to do or what to say so I just stood there.

The next few days were a blur. The doctor came to pronounce the death. The coroner came to get my mother's body. The police came to talk to first my father then to me. We must have told them over and over we had no idea what happened. She was fine, and then she was gone. Finally, they believed our story and left us to deal with our personal tragedy.

My father contacted Mr. Dimitri, the funeral director, and made the necessary arrangements to bring my mother to her final rest.

The visitation was held the following two days, Tuesday and Wednesday, as is traditional in an Italian funeral. This gave all the family and friends the time to come from near and far to pay their last respects to my mother and to visit with my father in this terrible time of tragedy. There were flowers and candles everywhere. My mother was laid out in her beautiful white Easter finery with a string of pearls around her neck.

My father and I sat in the front row and greeted well-wishers as they came by to express their condolences. We heard, over and over again, how this was "Just a tragedy." "A shame." "She passed too young." "She was too good to pass this way," and other trite platitudes designed to make us feel better. None worked. I shook their hands and accepted their kind words and gave the proper hugs and kisses. My heart, however, was empty and I knew the hole would never be filled.

My biggest concern was for my father. He seemed to sit sunk deep into the chair reserved for the husband of the deceased. He looked so small. He, too, accepted the hands of the guests, as they reached out to share their condolences, but there was no emotion in his eyes. He stared, unseeing, at each guest. He nodded his head as if a dummy on a string. When each one passed, his eyes would once again focus on the casket with my mother seemingly asleep. I knew he was devastated.

The next morning, Thursday, we went to the funeral parlor for the last time. We had a brief ceremony for just the family. Once everyone said their good bye, my father and I remained with my mother. I stood over my mother and the tears came in buckets. I could not believe she was gone. I held her hand for a moment until Mr. Dimitri came to my side and guided me away from the casket and back to my seat.

My father was last to visit my mother. He stood there for a moment and said a prayer. Then, he reached into the casket and held her hand as I had done just moments before. Again, my tears came flooding down. He just stood there for another minute, then finally bent down and gave her a kiss. I heard him whisper, "Wait for me. I will be there soon." He gave her one last kiss and left the room. I was left alone to watch my mother be lowered into the casket, and then I held my breath as they closed the coffin for the last time. As I let out my deepest sigh, I knew I would never see her face again.

The funeral Mass was held at Our Lady of Grace Church and was presided over by Father Murphy, the elderly priest, who was so much a part of my growing up. Since he knew my family well, he was able to make this a very personal Mass. He spoke of my mother with high praise, which brought many a tear to those attending.

Next came the drive to Long Island and the family gravesite located at the St. John's Cemetery in Queens, New York. When we arrived, the grave next to my grandmother was opened, and there was a pile of dirt next to the grave ready to be filled in. We all gathered round as Father Murphy read the final blessings that would help guide my mother into the afterlife. Slowly, the grave diggers lowered the casket into the bottom of the tomb. Once again, Father Murphy handed each person a white lily, a symbolism of the resurrection. Each mourner then passed the grave, said their final goodbye, and tossed the lily into the depths. Last to visit the grave was my father and me. I could see how deep in despair my father was. Here he was, for the last and final time, allowed a moment to be with his wife. Never again to be in her presence in this life. I was worried. He seemed to have shrunk before my eyes.

I steadied him as he approached the grave. For a moment, I was horrified to think he would fall in as he wavered at the edge. He said his final prayer and dropped his lily. I held fast to him as we walked away from my mother for the last time.

As soon as we were out of sight, the grave diggers commenced their job of filling in the grave and removing the debris left by the mourners. They whistled as they threw dirt over my mother. I was horrified, but this was how it was done, and I couldn't change anything.

We went back to the house to share a meal with the family as is tradition. We sat around the dining room table telling stories of my mother and remembering all the good times. We ate and drank until all were done. Soon it was over, and everyone bid their final condolences to me and my father.

It was not until everyone was gone and I was alone in my room, my father having turned in exhausted, that I remembered it was my twenty-first birthday. "Happy Birthday" I said as I tried to sleep. Unfortunately, the voices had different plans for me.

Chapter 56

We have all heard the voices. The voices inside our head. Those persistent, uncontrollable voices that won't let you sleep. They are there in the daytime as well. That voice that speaks to only us, that no one else can hear. The voices can only be described as that of a disembodied "other," dynamically interacting with and intruding upon the sense of self. The voices that always question or challenge what you're doing. They are often referred to as the "id" or the "ego" by psychologists. Some call them the conscious self, the subconscious, or the unconscious self, by those avoiding the issue with a joke. Many view hearing voices as imagination, while to others, hearing voices is often viewed with fear and suspicion, frequently vilified as a chaotic, corrupted symptom of illness. If you hear voices, you must be mad, yet we all hear them.

I remember that when I was in Catholic school they had a different view of the voices. I was told the voices in my head were a gift from God. You see, God loved us so much that he gave everyone a guardian angel that sat on our right shoulder. The angel was there to watch and see and hear everything you did. His charter from God was to make sure that we knew to do only good. He would do this by speaking directly into our head. Conversely the devil, not to be outdone, also gave us a gift. He gave each and every one of us our own demon. The demon sat on our left shoulder. The demon is blessed with a louder voice than the angel, and is more demanding. He wants us to do evil and will shout down the good angel, hence the voices of conflict circulating and arguing day after day.

I had my own idea of the voices. I believed the voices were the representative of the inner self or possibly the voice of our soul. We use so little of our brains that, perhaps, the voice is actually another part of our self and, hence, can represent an energy that is other than the conscious self. Whatever the truth, that day, the voices were loud and energetic so I had to listen.

The voices were relentless. I could not escape them. I tossed and turned, but the voices in my head kept up the questions. "Well, what are you going to do now? Who is going to take care of your father? What about school?"

On and on, the questions came, fast and furious. I didn't have any answers. I felt as if I had, not one, but two voices arguing and discussing my life inside my head. I could hear them going back and forth while I seemed to hover above it all as if I were a third party eavesdropping on a private conversation. Back and forth they argued. I couldn't seem to get a word in edgewise. I was helpless. Sleep would not come that night, no matter how hard I tried to tune the voices out.

As the voices pushed the discussion about what I needed to do, I began to see a possible solution beginning to form. What if I didn't go back to school that summer? What if I stayed home for the rest of the summer and helped settle my father? Then, in September, I could return and finish my senior year. Sounded plausible to me, but not to them!

The argument of the pros and cons of going back to school now or delaying for a few months continued. There were excellent reasons to go back now and equally excellent reasons to delay. It seemed like the discussions had gone on for hours. I tossed and turned as the voices continued arguing.

I knew there was no simple solution to my problem. I would have to choose the lesser of two evils. I decided the best thing to do was to stay home for right now (how long would be determined later), help my father deal with the loss of my mother, and then, when the time was right, return to school. I liked the idea and I guess the voices in my head came to like the idea as well, as they quieted down and allowed me to fall into a deep sleep.

I awoke the next morning rather refreshed and convinced that I had made the right decision to stay home and help my father cope with the loss we shared. I tossed back the covers and found that I couldn't move. My struggles with the inner voices resulted in my getting all tangled up in the covers to the point that my legs were twisted in the blanket so tightly I could not easily extricate myself. I unwrapped the covers from my legs and headed to the bathroom to perform my morning oblations.

After the struggles of last night, I felt pretty good about my decision to stay home for a while. I had not thought of what my father would say, but I assured myself that I could convince him this was the right decision for both of us and that I could easily pick up where I left off in September. The inner voice chimed in and said, "Who are you convincing: you or him?"

I actually wanted to shout, "Shut up," but I didn't and walked out of the bathroom, passing by father's closed bedroom door, and into the kitchen. I thought I would make breakfast before my father woke up. I figured this conversation would go much better on a full stomach.

I looked around and saw that the kitchen window, which should have been filled with the morning light, was almost pitch black. "What the hell?" I thought, until I recalled that Mom always closed the shades at night and opened them in the morning before I ever got up. Of course, it was dark; no one opened the shades.

Shaking my head at my own stupidity, I reached out and drew back the kitchen curtain until I remembered that the shades were never drawn closed last night. That was Mom's job, so no one did it. The shades were wide open and the kitchen window looked out into darkness. I was more than a little frightened.

I stepped back from the window and turned left toward the kitchen sink. I felt dizzy, unsteady. I reached out with both hands and placed them on the edge of the sink to steady myself. "What was happening to me?"

Then it dawned on me. I looked up above the sink at the cat eyed kitchen clock and saw that it was only 3:25 a.m. I stood there transfixed. I held on to the sink for dear life and stared at the clock, willing it to change and be seven-thirty, not three-thirty.

Quietly, I circled around the kitchen, closed the blinds and the curtains, washed my face in the sink, took a deep breath and headed back to my room to bed. I kept shaking my head to clear the cobwebs and try to understand what was happening to me. I guess I was just more upset about the loss of my mother than I thought. I felt that time was moving slowly, as if the world had moved on in some way.

Back in bed, I pulled up the covers, lay back down, and fell instantly to sleep. No voices in my head and no dreams. Just a deep and restful sleep.

I felt like I was asleep for only a few minutes when I heard a noise in the kitchen. It sounded like dishes rattling in the sink. I bolted up. No covers wrapped my feet but I felt as if I was drenched in a cold sweat. My room was filled with bright sunlight. How could that be, it was the middle of the night?

196

I sat on the bed unable to move, confused. I just went back to bed and now, what seemed like a few minutes later, the sun was up and there was movement in the other room. What was happening?

I swung around and my bare feet touched the cold floor, sending a shiver up my spine. Why was the floor so cold? It was bathed in sunlight and was normally warm. I got up and opened the door to my bedroom and stuck my head out just a peek.

"Well, it's about time you woke up," I heard my father call. "Would you like breakfast or lunch?"

Now I was really confused. I stumbled out of my room into a fully lit dining room and kitchen to see my father at the sink washing what appeared to be breakfast dishes. I stood at the entrance of the kitchen unable to say anything.

My father turned to me while wiping his hands on the dish towel. "I know you have had a rough couple of days, so I just thought to let you sleep would be a good idea."

I looked at him with confusion written all over my face. "What time is it?"

"Well, the clock says it's almost noon. Aunt Emanuella stopped by early this morning with some fresh baked rolls and fresh brewed coffee. She thought that we would need something to eat and she wanted to check that we were all right."

Stunned, I looked at the clock and, sure enough, it was almost noon. Time felt different. First it was slow, then it speeded up, and now I was not sure of anything that happened last night. Trying to come to grips with the events so far, I stuttered, "I'll have some of the rolls and coffee. We need to talk."

"Sure, ok. Let me heat the rolls and warm the coffee. I'll pour a coffee for me as well and then we can sit down and talk."

"Good, great," I stumbled and turned on my heels and headed to the bathroom to wash my face and get a grip.

I came back to the table a little calmer and more awake after splashing cold water on my face. I was still confused, but I knew I had to tell my father that I was not going back to school right now, and I wanted to get this over with.

My father placed a plate of hot rolls on the table in front of me, poured us both a steaming cup of coffee, and sat down at his usual spot at the head of the table.

I took a sip of coffee to bolster my courage when, before I could say anything, my father began, "I know what you are going to tell me, so let me go first."

I looked at him a little surprised and said, "How can you know what I am going to say?"

"Because I know my son, and I would be telling my father the same thing under these circumstances."

I looked a little puzzled and said, "Ok, you first."

My father took a deep breath and with a sigh began. "Robbie, I love you with every bone in my body. Nothing could ever change that. I know your mother felt the same way. She and I only want for you the best of everything."

"I know that, Dad, it's just..."

"Let me finish," he said continuing. "I know that you think it's best for you not to return to school right now and stay with me."

I was stunned. I sat there quietly as he continued.

You are the best hope your mother and I have for making a better life for our future generations. You are the first Mauro born in America. You will be the first Mauro to get a college degree and make a better life for his family. A better life than can come from being a laborer."

"Dad, don't say that. You did the best you could, and you never kept us back. You are a strong person and I appreciate everything you have tried to do. But I need to do this."

"No, you don't," he said sternly. "You need to go back to school and finish your work. My sister and your uncle live five houses away. She will be here more than I need. I still have to go to work. What will you do here all day except waste your opportunity watching me grow older? *No, I can't allow that.* You will go back to school as planned. I want you to visit often but I can and will take care of myself. Right now the toughest job you have is to finish your education and begin a new life and someday have a family of your own."

"But…", was all I could say when he slapped the table hard and said, "No buts, this is want I need you to do, and this is what is best for the whole family."

Well, when my father would lose his temper, even a little, people tended to listen, and listen I did. I spent the rest of the weekend at home and headed back to school on Monday morning. Although it was summer vacation, Dr. Grun had offered me a summer internship position for my senior year, helping him with his genetics research and paying me a nice stipend. This would carry me over until August and the beginning of my final year at college.

I knew it was right to listen to my father, but it was tough. I tried to visit some more that summer, but I was only able to get home once before school started. My internship with Dr. Grun was demanding of my time. It got even worse when classes started in August.

I was carrying a full load for my senior year, twenty-one credits, working with Dr. Grun and trying to take care of my father long distance. I thanked God that my aunts and uncles lived nearby to help him over some of the rough spots.

I did get home for Christmas that year. My father seemed to have aged ten years when I first saw him. He seemed happy, but I could tell something was missing. We spent winter break visiting our relatives and just talking about school and what I was planning to do when I graduated. He insisted I have a plan after graduation.

The rest of senior year went quickly. I was working hard on my genetics research and we even published a paper where Dr. Grun allowed me to be second author. When I showed the published paper to my father, you would have thought I had won a Nobel Prize. He was so proud of me that he took that paper with him everywhere. He would pull out the soon to be dog-eared pages and, point my name out to anyone nearby, and say that his son was famous.

Graduation soon came and the entire family took the three hour trek by subway and rail to Rutgers University to see me get my diploma. I remember it was a very hot spring day, and there were all the students, sitting in black caps and gowns, sweating. Our parents and families were sitting in neat rows behind us as the speakers droned on in ninety-degree heat. Some fainted, but my father was stalwart through the entire proceedings. He even called out, "Bravo, Bravo," when my name was called. I can say that I was not the least bit embarrassed as I faced the assemblage and called back, "Gracie!"

When the ceremony was over, we all headed back home to Brooklyn where, the next day, there was a celebration honoring my achievement. Everyone was there. Family, friends, and neighbors all assembled in the basement of my house. I could feel my grandmother and most of all my mother. Their spirits were there amid all the commotion.

I looked over at my father who was having a drink with Uncle Carmine in the far corner of the room. He looked older, frail. But I was too wrapped up in the commotion to give it a second thought. Perhaps I should have paid better attention. He caught my eye and lifted his glass in a toast. I acknowledged the gesture by lifting my glass in return. All seemed right with the world.

Unfortunately, that was not the case. My father, you see, never really recovered from the loss of his beloved. He put up a good show, but deep inside, he was never the same. He held on for as long as he could. Now, with my graduation behind me and a seemingly bright future ahead, my father could no longer bear the pain. Thirteen months to the day of my mother's passing, my father died of a broken heart.

Chapter 57

And so again we set into motion the ritual our family follows to bury our dead: notifications to family, friends, neighbors and co-workers, messages to the church to arrange the funeral, and of course, contacting Mr. Dimitri our family undertaker, who I am sure will bury us all. There were many decisions to make: burial clothes, flower arrangements, cards marking the event, what prayers will be said and by whom, and the purchase of a casket for my father. I was bombarded by decisions and requests for my time. I was torn one way then the other. I did not have time to grieve nor did I have time to understand what was happening. Then came the meeting with Father Murphy. He looked older than I remembered and frail, I was concerned that he would keel over during the ceremony.

Questions, decisions, more questions and more decisions. It was like I was on an out-of-control merry-go-round. Round and round I was spinning, my attention drawn from one issue to the next. I was confused, lost, and overwhelmed. It seemed I couldn't catch my breath.

During one of these hectic moments as I tried to stop a moment, Uncle Carmine came up to me and, putting his arm around my shoulder, said simply, "I know."

This simple act, and those two words, were enough to get me through. I breathed a deep sigh of relief, squared my shoulders and said, "Thanks."

The wake was a typical three day Italian event where the close family sat in the front row and person after person knelt at the casket to pay their respects, they came to each and every member of the family to wish their condolences. If I heard it once I felt like I heard it a thousand times "You poor thing, what are you going to do now?" I often replied with, "I don't really know." Unfortunately, that was exactly the truth. I had no idea what I was going to do I just wanted to get this ordeal behind me.

And so it was. Time did pass as it always does, even though I felt time had stopped and I was stuck in some loop for the past three days. Then came the final ritual of closing the casket, moving on to the church for Mass, and the laying of my father into the cold dark grave.

Uncle Carmine, the family appointed patriarch by virtue of the fact he was the oldest member of the family, asked me if I wanted him to stand with me as my father's casket was sealed for the last time.

"No, "I said thanking him for his offer. "I need to be alone with my father for the moment."

"Ok," he whispered as he once again held my shoulder. "I will be right outside. We can go together to the church."

I nodded and turned to see my father for the last time. I knelt at the head of the coffin, holding his cold hands. "You rest now. Your work is done. Go and be with Mama and watch over me. It is my job now to carry on." I held him for one last minute, stood, then bent over, oh so slowly, and planted a last kiss on his forehead. I stepped away and nodded to Mr. Dimitri to proceed and he slowly wound the knob that would lower my father into the casket and proceeded to seal the lid. I turned and walked away to be with the rest of my family.

We headed to the church where we were greeted by Father Murphy, who looked even worse than he did the day before. Father Murphy anointed the casket with holy water, whispered a simple prayer, and turned to lead the procession into the church.

Again, my senses were assaulted by the activities at the church. Some called it "smells and bells." These assailed me as Father Murphy and his two accolades prayed, released incense to accompany the prayers, and rang bells at appropriately important parts of the Mass. I was present in body, but my mind could not seem to take it all in. I was lost in my own thoughts until I suddenly snapped to attention as Father Murphy concluded the Mass saying, "And now let us take our brother Dante to his final rest."

The church was dead quiet when I suddenly stood in my pew and solemnly began to walk to the lectern. The silence turned to whispered murmurs as family and friends turned to one another to ask what was happening. Soon the silence returned as I stood before the assemblage and pointed toward the draped coffin and proclaimed, "Who was this man?"

I had not prepared a eulogy, nor did I know what I was going to say next, but the words seemed to assemble in my brain and flowed to my mouth.

I repeated loudly, "Who was this man?" Continuing in a more solemn tone I whispered, "Let me tell you. This man was once an infant born to a

202

loving mother and father in his home country of Sicily. He grew up in the tiny town of Piazza Armerina in the city of Enna with his older brothers and younger sister and infant brother." I looked down at the pews and I could see every head turned toward me and every eye looking directly into my own. They were riveted to my words. "When he was five, his mother took him on a journey that forever would change is life. His older brother, younger sister, and infant brother left the safety and comfort of their family home, accompanied by their mother, to a waiting ship, ready to whisk them off to the new world. A strange world where they knew not the language or where they would go." Pausing here to find the next words, I continued, "The journey was perilous. So perilous that his infant brother, Anthony, died along the way. The family carried on, they knew no other way." I could now hear the sounds of sobbing as the gathering hung on my every word with sad emotion.

I continued, "He grew up in a strange land. Together with his family he learned a new language and customs, never forgetting his own language and customs. He held on fast to these as he worked hard in school and later enlisted in the army, where he learned a trade which would later prove useful in helping him earn a living. He was a brave man, a kind man. He was not educated, yet he knew what was right and what was wrong. He fought for one and against the other." The tears flowed freely down the cheeks of those assembled as the sobbing grew louder interspersed with wailing.

Growing bolder, I said, "This man was not famous. He did not do anything noteworthy, yet he was something that no man ever was or could ever be." I paused and let the words sink in. There came a hush over the crowd. Taking a deep breath, I said, "He was my father and that is the greatest thing any man could be. Now, let us join together and take my father to be with his beloved wife as we gather to accompany him to his final resting place." Turning toward the casket, my eyes filled with tears for the first time, I said in a voice strong, yet like a whisper, "I love you, Dad." I turned and left the altar.

The scene at the grave was somber. The family gathered around the open hole in the ground as the priest said the holy words, sprinkled the holy water, and beseeched the good Lord to make room for my father in his house of many rooms. I heard none of it. I stood there in my silence, lost in my own thoughts. The voice in my head was insistent, "What are you going to do now?"

The ceremony soon finished, and the priest gave the final blessing. One by one, the mourners passed the grave for the final time, said their private goodbyes, and tossed in a lily, and turned away to go back to their lives. Soon I was the last one there.

I stepped closer to the grave and dared look down into the darkness, a darkness where my father's body would spend eternity. Except, it was not dark in the deep hole. It was if the sun had sent down a single beam to fill the grave with warmth and light. No, this was not a dark cold grave, but a warm, gently lit place of rest. I smiled for the first time in days. I called out, "Rest in peace, Dad, and say hi to Mom. I turned to walk back to the family when I heard a sound in the wind that I swear whispered, "I will."

Chapter 58

We all went back to my Aunt Emanuella's house to continue the traditional Italian funeral ritual with food and drink, much drink! You see, once the solemnity of the funeral is over and the body laid to rest, we celebrate life with a meal, drink and, of course, stories of the recently departed. By telling stories and recalling the name of the deceased, they never truly die; they remain with us in our hearts and minds forever. Sometimes, we even call upon them to help us in our lives. They may even visit us in our dreams; their energy is with us always.

And so it was. We celebrated my father with all of his favorite foods, lovingly prepared by hand. Breads, cookies, cakes and desserts galore. It was truly not a time to be on a diet. Along with the food came drink. Wines from Italy, Italian liquors and coffees were served to all, no matter age or level of infirmity. All would enjoy and drink until they could drink no more. We were celebrating for hours, but even this too would end.

With food still on the table and drink freely poured into empty glasses, the mourners, slowly said their goodbyes and trickled out the door. Soon I was alone with my Uncles, Carmine and Rosario, and my Aunt Emanuella.

The four of us, tired as we were, sat around the dining room table. I glanced at the kitchen clock astonished to see it was nearly nine p.m.. I took a deep breath to steel myself for what would happen next and, pushing back my chair and rising to my feet, I announced, "I think I better get home."

I could see a horrified look on my aunt's face. A quick glance from Uncle Carmine thwarted her attempt at comment. Turning toward me, he said, "Perhaps it will be better to stay here tonight."

As his words sunk in, it finally hit me. "What am I going to do now?" I was overwhelmed and it must have shown on my face for my uncle said, "Just stay here tonight and tomorrow you and I can talk about the future."

I looked up and chuckled. Puzzled, Uncle Carmine asked, "What's so funny?"

Still smiling, I replied, "You must be a mind reader. That was exactly what was going through my head at that very moment." We both laughed.

I continued to my feet and said, "I really need to go home and sort this out for myself tonight. I would very much like to discuss this tomorrow with you, but tonight I need to be alone."

My uncle said, "Well, you are the man of the house now and well old enough to make such decisions. Go home, rest. Tomorrow we talk."

I said my goodbyes, gave each of them a hug and a kiss, thanking them for their support, and headed to the door.

Aunt Emanuella and Linda walked me to the door. I knew they would try to get me to stay but my mind, although confused, was made up.

"Roberto," implored my Aunt, "stay tonight. You will feel better in the morning, please"

Linda chimed in, "Look, Bill and I are going home in a few minutes, you can stay in my room."

I looked at Linda and smiled. "Stay in your room? I can remember a time when you once told me that if I even so much as broke the plane of the doorway into your room you would give me a bloody nose! I was terrified you would really do it."

"Well, I might have then, but we are a little older. "She took a slow punch to my nose. "Really, you should stay."

I hugged them both, gave my thanks, assured them I would be fine, and turned to leave before they redoubled their efforts to thwart my escape.

Chapter 59

I bounded down the porch steps. The sun had gone down; there was still the cool evening light from a summer full moon. I closed the wrought iron gate, remembering how once Linda shut my hand in it, accidentally, and broke my finger. She told me they would shoot me since I broke my finger, just like they do horses! I laughed at the memory, turned, and headed home.

Some of the neighbors were sitting out on their porches, laughing and just enjoying being with family. 'Family,' I thought. 'My family was gone, I was alone. What am I going to do?' My mind was a tornado of thoughts and confusion. Round and round came the thoughts. 'What about school? Do I stay here? Move? Move where? What do I do now?'

I walked slowly down the street and soon came to my home; The home we all lived in for the better part of my life. A home so full of energy and life, now empty and devoid of sound. I stood there for a moment on the sidewalk and just stared at the darkened windows. Silent, empty. Taking a deep breath, to bolster my courage, I climbed the porch steps, closed the gate and headed to the front door. Pulling back the screen door, out of the far corner of my eye, I thought I saw a flash of light pass by the big front window. I was stunned. I knew there were no lights on in the house. It must have been a trick of the wind playing with the moonlight behind some leaves, making a quick flash across the glass. It was nothing. Nothing at all. I opened the front door and stepped into my home, alone.

I stood there for a moment letting my eyes get used to the darkness. I was afraid, for some reason, to turn on the light. I didn't want to disturb the darkness, yet I knew I had to move on, so I switched on the parlor light.

Light diffused in the parlor and streamed ever so slowly into the doorway of the living room. The light brightened the darkness as if the darkness had some power to keep the light at bay. I looked into the open doorway and, for a moment, thought I saw a shadow standing in the door. As quickly as it formed, the light finally penetrated the room and banished all the darkness from my sight. I was frozen to the spot, unable to move. I shuddered for a moment, caught my breath and said with the voice inside my head, "Robbie, get a grip. There is nothing and no one here. You're tired, confused, a little drunk and in need of some rest. Pull it together, man, and move on." I tried.

Stepping into the living room, I immediately turned on all the lights I could find. My father would have given me hell for wasting electricity, but right now all I could do was make sure there was not a dark spot anywhere in the house. I turned on every switch and table lamp from the front of the house to the back bedrooms.

My nerves began to settle, so I sat down in the dining room at my usual spot. I looked around the room. From my perch I could see the kitchen, empty and quiet. I could turn my head and look down the dining room past the doorway into the family room. Quiet. Turning fully around I could look down the hallway toward my bedroom, the bathroom, and my parent's room. Silent. For the moment, I was alone.

I decided that a drink would be in order to calm my frayed nerves and help put me to sleep. My father would always have a bottle of Chianti from Tuscany. We often enjoyed a bottle on Sunday with the main meal, so I knew there was always a bottle or two on hand. I got up from the table, pushed my chair in, as I was always told to do, and opened the closet to get the bottle.

As I reached in, I heard a noise at the dining room table. It was the same sound I had just made pushing my chair against the wooden floor. The hair on the back of my neck and arms began to rise. I could feel a new energy in the air.

I grabbed the bottle, jumped back from the closet, stood up, and surveyed my surroundings. Everything was exactly as I had left it. "Of course it is as you left it, you are the only one here," said my inner voice. "Have a drink."

I went to the dish closet to get a wine glass and, without waiting another second, poured, then drained, two fingers of Chianti from the glass. I could feel the warmth as the dry wine slid down my throat. I felt suddenly warm and calm. I headed to the dining room table, placed my glass down, and poured a full glass. As I was putting the cork back in the bottle, I could once again feel the room fill with energy, and I suddenly heard a distinct "chink" the sound that two wine glasses would make as if we clinked in a toast. Except there was only one glass. I figured my mind was playing tricks on me again so I sat down and sipped the rest of my glass as I began to contemplate my next move.

I sat there for a long time, sipping and thinking, coming up with nothing. I poured another glass. I knew I was feeling the wine, but I needed to calm down and the wine was producing the desired effect. I was calm, but my senses were heightened. I could feel the hairs on my arms rise again. Suddenly, out of the corner of my eye, I saw a quick movement in the kitchen and heard a voice.

The pitch was female and far away. It may have been the wine playing tricks or voices from outside as neighbors said their goodbyes for the night.

I tried to clear my head. Deciding I already had too much wine, I stood up to go to the kitchen to pour the remainder into the sink when I heard a deeper voice say, "Such waste." I froze again.

The mind is a strange engine. The senses of sight, touch, and hearing are what the mind uses to make sense of the world. The mind wants to make order out of chaos and so psychologists have concluded that, when the mind hears something that it is not familiar with, the mind tries to make it familiar, and so, many sounds that are not really voices are actually heard as voices. Therefore, I decided, what I heard was not a voice, but my clouded mind trying to make some sense out of chaos. Yeah, that was it. I was having an auditory hallucination. Too much drink, exhaustion, and being alone were conspiring against me. I poured the rest of the wine into the sink.

I turned quickly to head to bed and I must have been drunker than I thought because my head spun fast and my eyes moved slowly, giving me an immediate sense of vertigo. I reached out toward the sink to steady myself and, out of the corner of my eye, I saw another flash and another shadow. I stood there for a minute, my head spinning and my body weaving, firmly convinced I was not alone. Maybe the drink was to blame or maybe the drink opened me up somehow to something in the house. I don't know which, but I had to get out. Suddenly, this was a mistake.

I steadied myself as best I could, and left the kitchen heading towards my room. I needed to get some things I needed for the next couple of days, but I didn't know what they were. I was really confused, drunk, and damn scared.

On my way to my room, I opened the closet door to see if there was a bag or something I could throw some things into. The closet was pitch black. I fell to my knees and rummaged around trying to find something. I couldn't see a thing. My sense of touch was clouded and I was getting more crazed by the second.

Suddenly, it was as if a light came on in the closet. Not an electric light or even a flashlight, but a glow. I can't explain it other than maybe my eyes adjusted to the darkness or some light that was in the dining room had filtered down the hall giving me just enough light to see. Either way, my hands felt the rough surface of a cloth canvas bag. I pulled and tugged, but it was stuck. "Oh, come on now. A little help, please," the voice in my head pleaded. I tugged once more and the bag slid out as easy as could be. I was tugging so hard I fell over on myself and lay there on the hall floor. Panting from the strain and stress, I looked up and stared right into a light bulb. The bright aura almost blinded me. Then I thought, "Why the hell was the closet so dark when the hall light was on?"

Lying frozen and still staring into the light, I closed my eyes for a split second and then opened them. Instead of a bright light, I could see a face, the face of my mother, brilliantly lit from behind. I was in shock.

I knew from my psychology class that seeing faces where there are none, is again a safety mechanism the mind uses to make order out of chaos. They even have a term for the phenomenon, pareidolia. Minds games or not, I was terrified. I was not alone. I heard sounds, voices, and was seeing things. I had to get out and fast.

I crawled into my room, refusing to look again at the face in the light, and quickly threw some things in the bag. I pulled some of my textbooks off the shelf, threw some clothes next into the bag, and looked around at what was left. I know I wasn't thinking clearly, so I opened and closed several drawers, tossing things into the bag and moving on. Soon the bag was full. I zipped it closed, and started as fast as possible through the house, shutting off lights, and heading for the front door.

As I reached the parlor, I heard my name called from the living room. Against my better judgment, I stopped and turned to see who it was. There in the far corner of the room, in the darkness were, not one, but two shadows. They were frozen there against the wall as if they were looking at me. Turning, I heard one last voice, "We love you."

I headed for the front door. Not turning around, I put my bag on the top step of the porch, closed and locked the front door and, picking up my bag, headed down the steps to the sidewalk. I never returned to the house again.

Chapter 60

I stood there, rooted to the sidewalk. I was panting, my breath coming in short bursts. Although there was a cool evening breeze, I was sweating profusely. My arms were shaking and I was off balance. "What the hell was happening?" I said to myself.

I took a step and leaned against my Sycamore for balance, longing to feel something other than my own body. I tried to catch my breath but was unable to suck in any air. The panic grew. I stood there for a minute, my right hand against the soft wood of the tree, bent at the waist trying to calm my nerves. Slowly, ever so slowly, I felt as if there was an energy coming from the tree, a calming energy. I stood up, took in a deep breath and filled my lungs. I followed this with a long, deep exhale as if I could empty my lungs twice without the need to fill them. I could feel a change coming over me.

I was able to stand and, as I did so, I turned toward the house and looked at the place I once called home, as if for the first time. It looked different but, of course, it was exactly the same. I stood there for a moment and shook from head to toe as if to shake off some outer skin that was covering me. I could feel the heat from my arms, my head, and my entire body leaving me. I could almost "see" the waves of heat energy as they lifted from my body and seemed to flow into the house. I shuddered once again, this time involuntarily.

I continued to look at the front of the house, looking for something but not knowing what. Suddenly, my heart rate slowed, I could feel the cool evening breeze blow on my now cool skin. I felt calm, at peace. I turned on my heel and started to walk to my aunt and uncle's house, trying to figure out what I was going to tell them.

With each step away from my own home, I felt better, calmer, more in control. It was as if there was something in or about the house that had invaded my mind and body. With each step I put distance between me and whatever it was until the distance was enough to completely break the influence. By the time I reached my uncle's driveway, all was good.

Truth be told, I loved my Uncle Rosario more than any of my other uncles. I took his name as my confirmation name. I recall the day he stood behind me, strong hands on my shoulders, as the priest gave me the sacrament and slapped my face proclaiming me a "soldier of Christ." He was my pillar of strength. Unfortunately, the years took that strength from him.

My stalwart uncle suffered from a most horrifying form of dementia. There were times when he was lucid and engaged in all around him. Then, there were the times when he was lost in a world within his own head. It was sad and painful to see him go from one phase to the other for he was confused and scared when he lost his hold on reality.

Like most things, however, the condition was a double edge sword. When his mind retreated into its own world he seemed to be more open to the unseen world around him. He claimed to have conversations with the dead. He saw his mother and father as they were some fifty years ago. He was visited by those "who need his help" to give a message to some living relative or just needed help in moving on. Of course, no one believed he could commune with the dead. We all accepted that it was only a figment of his imagination. It kept him calm to think this condition gave him purpose even though it scared the hell out of the rest of us. If this "reality" made him feel better, then there was no harm.

So I walked past the driveway and headed to the porch at my uncle's house. For some reason, my eyes were pulled toward the front window. There, in the shadow of the parlor, lit from behind by a small lamp in the living room, stood my uncle. He was standing alone in the darkened room, staring out into the night, looking directly at the full moon, his lips moving as if in conversation. His face was blank and relaxed, almost to the point of catatonia. His left hand rested on the back of a wing back chair, seemingly to steady himself. His shoulders were slouched and relaxed. It looked like he was asleep standing up. I stood there a moment as I looked at my beloved uncle lost in his own world. I was both saddened and pained. Saddened to see my uncle in such a state. Pained to think of my own troubles in comparison with what he must be going through. I looked up for another minute, said a brief prayer, an old Catholic habit, took a deep breath and headed up the stairs to the front door.

The door was unlocked, normal for no one left their door locked in this neighborhood. Carefully, trying not to frighten my uncle, I quietly opened the door. As I stepped into the parlor, turning to close the door, I heard my uncle say, "I was expecting you."

Turning away from the door I stood frozen in the parlor as I tried to digest his words. Expecting me, how? Why? As I was contemplating what was going on, he continued in a far off voice, "It must have been noisy over there."

Now, I was frightened. What was he saying? Before I could say a word he spoke again, "Sometimes they are not ready. They need time."

Stuttering, I asked, "Who needs more time, Uncle?"

"The dead, sometimes they are not ready to be dead," he muttered. At the same moment he finished this utterance, I saw him physically change. First, there came a light to his eyes. His blank stare went away as the muscles in his face seemed to tighten into almost a grin. The sag in his shoulders rose to the point where he stood up straight and proud. He shook off the malaise he was under and, looking directly at me with clear bright eyes said, "Robbie, what are you doing here?" as if the last few minutes never happened.

I stuttered a response, "I couldn't sleep at the house."

Without skipping a beat, he smiled a broad smile, walked over to me and, putting his hand on my shoulder said, "That's fine, there is no need to be alone tonight. You are always welcome here. Come on, let's get you settled."

He took me through the house and down the hall to Linda's old room. He turned and bid me good night and headed to his own room and to bed. I stood there for a minute trying to comprehend what was going on, but exhaustion seemed to overtake me. I tossed my bag into the corner and sat on the bed. I was going to get changed, but the sight of the pillow pulled me down. Fully clothed, I fell fast asleep. It was the best sleep I'd had in a long time.

Chapter 61

I awoke the next morning, well-rested, clear-headed, and feeling better than I have in a very long time. It was as if I had a new purpose in life. I just didn't know exactly what the purpose was. I knew that I had to return to school, to complete the summer project that I was obligated to complete for Dr. Grun. Once there, perhaps, I could secure a job in one of the university or local labs as a lab tech. I had my degree and I was sure Dr. Grun would vouch for me. It was way too late to apply to graduate school; I missed that boat a long time ago. I could work for a year, save up some money and apply for grad school, and get on with the rest of my life. It seemed like a good idea at the time.

I came into the dining room after cleaning up Linda's room, I was somehow afraid to leave a trace that I was in the room. She once threatened to cut off my hand if I touched anything in her room; imagine what she would cut off when we were younger if she knew then that I slept in her bed!

I joined my aunt and uncle who had already sat down to breakfast. Over a hot cup of espresso and some freshly baked breads, I shared with them my plans to return to school.

Since I was an adult, my choices were my own, so they listened with great patience, asked some questions on how I would get along, and finally gave me their blessing. In an Italian family, no matter how independent you think you are, it is always a great feeling and, a deep-seated need, to get your family's blessing. So, I was genuinely happy when they gave me theirs. I decided it was best that I leave the following morning. Since it was Sunday, my aunt decided to call my Uncle Carmine, Aunt Sandra, and my cousins Lillian and Annette. My whole family would be there for a grand farewell.

Aunt Emanuella outdid herself. The meal was cooked from scratch, and the menu was filled with all my favorites. Freshly baked breads, Italian chicken parmesan, lasagna, fresh salad, and an array of Italian baked sweets to make a bakery jealous. It was a perfect send off.

At the end of the meal, Uncle Carmine, the de facto head of the family, called me to the parlor for a talk. He asked me my plans, to which I reiterated all the plans I had discussed earlier with Aunt Emanuella and Uncle Rosario. He, too, listened intently, asked a few questions, and agreed that this was a good plan. I was feeling pretty good that maybe all things would work out.

"OK, then so what about the house and all the contents of your home? What do you plan to do about that?" he asked.

"I don't know," I stammered. "I really have no idea."

"Well, then, let me suggest that since you have plans that do not include Brooklyn for the near future, you give me the authority to sell the house and the contents. We can put the funds in a secure account, from which you can draw as you need, to get your future in order. This will give you a head start, and I am sure it is what your father would want. In this way, your father can make a last effort to help you begin a new life.

"I think that would be perfect. How can I thank you for taking on such a task?"

"Just promise me you will never do anything the family would be ashamed of and that you will always keep close to us all and that would be enough for me."

I readily agreed and stepped forward to shake his hand and seal the deal.

Chapter 62

The next morning, bright and early, I headed to the train station for the ride back to New Brunswick. I had my father's old duffel bag, packed with all my belongings slung over my shoulder. I was ready for anything, or so I thought.

Once I got to the station in New Brunswick, I headed over to my rooms on Seamen Street. As I bounded up the porch I happened to see what looked like an envelope stuffed in the screen door. Since most of the residents were gone for the summer, I had no idea who would leave a note, so I plucked it from the door.

At once I knew the envelope was in the door for some time. It was a little wet and soiled as if it had been subject to some bad weather. I could hardly read the outside of the envelope, but I could make out a capital R as part of the name on the front, so I tore open the envelope and read the contents.

Sure enough, it was sent to me, sometime late in June. It was from Dr. Grun. The note read:

"Robbie, I heard about the passing of your father. Please accept my sincerest condolences for your loss. I need to see you about a pressing matter. Please come to the office at your earliest. Dr. G"

I had no idea what could be so urgent, then it came to me. I must be in some deep trouble for having left the lab in a rush. I knew I should have contacted Dr. Grun to let him know what was going on but I forgot with all the turmoil of the last several weeks. I failed to keep up the research as I committed to him and now, having let him down, he would not be likely to give me the reference I would need to get a lab position. My plans were falling apart before I even had a chance to begin.

I headed over to his office immediately, hoping to catch him in a good mood, and see if I could throw myself on his mercy. I was a nervous wreck as I headed through the doors of Thompson Hall and down the long hall to his office in the far corner. I could see that there was still a light on in the office. I stopped outside the glass door for a moment, to slow my racing heart and steal my nerve against what was to come. I took a final deep breath and opened the door, forming a huge smile on my lips.

I was greeted by a stern looking secretary. Rita was about fifty-eight years old and a fixture in the Biology Office working for Dr. Grun forever. She has always appeared stern to every student who ever walked into her domain. However, it was an act. If she liked you she was the nicest person in the world; if however she didn't, look out. I was one of the fortunate ones. She loved me.

As soon as Rita recognized it was me who had the audacity to enter her domain, I could see her face transform right before my eyes. From the stern scowl reserved for all undergraduate students to the light smile reserved for some graduate students to the happy bright cheer reserved for the select few.

"Robbie Mauro, where in heaven's name have you been?"

"It's a long story," I replied and proceeded to give her a blow by blow description of the last several weeks, hoping to further garner her favor so I could beg her to help me smooth over any issues with Dr. Grun.

She listened intently as I went over my troubles and travails one by one. She appropriately sighed and tut tutted, shaking her head in sympathy. When I was finished, she declared, "You poor thing," and, most uncharacteristically, left the safety of her desk, walked over to me, and gave me a big hug. I was stunned.

After a moment, she released me and, smoothing her clothes, regained her composure and her position of authority behind the desk and asked, "Well, what can we do for you today?"

I explained about the note from Dr. G, handing her the somewhat soiled document to prove, in effect, that I did not get the note earlier, but went straight to the office as soon as I had.

She took the note and read the words in silence. Looking up she said "I see. Well Dr. Grun is not here today, but I am sure he still wants to speak with you." From this I gathered she knew what he wanted to talk to me about. Rita knew everything. However, try as I might, she would only say, "Dr. Grun is at a conference until Friday. I will let him know you are back in town and I am sure he will see you when he returns. Come back here on Friday and we will take it from there." I was dismissed. There was nothing else to say or do, so I thanked her and sheepishly left the office, trying to close the door without a sound, I did not want anything to disturb her.

"Now what?" I said to myself. I stood on the steps of Thompson Hall looking over the common that led out to Passion Puddle trying to determine my next move. "I have a week to get things right with Dr. Grun," I thought, so I decided to head over to the lab to see what damage control I could do on my research. I hoped that if I could get things back in order and write a stellar lab report, I could worm my way back into his good graces and still get that much prized reference. So, off I went, back into Thompson Hall and into the bowels of the basement where my lab was. Unfortunately, the lab was a mess, just as I had left it.

I assumed that Dr. Grun, who was fastidious in his desire for order in the lab, must have stopped by the lab, saw the sorry state of affairs and became angry with me for not only leaving, but leaving a mess. I hoped that if I cleaned up the mess, put everything in order and compiled a stellar report, I could quickly return to his good graces.

I spent the better part of every day for the rest of the week working in the lab. Except for food and four hours sleep a night, I was busy in the lab running and rerunning experiments and trying to do four weeks of work in four days. I must have been very lucky for every experiment went perfectly and all the results were exactly as predicted. That rarely happens in science; if something can go wrong it will. I wrote an exceptional lab report complete with charts and references. It was, by far, the best work I had ever done.

On Friday afternoon, as instructed, I returned to Dr. Grun's office with my completed study, bound and ready for presentation. Rita again greeted me with her stern look, which quickly melted to a smile. "Welcome back. I hear you have been busy." How did she know? I never said anything to anyone; in fact, I hardly saw anyone all week as I buried myself in the lab.

"I have good news and bad news, "she stated matter-of-factly. "The bad news is Dr. Grun is not here. The good news is he has invited you to his farm on Sunday precisely at two p.m., so don't be late" She smiled and looked down at her desk. Dismissed again. I stood there for a second with my mouth open. Before I could say a word, Rita looked, up, smiled, and said, "That is all." A final dismissal. I knew it was no use to say anything, so I uttered a goodbye and quietly left the room.

There was nothing I could do but wait until Sunday. I headed back to Seamen Street and a much needed rest.

Chapter 63

Dr. Grun lived on the north side of campus about a ten minute walk from Thompson Hall. At one time, the property was a vast horse farm but, many years ago most of the property had been donated to the university except for about twenty acres which comprised the current residence of Dr. Grun and his wife Elizabeth.

The house itself could only be described as "grand" in every sense of the word. The fresh coat of white paint stood in contrast to the dark blue shutters surrounding each large front window. The front of the house was preceded by a large porch, with a gray painted wooden floor, white side rails and comfortable chairs for family to sit and enjoy the peace after a hard day's work in the field. The front door was guarded by a light screen door painted the same color as the shutters. The front door was decorated with a beautiful summer wreath hand fashioned with colorful and fragrant flowers. The scene was very open and inviting.

I arrived promptly at two p.m., as instructed by the ever punctual Rita, dressed in a fresh white shirt and dark black pants. I had a bottle of red wine, another suggestion from Rita, under my arm. I bounded up the steps to the expansive front porch and reached out to ring the bell when the front door suddenly opened and there stood Dr. Grun himself, smiling broadly.

"Come in, come in young man. We were expecting you," he said, putting his arm around my shoulder and calling to his wife, "Lizzy, we have company."

He ushered me into the front parlor, which was filled with an array of farm antiques and other implements of his trade. From the ceiling hung a two horse yoke, once used to pull a plow. On the inside wall were photos of the farm over the years, showing various seasons rich in the colors of summer and spring. The autumn photos showed the large trees that bordered the horse paddock, bespeckled in bright reds, oranges and yellows; while the winter shots showed snow bound fields and the home in various Christmas decors over the years. As we walked through the room I admired the decor when Dr. Grun noticed the bag in my hand and said, "Let me guess, Rita suggested a fine red wine for dinner? "

I stammered, "Yes sir." I didn't know if I should feign ignorance and claim that I thought of it myself.

221

"Good, I can always count on Rita to council my guests properly." He laughed and ushered me further into his home. He introduced me to his wife of thirty-four years, Elizabeth, who took my hand and led me to the dining room where she had set a fine table of hot dishes. The room smelled of meats and a variety of vegetables. "I hope you brought an appetite along with that wine." She led me to a seat at her side.

I was somewhat overwhelmed. I was told that Dr. Grun wanted to talk to me, not that he had invited me to dinner. Without thinking, I said, "Dr. Grun, sir, Rita said you wanted to talk to me."

"Yes, yes, of course, we will talk. Indeed, but first dinner and wine. What do you say, lad?"

"Yes, of course," was all I could say.

So there we sat, the three of us enjoying a fine dinner and light conversation. Dr. Grun expressed his deepest condolences on the passing of my father and asked me if I was okay. I assured him I was fine and I began to tell him of my plans when he politely interrupted by saying, "In due time, son. We will discuss in due time."

So, we finished dinner and were treated to a fine dessert of biscuits with lemon, an old Romanian favorite. I was informed that Dr. Grun and his wife were born in Romania, hence the recipe.

With dessert completed, I paid my most humble thanks to Mrs. Grun for an outstanding meal. Dr. Grun and I retired to the front porch for a talk. He hit me immediately with "Robbie, I was very disappointed to learn that you had not applied to graduate school upon completion of your undergraduate work. As a member of the admissions committee, I was looking forward to getting your application. What happened?"

"Sir, I was planning to apply, but when my father died, I was somewhat at a crossroad as to what I was going to do. By the time I figured it out, it was too late. I was hoping to ask you for a reference, so I could apply for a lab position at the university and then apply to graduate school later," I said, hoping to obtain his approval.

"Young man, I can do better than that. First, it is never too late to apply to grad school, especially if you know the head of the committee. Second, if you promise to get your application into the university system by the end of the week, I can assure your acceptance into my program. Will that work for you?"

"Yes, yes that would be far beyond my expectations, but..."

"No buts. There is one more thing." Rising from his chair on the porch, he said, "Follow me."

I rose in obedience and followed him off the porch and down the front steps toward the far end of the yard.

"You remember Robert Berkowitz, now Dr. Berkowitz, my former graduate student?" he asked.

'Yes sir, of course I do. I was working with him on some of your projects."

"Yes, yes, of course you were. Well, he told me that you might be an exceptional person to replace him as my graduate student. He liked your technique and your dedication to your studies."

We stopped walking and stood in front of a large carriage house. The kind of carriage house that, at one time, might have held up to twenty horses. The building was immense, with large front doors and a hay loft above. There were no longer any horses on the farm; the stalls had been converted to storage and a fully stocked lab. I followed Dr. Grun around the side of the building to a stairway along the outside of the building.

"If you are going to replace Berkowitz, you should enjoy all the amenities he did. Follow me," he said, heading for the stairs.

When we reached the top of the stairs, he drew a key from his pocket and opened the door. We entered a loft apartment, replete with bedroom, kitchen, study, and private bathroom. Dr. Grun turned to me and handed me the key saying, "Welcome to your new residence."

I was stunned. "Sir, there is no way I could afford such an apartment."

"Nonsense. Berkowitz, and now you ,will reside here while in school and all that I ask in return is for you to study hard, work hard in the lab, and, from time to time, help me with some chores around the farm, I am getting a little older you know," he said chuckling, much pleased with himself.

"I don't know what to say."

"Yes, would be a good start."

"Well, then, yes" I said, as I shook his hand to seal the deal and looked around at my new residence. This was much better than I could ever have hoped. I guess my parents were indeed smiling down at me.

Chapter 64

After all the crazy things that had happened in my life, things were finally looking up! I was moving into the loft apartment vacated by the recently minted Dr. Bob Berkowitz. He left me with a complete library of research books, and many of his personal notebooks concerning the research he was working on for Dr. Grun. Since I was going to take on the task of replacing him in the lab, these notes would prove to be very valuable indeed.

I learned from Rita that I was the fifth graduate student allowed to live in the loft. It seemed Dr. Grun offered these accommodations to a very select few. I was humbled to be one of them.

The loft was very well appointed with some nice antiques and some very modern yet functional furniture. It seemed that the antiques had come from different grad students over the years. Each student added some personal touch or arrangement and left these in the loft as part of the history of each one.

Although really one large open space, the loft was nicely divided using furniture and bookcases to form a well-appointed dine-in kitchen, reading/living room with antique lamps on chestnut tables, a study area replete with roll top desk and dark green banker's lamp, and finally a spacious sleeping area with full size bed and private bath. Not bad for a city boy from Brooklyn, not bad at all.

Of course, I was still mourning the loss of both parents within the last year, a deep loss that would never truly be cleared. But, even from this loss came some good news.

When I went home the next weekend to tell my family of my good fortune and to get my remaining personal effects, Uncle Carmine told me he had been able to sell my parents' home for a very handsome profit. He paid some expenses and there was still a significant amount of money left over. Being the wise man that he was, he informed me that the extra money was put into a fund, one that would pay me money every month for the next fifteen years. It was not a fortune, but the money would go a long way to helping pay my expenses. Coupled with the free rent from my new apartment and the salary from my teaching position, I would have no money worries for my full graduate school career. I am sure the souls of my parents would be pleased that they were still able to help me even after they were gone. I went to Mass that Sunday and lit a candle for each of them to thank them for all they had done for me. I promised to make them proud.

My uncle was even able to salvage a few personal items from the house before it was sold, the most important of which was my grandmother's bentwood rocker. I loved that chair. It had a very special place in my heart. I would often sit in my room in the dark just before falling asleep and imagine my grandmother, wrapped in a blanket, rocking slowly, watching over me as I fell asleep. I was comforted to know she was there watching over me. I had to take the chair with me in memory of her.

There were some other items from the house that held a special memory of my parents that I also had to have. When I put everything together, however, I had no idea how I would get them to my new home. Once again, Uncle Carmine to the rescue. He seemed to have some friends who owed him a favor. I never asked any questions, I was just pleased when the items arrived the next week to my loft at school.

School started that September and I was enrolled in four graduate courses. One in genetics, my major field of endeavor, another in statistics, and two additional courses designed to help me in my research.

I also taught a freshman class in General Biology for Dr. Grun. It was amazing to see the faces on these freshmen, many of them away from home for the first time in their lives. It was like looking at deer frightened by a flashlight in the woods. That sort of blank stare with large black eyes just staring into space. I am sure, just four years ago, that was me. I had to shake my head and laugh at the sight. I committed to being the best teaching assistant I could be. I wanted to make a difference, and I was going to work hard to be a success.

Besides my classes and teaching, I was involved in my own research. I was continuing the research on Avian Infectious Bronchitis Virus where Dr. Berkowitz left off. New Jersey is known as the Garden State because there are many acres devoted to agriculture and livestock. The poultry industry in New Jersey is very strong, especially in the Vineland area, south of New Brunswick. Each year tens of thousands of chickens are infected with the virus. Birds so infected fail to thrive or succumb to the disease. The cost to New Jersey poultry farmers can be devastating. Dr. Grun and his team had been working on developing a vaccine to treat the birds before the infection set in. I was to continue this work where Berkowitz left off. I was to work on determining the different serotypes present in the virus so that we could develop a vaccine, depending on which specific species of virus was infecting the flock. I had my work cut out for me. When I was not busy with these endeavors, I was helping Dr. Grun at the farm, for which I was rewarded with a standing invitation to Sunday dinner, a feast that gave me leftovers that often lasted four days.

For the next several years, I was busy and loving it. I excelled at my classes, enjoyed teaching, and was making great progress with my research. I was happy and looking forward to the future. Yes, things were looking up, but it never seemed to stay that way for long.

Chapter 65

Mark

I don't know why I never told Robbie the truth. I knew I should have, but he was so mad that summer seven years ago, when I told him about the piece of the Ouija Board I found. He was so mad he swore and then punched me to make the point to stop talking about it. So I lied. I told him I buried it with the rest, but I didn't. I kept it. I don't know why, but I kept it all these years. That damn eighth piece, the infinity piece, Robbie called it. Now it was almost Robbie's twenty-fifth birthday.

For the last three months I was having nightmares. Well, not exactly nightmares, but the *same* nightmare. Sure I was stressed out. I was completing my last term at law school; I was in the top ten percent of my class. I was studying for the NY State Bar Exam, while working as a clerk for Judge Frederick Collins, Presiding Judge on the New York State Court of Appeals. Yes, I was stressed.

I had gotten to the point that I was afraid to fall asleep at night. This only made things worse. When I did fall asleep, I was so tired that I was unable to wake from the dream. I was forced to relive the same vivid full color dream, night after night.

The dream always began the same way. I would be back at home, sitting on the front porch waiting for my brother Roger and Robbie. Suddenly, out of nowhere, I would hear a screech as if someone was torturing a small animal. The sound was horrible as if the insides of the animal were being ripped out. As soon as the sound died away, I was no longer on the front steps, but I was on a dirt path in some kind of fog or mist. I would look around and couldn't see anyone or anything, the fog was so thick, but I was not alone.

I could sense, rather than see, I was not alone. There was someone just out of reach in the fog, taunting me. Whoever, or whatever it was, was moving around in swift circles, around and around, so that the fog swirled about, revealing a glimpse of solid form but nothing to identify who or what was there.

I called out, "Who's there? What do you want?" Then I demanded, "Show yourself." Instead of getting some clarity of the figure, there was another desperate screech, worse than before, louder and more pitiful. I could feel myself sweating in bed, but I could not force myself to awaken. I felt trapped and unable to move. I knew the dream had to play out.

As the fog swirled about me, I could begin to see the ground more clearly. There was a path and some grass near the path. I could smell the scent of fresh flowers, lilies I think. Eventually, the fog cleared and the path and the ground became suddenly clear, I was standing on the path in the middle of the Gravesend Cemetery, right near the spot Robbie broke his arm back in high school. I was terrified. I knew it was a dream, and I told myself it was a dream and demanded I wake up. But nothing, the dream went on.

Once again the venue changed. This time I was in the garage back in Brooklyn. Robbie and Roger were there. We were standing around an old barbeque grill. Robbie was lighting a match and Roger was dousing something with lighter fluid. I knew exactly where I was, back on the day we destroyed the Ouija Board.

The scene changed again. Now I was alone in the dark, someplace outside, because I could feel a breeze and could hear a sound that I couldn't identify. It sounded human, but was not words, more like a guttural sound that could become a laugh or a growl. It became both. First a growl, which morphed into a laugh, and back to a growl. Back and forth it went. My dream self put hands to my ears to stop the sound to no avail. It only grew louder. I was frozen in my bed, sweat dripping, trapped in my dream.

After what seemed like an eternity, there was silence. A silence so profound that I thought I was dead, but I could feel my heart beating wildly in my sleeping body. I was still trapped. I could not move a muscle. I was being held to the bed by my own dead weight. Then, another sound. This time it was a voice. It was a woman's voice, not the sweet sound of a chaste woman, but the horrid guttural bay of a despicable hag. One word, said once, "Soon." Then it was over. My body was drenched in my own sweat. I could move again, and so I jumped out of bed and headed to my dresser. I reached into the drawer, and all the way to the back. I clawed at the back of the drawer until my fingers found what I was looking for. I pulled my hand back, my fist closed, too scared to open my hand and gaze on the object within. I didn't need to see the item; I knew exactly what it was. Once my nerves settled, and my courage returned, I opened my hand to reveal the piece, that damned piece, the eighth piece of the Ouija Board. Worn, broken, but not destroyed, the eighth piece. Infinity. Freedom.

Chapter 66

I had successfully completed four years of graduate study. I was finished with all of my coursework by the end of May. During the past four years I had made significant progress with my research. I was even able to publish three separate peer-reviewed articles, allowing me to bask in the scientific limelight, at least for a little while. Even Dr. Grun was pleased with my progress. The only thing I had left to do was some additional final research and submit my dissertation for review. I planned to complete my PhD degree by January next year.

Since all was going according to plan, I decided to take a little time for myself this summer. By the end of May, the undergraduates had left the campus. What was once a crowded environment quickly morphed into a quiet peaceful campus. There were only five graduate students who planned to stay over the summer. Since I really had no place to go, and my lodging was free, I decided to stay and enjoy the summer. Even Dr. Grun decided to do some vacationing. He was planning to celebrate his fortieth wedding anniversary by taking the affable Mrs. Grun to Romania, the land of their birth, for the summer. I would have the farm all to myself. I would miss Mrs. Grun's meals, but the peace and quiet of the farm would be a just reward.

It was the second week in June, and it came time for the Gruns to leave. After sitting me down and giving me a list of do's and don'ts for managing the farm, Mrs. Grun finally pulled the good doctor away from me by saying, "John, Robbie knows what he's doing, so let him do it." Dr. Grun shook his head, laughed and said, "What's the worst that could happen?" How prophetic those words were to become.

Soon after the Gruns left I settled into a routine. I rose early, to feed the horses and muck out the stalls. Next came the chickens, feed two family hogs, and turn the horses out for a run in the paddock. By noon the chores were done and the rest of the day was mine.

Often I would sit in the hammock in the front yard and read a book. Most of the books I had been reading were textbooks or works of a scholarly sort, not the kind of thing one looked forward to. Now I enjoyed a novel or two and was looking forward to reading some nonfiction just to pass the time. I often fell asleep while swinging in the hammock, Yes, it was a very peaceful start to the summer.

It was around the middle half of June that things changed a little. One day I fell asleep in the hammock as usual when, instead of a peaceful nap, I was caught up in a nightmare. I could hear a voice calling me from a distance. I assumed someone was in the yard calling on Dr. Grun. Not all of the graduate students knew he was gone for the summer, so some still stopped by for a chat or some guidance with their research. I tried to help one or two in his absence. So, I heard the voice calling and getting closer, but I couldn't wake up.

Not only could I not wake up, I couldn't move either. It was as if I had fallen into a very deep sleep, but I was still aware of my surroundings. I heard the voice getting closer, as if a female were approaching the hammock, but I still could not open my eyes. My arms and legs were like lead weights. My breathing had become shallow, and I was sweating. I was consciously aware of all of this, but I could not change the fact that I could not open my eyes.

Again, I heard the voice, a single sound, but I couldn't understand what she was saying. Now, my heart started to pound in my chest. I could feel my eyeballs moving behind lids that seemed cemented in place. My hair was plastered to my forehead. A slight breeze rocked the hammock, but I could feel no wind. It was as if a hand were slowly pulling on the hammock and releasing it so that it rocked slowly from side to side. I tried and tried but could still not open my eyes. I began to panic.

Finally, the sound of the voice was so close I could swear I could feel the breath of the speaker brush my right ear when I heard the word "Soon" whispered directly into my brain. Suddenly, I was released from the trance and I startled awake. I forgot where I was for a moment and tried to jump up but found myself sprawled on my back as I tumbled out of the hammock and onto the front lawn. I jumped up in my indignity, and looked around, ready to pick a fight with whoever was so rude as to cause me to fall, but there was no one there. I stood in the front yard, turned a full circle once, twice, but there was no one. I was alone and scared. I headed back to the loft, took the stairs two at a time, and locked the door behind me. As I stood alone in the safety of my home, I heard another sound. It was the sound of far off laughter. Not the happy laughter at some joke or someone having a good time. No, it was the sinister laughter of someone who enjoyed torturing small animals. It was the sick laughter of the deranged.

Chapter 67

Mark

The dream continued but, each time, it seemed to be a little more real, a little more frightening. At first I really didn't understand what was happening. I knew it had something to do with the eighth piece of the board. Then, suddenly, it came to me all at once. This June 18th was Robbie's twenty-fifth birthday! That had to be it! The dream was telling me something bad was going to happen. But what? And what could I do to prevent it? I had no idea, but I had to do something.

Although I still counted Robbie as my best friend, I really had not seen much of him since his mother and father died. He was in New Jersey and now I was in upstate New York. Sure, we corresponded a few times and, once last year, we both were home at the same time. We tried to catch up, but family obligations intruded, so we just didn't have the time to do much together. He went back to New Jersey and I headed to the city. We really had not talked since.

I knew the dream was somehow telling me I needed to do something. I had a ton of work to do for the judge, but what if Robbie needed me more? I had to do something, so I headed over to Judge Colins' office to see if I could have a few days to "visit a sick friend."

Now the good judge was not one to care about your problems. He was a man of principles and, if your principles did not include devoting your life to his whims, he could be a bastard. There was no way I could tell him I was having nightmares and I needed to go help out a friend on some unknown quest. I needed a miracle. I was heading over to his office, trying to come up with a reason he should give me a few days off. I played over several scenarios in my head and discarded them before I had completed the thought. I was doomed.

I entered the judge's office and just stood there for a moment, trying to get up the courage to open the door to the outer sanctum of his chambers. I stood there trying to gather some courage when Mrs. Carlton, Judge Collins' personal assistant, called out, "Mark, are you coming in or are you going to stand there all afternoon?"

I was stunned. How did she know anyone was there? The door was a solid wood door with no windows. Better yet, how did she know it was me? I had no choice but to proceed.

"Well, I am glad you finally chose to come to the office." she admonished without looking up from her desk. "The judge has given me a great deal of work he wants you to complete while he is on vacation," she stated dismissively, handing me a stack of legal files.

Stunned I took the files, hearing for the first time the judge was on vacation. "Vacation?" I stammered. "The judge is on vacation?"

Looking up from her desk for the first time, Mrs. Carlton removed her glasses, pinched the bridge of her nose in exasperation, a move I had seen the judge perform countless times when he was irritated at some lawyer, and sighed. Blowing out the last bit of breath as if she were blowing out candles on a birthday cake, she said, "Of course, he is on vacation. That is why he has interns. Now get out and get busy, I have work to do." I was dismissed.

As I spun on my heels to leave, the thought crossed my mind, "These two were made for each other." I headed out the door and realized, I had my miracle. I could leave Sunday morning, head to New Brunswick by train, and spend all day with Robbie making sure nothing happened on his birthday. I had five days to prepare. "For what?" I asked myself as I headed back to the apartment to get working on the judge's assignments.

Chapter 68

Monday June 17 dawned bright and early. It was going to be a beautiful day. I awoke with a slight headache, perhaps a remnant from the previous night's bad dreams. I made myself breakfast of fresh fruits and orange juice, trying to get a sugar load to cure my headache. It was not working. With the Gruns still out of the country, I had the whole farm to myself. There was much work to do, however. Fortunately, in the last few days I had developed a routine allowing me to complete the farm chores by ten a.m., giving me the rest of the day to myself. Unfortunately, with the farm chores done, my headache was worse.

I brewed a fresh pot of coffee and enjoyed a cup on the front porch, hoping the caffeine would help. As I sat there enjoying the brew, it dawned on me that today was the day before my twenty-fifth birthday. I really had not given it thought until now. I had no plans to celebrate this milestone and no one to celebrate with. I felt kind of bummed out that such an important event would be spent alone. I needed to find a way to change that.

I thought I would head to the lab to get some work done on my research. Since the semester had ended, I was free of classes and teaching, so I had a great deal of time to devote to my dissertation. Dr. Grun, in an effort to help me, had relieved me of my teaching duties for the next semester. In addition, I was finished with all my coursework, so I expected I would have all the time I needed to finish my research. I wanted to be done by next year so I planned to focus my efforts to get things done.

My lab was in the basement of Thompson Hall, a 10 minute walk from the farm. The weather seemed to be getting worse as I walked down the path toward campus. As I rounded the corner and entered Campus Drive, I looked up and noticed something strange. The sky directly overhead was dark, with ominous clouds swirling directly above me. The wind blew high in the sky, but the air around me was calm. When I looked in other directions around me, the rest of the sky was bright and sunny. There were some clouds, but they were light and wispy and floated in a calm sky. It was really odd to see the focus of a storm directly overhead while the rest of the sky was so clear. I guessed it was an errant storm cloud that would soon pass. It didn't.

I headed down to my lab, which was located in the basement. As I entered the stairwell I felt a shudder run down my spine. I stood there for a second, shook off the feeling, and headed the rest of the way down.

I was in the lab for a few hours when suddenly I heard a noise. Usually the building was filled with students and faculty, but it was June and no one was in the building except for me, so it was really odd to hear sounds. I stopped working and listened. Dead silence. I knew it was someone or something playing with me, so I waited to see if the noise would come again. Sure enough, there it was again. This time it was clearly the sound of a door opening and closing.

Someone, for sure, had to be in the building. I opened the door to my lab and looked down the hall. Empty. No one was there. There were only two other doors in the hall, one to the lab next door belonging to Dr. Tudor and one to the locked janitor's closet. Dr. Tudor was on sabbatical for the summer, so I suspected it wasn't him. "It must be the janitor, Mr. Sanchez coming to do some work," I thought.

I took a few steps down the hall and called out, "Is anyone there?" Silence. Shaking my head, I turned on my heels and headed back to my lab when I heard it again. The sound of a door closing. This time the sound was right in front of me and came from the area past my lab. But there were no doors there. My lab was the last door in the hallway. Now, I was confused and a little scared. I called out again, "Ok, quit clowning around. You got me. Who's there?" Nothing. I stood there for a few minutes, waiting to hear someone or something but nothing. "Damn," I muttered to myself. I looked around once more, saw nothing, and headed back to the lab.

I spent another hour working in the lab with no further disturbances. Soon, I had pushed the whole ordeal from my mind and decided I was done for the day. My headache never really went away, so I assumed my headache contributed to the experience. I packed up the lab, shut the lights, and headed for the door. I looked over my shoulder to make sure the lab was secure and walked out. Pulling my keys from my pocket, I closed the door and prepared to lock it. As I did so I, once again, heard another door close and lock, just like I had done with my door. It had to be an echo or my imagination or a delayed reaction from the headache. Whatever it was, I ignored it and headed home.

The strange weather had cleared up to the point that I was walking home in a bright beautiful warm summer day. The breeze was blowing from the west and was filled with the fragrance of fresh mowed grass from the common area around the lake. It was a beautiful day.

When I got home, I decided to open a beer and get ready to cook some chicken on the barbecue for dinner. I lit a fire and sat back with a cold one or two waiting for the coals to get hot. My headache was finally going away, and I was getting real hungry.

As soon as the coals were ready, I put on half a bird and some corn on the cob and relaxed under the bright sun, waiting for the food to cook. I was so relaxed, with the warm sun beating down on my face that I must have dozed off.

The beer bottle slipped from my hand and startled me awake. I had fallen asleep under a bright warm sky and woke to another storm cloud directly overhead. "What the hell?" I said to myself. It was as if bad weather were following me. The food was cooked, so I grabbed my dish, piled on the food, and covered the coals. I headed up the stairs to the loft in case it really was going to rain. The way my day was going, anything was possible.

After dinner I did the dishes, grabbed another beer, and headed to my favorite chair to continue some reading on virus identification. I really had some trouble concentrating. Maybe it was the headache, maybe the beers, or maybe the boring subject matter. Whatever it was my mind kept wandering. Tomorrow was my birthday, and I still had no plans to celebrate.

As I sat there brooding on my misfortune of celebrating a milestone birthday alone, I thought I heard a noise outside. I clearly heard someone coming up the steps. Before I could react, I heard a knock at the door. Not expecting anyone, I had no idea why anyone would be knocking at my door. I thought it was my imagination again; I was a little drunk for sure. Before I could react, I heard the knock again, this time a strong knock, which was indeed insistent.

Struggling out of my seat, I was a little wobbly from the beers, I headed to the door. I opened it, half expecting to find no one there. But instead, there was someone there, someone who shouldn't be there. "What are you doing here?" I exclaimed as I stepped back from the door and gazed at my unexpected visitor.

Chapter 69

Mark

Monday June 17 dawned bright and early. It was going to be a beautiful day in Elmira, New York. I had planned to travel to New Jersey to be with Robbie for the fateful twenty-fifth birthday. I was able to get most of the work for Judge Hardass completed, but I had to make a deal with my roommate to get the rest of the work completed on time. I had to do three future briefs of his choosing, and he would complete the rest of my work. It was a lousy deal for me but, if I had any hope of getting away to be with Robbie, I had to make do.

There was no direct route from Elmira to New Brunswick. My only option was to take a bus from Elmira to Binghamton, then another bus from Binghamton to New York City and finally a train from New York to New Brunswick station. From there I still had to get local transportation from downtown to Rutgers University and then I had to find Robbie's residence. If everything went perfectly, the route would take nearly seven hours. Needless to say, it did not go perfectly.

My plan was to arrive in New Brunswick before eight p.m. and head over to Robbie's place. So, I decided to take the first bus out of Elmira at seven a.m. I arrived at the bus station with forty-five minutes to spare and bought my tickets to both Binghamton and on to New York. As soon as I had the ticket in my hands, there was an announcement over the loudspeakers indicating the bus to Binghamton was delayed due to mechanical issues. We were told to "please stand by." Further information would follow.

After nearly two hours, there was no information forthcoming, so I got up and asked the ticket seller for some information as to what was happening with the bus to Binghamton. He looked at me quizzically through the grating and said, "Young man that bus left right on time nearly two hours ago."

I was aghast. "What?" I exclaimed. "There was an announcement over the loudspeakers saying the bus had mechanical troubles and to "please stand by," I said. "I really need to get to New York. Can you help me please?"

"Yes sir, I am sure we can get you to New York. Let me check the schedules," he said calmly.

The ticket agent spent several minutes looking over the schedules, making notes on a notepad, and then scratching them out and starting over again. Removing his agent hat and scratching his head in confusion, the agent looked at me through the grate and said, "It seems that our bus schedule and your train schedule do not mesh at this point in time. The only bus that could have gotten you to New Brunswick, per your schedule, was the one that left at seven a.m."

"That can't be," I said in a near panic. "I have to get to New Brunswick today."

"Well, there is a longer route through Syracuse that gets into New York about seven tonight and into New Brunswick around nine," he said, flipping some more pages through the bus schedule.

"Book it," I said, reaching into my bag to return the previously purchased tickets.

I boarded the bus to Syracuse and resigned myself to the fact that I would still get to Robbie before midnight on the eighteenth and, therefore, still be there before his birthday. I found a seat near the rear of the almost empty bus, settled in, and fell asleep.

I woke up a few hours later to find that I was only twenty minutes outside of Syracuse. We pulled into the bus terminal, and I headed to my connection. I read the gate number on my ticket, Gate 18, and saw that I was at Gate 1. "Great," I thought. "I have ten minutes to catch the bus and I have to go all the way to the other end of the terminal." So I grabbed my bag and double timed my way down the crowded terminal. Apologizing my way through the crowd as I bumped my way past fellow passengers, I finally arrived at Gate 15. I stopped, mystified. I looked around and saw I was at the end of the terminal.

'What the hell," I thought, "where is Gate 18?" I stepped up to the counter at Gate 15. "Excuse me," I said to the counter person, "but I'm in a hurry, and can't seem to find Gate 18."

The cute young girl at the counter looked at me with surprise and said, "Well, that's because we only have 15 gates. There is no Gate 18."

I had my ticket in my hand and thrust it at the counter girl, who took a step back as I cried out in a panic, "Look, my ticket says Gate 18!"

"Calm down, sir, let me take a look," she said as she reached for the ticket, her hand trembling. I must have frightened her in my panicked state.

She took the ticket and pronounced, "Sir, the ticket says Gate 1, not 18. Gate 1 is at the other end of the terminal. Your bus is scheduled to leave right now, so I suggest you hurry." Handing me the ticket, I took a look at the printed gate number and, what once said 18, now said 1.

With no time to lose and not having a second to spare, I took off at a run toward Gate 1. She called out sarcastically, "You're welcome."

Now, I was in a panic. I had to catch this bus. So, I ran with my bag slung over my shoulder. This time I did not even have the time to apologize as I bumped and rolled my way all the way back to where I started.

Huffing and puffing, I got to the gate and looked at the closed door, only to see there was no bus in the station. Suddenly, out past the door and in the flow of traffic, I saw my bus. It was stopped in a line of busses queued up to make a left turn out into the city traffic. I panicked and slammed through the closed terminal door and ran into the bus lanes. I heard a ticket agent call out behind me, "Hey, you can't go out there. It's dangerous. Stop!"

At this point, stop was not in my vocabulary. I ran up to the bus and banged on the door of the bus calling to the bus driver to open the door. The driver must have thought I was a madman. At first it seemed he was not going to open the door but, since he was still far from the corner and free to make the turn out of the terminal, he relented and reluctantly opened the door.

Huffing and puffing, with sweat running down my forehead, I jumped on the bus before the driver could close the door in my face.

"Son, I can't pick up passengers on the road. I am afraid you will have to exit the bus," the driver said.

"Sir, I am very sorry but I have to see a friend in the hospital," I lied. "I am afraid he might die," which was not entirely a lie.

I guess, since I was already on the bus and I had a valid ticket, the driver must have felt it was easier to take me on rather than try to get me off. He shrugged and shook his head and said, "Look I want no trouble. Sit down and shut up."

"Yes, sir," I replied, as I found the first open seat and fell into it as he pulled out into traffic.

It may be hard to believe, but the rest of the trip was more uneventful. I arrived in New York with enough time to walk the five blocks to the Grand Central Station, the main train terminal. The train bound for New Brunswick and beyond was waiting for me and I boarded without incident. Whatever forces that were trying to keep me out of New Brunswick must have given up. The train left on time, and I was on the last leg of what was now a fourteen-hour journey.

The train arrived into New Brunswick station a little after nine. I headed down to street level and was faced with a conundrum. I really did not know exactly where Robbie lived. I knew he lived in a loft that was on the property of one of his professors, Dr. Grun, but exactly where, was a mystery. So I decided to take a livery to the college campus and see if I could find someone who could help me. After all, how big could the campus be, right?

I was dropped off on Lipman Drive in front of the Administration Building. I was at the right campus, but still in the dark, literally, as it was nearly ten and no one seemed to be around.

I stood in front of the building for a few minutes when, out of the shadows, a female student appeared, walking directly toward me. Trying not to look like a stalker, I said, "Excuse me, but I am looking for some directions to a Professor Grun's house."

Before I could explain further, she said "Follow Lipman Drive to College Farm Road to Dudley Road. Take Dudley Road all the way out to the farms and Dr. Gruns' house will be the only house on the right."

Before I could say anything, she walked away. I picked up my bag and turned to at least call out a thank you, but she was gone. I turned onto Lipman Drive and followed her directions, eventually coming to a large farm house just off the end of campus, exactly where she said I would.

I bounded up the stairs, glad this ordeal was over but, before I could ring the bell, I noticed something odd. There were no lights on anywhere in the house. Then I remembered that Robbie lives in a loft. I stepped back and looked around the house, but I saw no loft entrance. I looked around and, out of the corner of my eye; I saw an old carriage house off to one side. Looking closer, I spied a light on in a window on the upper floor.

I headed down from the porch and over to the carriage house. As I came around the corner, I noticed a set of stairs on the outside of the building leading to the second floor where the lights were on in the window. This must be the loft Robbie was talking about. I grabbed my bag, tossed it over my shoulder, and headed up.

At the top of the stairs, I took a deep breath and knocked. Nothing. I knocked again, this time a little harder. I heard someone move inside. Suddenly, the door swung open and there stood Robbie, from the looks of it, a little drunk.

"What are you doing here!" he exclaimed, stepping back from the door.

I reached down into my bag and pulled out two six packs of beer and said, "Well, I came to celebrate your birthday, but it looks like you had a head start!"

Chapter 70

I stepped aside, still a little confused at Mark's arrival. "Come in, come in," I said with a slur. "I didn't expect to see you." Mark entered and stood for a second before dropping his bag and throwing his arms around me in a classic Italian male greeting. He patted my back the requisite three times and I returned the gesture.

We pushed back at arm's length, stood, and looked each other over from top to bottom. I was still in shock seeing Mark in my room. I didn't know why he came, but I was really glad he did.

I welcomed him into my loft and bid him sit down. Instead of sitting, he looked around the loft and exclaimed, "Not bad for a city boy in the country."

I laughed and told him that the loft was part of my deal with Dr. Grun. As long as I did some work for the good doctor and studied, I had a place to live.

Mark laughed and said, "Well, Judge Pain in the Ass would never make such an offer, even if I licked his shoes daily." We both laughed and sat down.

Opening a fresh beer, I handed it to Mark and asked, "Really, why are you here?"

"To be honest," he began, "I have been having dreams that something was wrong, or going to be wrong. It has been a long time since we were together and, besides, you only turn a quarter of a century once, so here I am."

We spent the next several hours drinking and talking about old times, swapping stories and lies. The clock over the kitchen sink struck midnight and Mark offered me a toast. "Here is to your birthday. Tomorrow we celebrate like there's no tomorrow."

I wonder if Mark knew how prophetic he was.

Chapter 71

I woke early, as usual, the next morning. My head was pounding from the late night beer fest. I padded over to the kitchen to pop a couple of aspirin, hoping to clear my head a little. Mark was fast asleep on the couch, wrapped in a blanket and looking exhausted. I headed out of the loft to do the morning chores, careful not to wake Mark. By the time I was done, a few hours later, Mark was just rousing from sleep.

'Well, good morning. How are you feeling?"

"A little like the Prussian army was using my head as a marching field all night. My mouth tastes like an old mud boot," he groused as he tried, and failed, to get off the couch. "What time is it anyway?"

'It's nearly eleven. If you can manage it, we can take a walk around campus, and I can show you my lab."

"Sure, just give me a minute to screw my head back on."

Mark
I was a mess. My head hurt like hell and my stomach was ready to wretch, but there was no food to let out. I sat there on the couch a few minutes thinking. "Well, it's eleven o'clock. I only have to make sure nothing happens for the next thirteen hours." I had to think of things we could do that would not raise Robbie's suspicions, but were absolutely safe. A walk around campus would be perfect. All I had to do was get off the couch, which turned out to be harder than I thought.

Shortly thereafter, I got dressed and, having chowed down on some dry toast, we were ready to leave. Robbie led the way. As we left the loft in the bright daylight, I got a chance to see for the first time really how beautiful the farm was. It was a bright June morning. Birds were everywhere, picking on the ground for seeds. Nothing like the drab mornings in Elyria. I was pleased that things were working out for Robbie. Now, I had to make sure nothing changed.

Chapter 72

Mark looked a little better after a hot shower, change of clothes and some dry toast. We headed out and I showed him around the property. From there we headed off down the path for the mile walk to the campus and my lab. It was nearing noon by the time we got to the main campus. We were both starving, so we decided to head over to the dining hall for lunch. After a typical college lunch of cheeseburgers, slightly overdone and French fries, undercooked, we headed back to Thompson Hall for a tour of my lab.

We took the long way around so I could show Mark more of the campus. As we rounded the corner near the campus student center, Mark stopped.

"Is that what I think it is?" Mark said as he grabbed my shoulder with one hand and pointed with the other. "Is that a handball court?"

"Yeah, why?"

"I didn't think that out in the country they played a real city game like handball," Mark teased, like we were all country bumpkins. "Come on, I bet I can still kick your ass."

"Kick my ass? That's not how I remember it. I recall I was the kicker of your ass," I said, pushing into his shoulder, catching Mark off balance.

"Well, we can do the lab later. Right now, let's play," he called, starting to trot over to the courts.

'Well, if you want me to beat you on my birthday, I am up for that," I called after him, breaking into a trot.

As usual there was no one on the courts. It was true that handball was more of a city game and the locals really did not appreciate a good hard game. Oh well, more room for us to play. We bought a fresh can of balls from the student center and headed out.

It was a beautiful day. The sun was shining at our back, so there was no interference from the bright sunlight. The temperature was a cool seventy-two degrees. It was a perfect day.

Mark opened the fresh can of balls with a pop and a hiss and trotted out to the service line and hit a light serve to warm up. We volleyed back and forth, not trying to score, just trying to limber up and get the old muscles working. After about fifteen minutes Mark shouted, "Ready, loser?"

"We'll see at the end who's who," I shouted back. And so we began the first of many games.

I was a little out of practice. The last time I really played was years ago in Brooklyn. Obviously Mark was playing much more and he had vastly improved.

Whether Mark was serving from the service line or I was serving, Mark would always fight to get in front of me to allow for better control of the game. Or, at least, so he thought. You see Mark had a tell. If you watched him closely, you could always tell to which side of the court he was going to hit the return.

If he stood with his shoulders squared to the front wall, he was going to hit the ball to his right. If he turned, so that his left shoulder was facing the wall, he was going cross court and hitting the return to the left. This allowed me to know a half step in advance where Mark was going to place his next shot. I used this to my advantage and was able to keep ahead of him by two games to one.

We had been playing for quite a while. I was more than a little sweaty and, frankly, my hand was killing me. So, I said, "Look, we are about even. How about one more game, and loser buys the birthday dinner?"

"Sure," he called back, "bring your wallet 'cause you are going down," and he slapped a wicked low serve for his first point.

We went back and forth, point after point, staying evenly matched. I took the lead after an exceptionally long volley, when I switched hands and hit a lefty just outside of Mark's reach. One more point and the game was mine.

"Would you like to give up now, or are you enjoying the pain?" I called out, trying to buy a few seconds to catch my breath.

"Wah wah," he retorted and took a service stance.

247

At that very second the atmosphere changed. The bright sun, which was in clear blue skies all day, hid behind a cloud. Birds, which were chirping and flying about all day, seemed to settle down and become silent. The feeling was chilling, ominous. Mark had just bounced the ball in his service stance, so I had to focus on that.

It was a typical low serve, which I easily handled. We had gone back and forth a few volleys when Mark got into his "tell "stance with his left shoulder facing the wall. I knew then that the ball was going cross court. I started to make my move to the left side of the court when Mark spun in the air and into a full squared stance and hit the ball low and hard to the right. I didn't expect the move, but in the split second it took him to make the move, the world changed.

I knew I had to reverse direction, something I was well capable of doing. So I twisted to my right, and pushed off with my feet and stretched out just in time to ……

Chapter 73

Mark

When I saw the handball courts, I was elated. I knew this was a great way to keep Robbie right next to me so I could make sure nothing happened and we could have some fun at the same time. When I made the suggestion, he readily agreed, and so we began.

Robbie was always a little better than me, but I still played often and I assumed Robbie was out of practice. One of my friends once told me I was predictable. I asked what he meant and he told me I had a 'tell.' It seemed that when I was going to volley right, I faced the wall. If I was going cross court, I led with my left shoulder. I had to use this to my advantage today.

Unfortunately for me, Robbie was not as out of practice as I had hoped. He took my wicked low serves and spinning returns in stride. After a while I was growing tired and my right hand was swollen so much I could hardly close it. Robbie called out, "Look, we are about even. How about one more game, and loser buys the birthday dinner?"

I was relieved and took a stance to serve, low and hard for a winner, but Robbie easily returned the volley. This went on for most of the game when suddenly I found myself at game point, and I was on the losing end.

I knew I had to do something, so I hit my serve low and hard. Robbie returned it handily. This was my chance. After the serve, I moved my left shoulder toward the wall, signaling a cross court shot. Soon as I heard Robbie return the volley, I knew he would be heading left. I spun my head around in time to catch Robbie making his move left. I jumped and spun, squaring my shoulder for a low hard right kill shot. Kill shot it was.

I waited a half second to see if by some miracle Robbie could return the shot. When nothing happened I spun around and everything changed.

Chapter 74

...watch the ball fly by my outstretched fingers. At the same instant, I felt, and heard, a snap in the back of my head. It was the same sound made when a rubber band is snapped on your wrist. The pain at the base of my skull was excruciating. I could feel a hot liquid pouring down the back of my neck, not on the outside, but on the inside of my skull. My ears felt as if the pressure had built to the point of bursting my eardrums.

Time seemed to pass slowly. I could feel my body floating in the air as if time was slowing down. I seemed to be able to control my fall. As if I had all the time in the world, I twisted my body so I would land on my back and not on my head. As I twisted in midair, I looked up and caught sight of the sky above. What was once a clear blue sky was now a dark and foreboding swirl of storm clouds. The weather had changed in an instant. I felt my body hit the ground, hard. Bounce and hit the ground again. I didn't, couldn't move.

As I lay frozen to the spot, I looked up once more to see that the clouds had completely cleared. The sky was a bright blue once again. The last thing I remembered, before passing out, was the sound of laughter. Not a happy laughter but a more sinister cawing. Then everything went dark.

Chapter 75

Mark

I saw that Robbie had made a desperate attempt to change direction and lunge toward the return shot floating just outside of his reach. My reaction went from happy to horror, as I saw him in what could only be described as "floating" in midair. I tried to run toward him, but I moved as if in slow motion. I was moving as fast as I could, but my feet felt like I was running through thick molasses. I strained every muscle I could to gain speed, but it was no use. I knew I could do nothing to prevent Robbie from smashing his head onto the hard concrete playing surface.

I doubled my effort, but as I moved forward, Robbie turned a full quarter twist and came down on his back, not once but twice. Incredible, I thought. I was only three steps away from where he lay, but it felt like it took me forever to reach him. When I got there, he was limp and not moving.

I had no idea what happened, but I knew enough about head and neck injuries that I didn't want to move him for fear of making things worse. I dropped hard to my knees and put my hand on his stomach and bent my face to his to see if he was breathing. Thank God, he was. I called to him several times, but got no response. I knew I needed help but didn't want to leave him there alone.

After what seemed to be an eternity, I knew I had no choice, Robbie needed help and quickly. I got up, ran as fast as I could to the gate at the end of the court, and started to run toward the student center to get some help. As I flung open the gate, I was stopped by a murder of crows.

They must have been feeding in the tall grass surrounding the handball court. When I ran through the open gate, I startled them, and they in turn, startled me. I was blocked, as they flew in every direction including some right at me. There must have been hundreds of them, screaming and flapping every which way. These were huge black birds, which flew cawing and cackling as if mad, around and around, almost intent on keeping me from getting help.

I quickly regained my composure and ran through the screeching birds heading toward the student center. When I arrived, I was out of breath, sweaty and looked a little crazed myself. No one was there. I called for help, but heard no reply.

I ran to the student post office, which was inside the student center, and saw two office workers chatting at a table behind the counter.

"That's a shame what happened, such a nice boy," I heard one say.

"True, he was so nice."

I couldn't believe what I was hearing. I stopped in the middle of the room, stunned. I knew they couldn't be talking about what just happened to Robbie. I snapped out of my reverie and called out, "Help, please help. I need an ambulance."

One of the two ladies looked up at me, over her reading glasses, and said in a motherly tone, "Now calm down, young man, and tell me what happened."

I took a deep breath and all I could say was, "My friend is badly hurt on the handball court outside and he needs help."

She instructed me to return to my friend and she would call for help, so I spun on my heels, and, as fast as I could, ran outside, across the tall grass, and back to Robbie. He hadn't moved a single muscle from the time I left him. I knew this wasn't good, so I fell again to his side and held his hand. Tears came to my eyes because, as I touched him, I knew things would never be the same again.

Chapter 76

The pain in my head was excruciating. It felt like it would explode. I could still feel a hot liquid pouring down the back of my neck, but from the inside, inside my skull. I couldn't open my eyes or move any part of my body. I felt like I was frozen to the spot.

Suddenly, my eyes began to see bright spots flashing behind my closed eyelids. The lights were intense, causing my head to ache further. The optic nerve can only send one signal to the brain, that of seeing light. Since the nerve can't send a pain signal, it can only respond in one way. The intensity of the light was a strong indication of the amount of pain this section of my brain must be feeling. I was worried. Actually I was terrified.

As I lay there I could feel the energy draining from my body. I knew I was hurt, bad. I could only guess how badly. I fought a losing battle to remain conscious. As I drifted away, I could hear Mark calling my name. Then I was gone.

Mark
Within minutes the ambulance arrived and the medic ran to Robbie's side and checked his pulse. He asked me what happened and, through sobs and tears, I told him the best I could.

The medic called for his partner to bring the stretcher. He came running with the stretcher and some other medical equipment. In no time, they had Robbie strapped on the stretcher and were carrying him to the ambulance. Since I had no other options, I asked the medic if I could ride along with my friend. After a brief hesitation, he said, "Of course, hop in," and we were off to the hospital.

I could feel the presence of another person quickly come next to me as I wavered in and out of consciousness. I knew Mark was at my side and he was sobbing, but I had no way to communicate to him that I knew he was there. I wanted him to know I was right there with him, but I had no way to communicate. The strange part, however, was that when Mark touched my hand, I could feel a burst of energy pass from him to me. It was as if I were getting a charge of energy from his body into mine. It was both exhilarating and painful.

I could hear Mark and another person talking, but I wasn't able to stay focused enough to catch every word. I guessed that the other person was a medic, based on snippets of what I was able to hear, and that he was here to help. When he touched my hand, I got another high voltage jolt. I had no idea what was happening.

After a few minutes I felt like I was floating away. I tried to focus and keep in the present, but it was no use. The world went black.

Chapter 77

I had lost all track of time. I regained consciousness. Well, not exactly full consciousness. If any of you have ever been in a coma, or known someone in a coma, perhaps you can relate to what I was feeling. I couldn't move. I could feel that I was lying down in some kind of a room with intense light, but I couldn't feel any part of my body. There was no pain, no sensation of hot or cold, just the feeling of being present and nothing more.

As I lay there, I tried to take stock of my body. I knew I was flat on my back. I couldn't feel my hands or feet. I couldn't turn my head or any part of my body. It was as if I were a sack of meat. I couldn't open my eyes, yet I could see light and dark as if someone was moving in front of my eyes and passing in front of a bright light. I could, however, hear what was going on around me. It took a lot of energy, and I didn't have much to spare, but I was able to hear the doctor and someone else, perhaps a nurse commenting as they passed by my room. I couldn't hear the whole conversation but I did make out the doctor saying "caused by a severe head trauma with internal bleeding" before I passed out again.

Sometime later, I had no idea how long; I once again came to a low level of consciousness. I knew I was weak. It took all my energy to stay at even this low level of consciousness. I was, however, able to think clearly. It was the only thing I could do. I remember the doctor saying I had a head trauma, so that would explain why I had large gaps in my memory. I had some clear memories, some foggy memories and some areas where there was nothing. This is very common in head injuries, but this didn't make me feel any better. Strange thing though, I was not frightened. I was more like at peace. I don't know why, but I was accepting of my condition more than I could have imagined.

As I lay there, in what I assumed was my bed, I could tell I was in a darkened room since I couldn't detect any bright lights through my closed eyelids. I guessed that in my coma state the doctors felt that resting in the dark would not be a problem. I did notice, however, that my body was cold. This was my first sensation of hot and cold, so I thought that was a good sign, that maybe some of my senses were coming back. My bed felt hard and cold as if I was lying on a metal sheet. I also noticed a distinct lack of sound as if I were in a closed room devoid of outside influence. I was actually thankful for the lack of stimulus; it didn't drain my energy so fast, so I was able to hold on a little longer. I still couldn't feel my arms or legs, but I knew, in a general sense, where my limbs were. My arms appeared to be folded across my chest in repose of deep sleep. As my energy level was spent, I drifted off again into a deep coma.

The next time I became sentient, I knew I was getting better, because I could sense the room was filled with people. I thought that if I were getting worse they wouldn't let people into my room to disturb me, so this was a good sign, right? I began to feel stronger. I still couldn't move my body, nor could I open my eyes, but my sense of hearing was fully returned and I could hear people talking. As I focused my energy to hear what they were saying, I was a little shocked to hear sobbing, and people talking in hushed tones, so low I couldn't make out what they were saying. I became agitated and felt my energy draining fast. I didn't want to slip away again so I fought hard to keep focused. I had to know what was happening.

Soon, I sensed someone come up to my bed. It was my Aunt Emanuella. "Why was she here?" Was I that sick? Who told her I was injured?" There were a hundred questions floating in my head. I could feel myself slipping away, but suddenly she bent closer to the bed and took my hand in hers. I felt the intense electric shock again and could feel my energy level jump up a notch.

Many people believe in the healing power of touch. By touching the hand or laying your hands on the forehead or even over the heart, it is said that the energy from the healthy person can flow into the injured person and help them with the healing process. Well, I believe it now; I could feel the exhilaration in my body as my aunt's energy flowed into me. I felt stronger and an overpowering feeling of love and well-being. I never wanted her to let go.

My aunt held my hand and said a prayer asking God to take care of me and then she kissed my forehead and turned away. I wanted to scream out, "Don't go, stay. Hold my hand I need you. Please stay," but alas I was unable to open my mouth and shout. I was despondent, but there was nothing I could do.

Over the course of the next few hours, as I lay there in my bed, I could feel people, as they came up to me to say a prayer or hold my hand. Many of them kissed my forehead or brushed my hair out of my eyes. They told me how good I looked. I knew they all loved me and I could feel every one of them as they took my hand and sent a powerful jolt into my comatose body. But there was nothing I could do. I had lost the power of communication. I tried to shout, move my foot, my little finger, anything to show them I was there and that I knew they were there, but nothing. I was powerless. My coma was too strong. I could sense they were there, but they could not sense I was there as well.

Soon, it was too much for me, and I once again drifted off into the deep recesses of my mind and into a deep blissful coma. "Will I ever recover?" I thought as the last vestige of my consciousness surrendered to the blackness.

Chapter 78

After a few days I was left alone, completely alone. The few times I regained some level of consciousness, I could only tell that I was in the dark, lying flat on my back with a deep sense of quiet and peace all around me. Being left like this was actually a blessing.

When I was in a room with distractions, my energy level would drain very quickly. When I was alone in the dark, I was able to hold onto my energy longer, and in fact over time I noticed I was getting stronger.

I have no memory of my time in the hospital, nor do I really remember how long I was treated. I only knew that it took a very long time before I could muster the energy to leave. When I did leave the hospital for the first time, I was weak but happy.

I soon found myself back in my loft apartment resting quietly. I may have rested a few days, maybe longer, I lost all track of time, but each day I felt stronger. I could stay awake longer but I still had a myriad of problems.

For one, the feeling in my extremities never fully returned. I had no feeling at all in my hands and feet. If I tried to move something with my hands, I couldn't feel it, so I sometimes knocked it over or pushed it along the table. I had a real hard time trying to grasp something as my fingers seemed beyond my control.

I also couldn't feel when my feet hit the floor. It was as if they were asleep. This made moving very complicated. I would move slowly across the floor. It felt more like floating since I never felt anything with my feet. It was unnerving and caused me to move very slowly and silently.

My head injury was indeed severe. There must have been a buildup of blood into my cerebral cortex, the area of the brain responsible for memory, because I had significant memory loss. Fortunately, the damage was manageable. I remembered things before the event clearly, as these memories were deeply fixed in my brain. Memories of the event and the subsequent time just after were sketchy at best. When I tried to remember, I couldn't, so eventually I just stopped trying. I assumed if these memories came back, I would deal with them then. Until then, it wasn't worth the energy to try to recall.

I was now ultra-sensitive to light. Sunlight caused me to experience pain and confusion, as if I were getting too much input through my eyes. If I avoided direct sunlight, I could manage the pain, so I often kept to the shadows.

When I was alone, I could manage very well. I stayed in the shadows and focused my energy on what I needed to do. The problem was when I was in the presence of other people.

The sensation of getting "jolted," when I came in contact with another person had not abated; in fact, it had gotten worse. I didn't actually have to touch another person to get jolted; I only needed to come into a crowded room to feel assaulted by the energy given off by those present. Sometimes, I could feed off this energy but, if the room were too crowded or too energetic, I couldn't handle the input. I needed to stay away from crowded spaces. Since I was finished with my classes and I no longer had to teach, I could basically stay away from people. I was able to work in my lab since this was a very quiet space. I could work in the early evening, so I could stay away from sunlight. So with some major accommodations I could continue my studies, and, hopefully, over a period of time, more fully recover to allow a more normal existence.

So, I became like a monk in a cloister. I rested most of the day in the loft, went to the lab early evening, and worked most of the night. I avoided people as much as possible and essentially developed a routine that could accommodate my condition. I was feeling in control and getting stronger. That is, until I met HER.

Chapter 79

I had fallen into a routine, suited to my condition. Early evening I would leave the loft, and travel down through the path in the woods and come out at the top end of the commons near Passion Puddle. Passion Puddle was actually a small drainage lake near one end of the common, and was the center of campus life for lovers.

The old tradition said if you walked hand in hand with your lover three times around the puddle without stopping, you were destined to spend the rest of your lives together. I always made it a point to arrive at the puddle alone and leave alone.

I would pass along the side of the puddle, and travel across the common to Red Oak Lane. A short distance from there I would cross Lipman Drive and enter Thompson Hall, through a side door, that led directly to the basement and to my lab. Thus, I would never have to come in contact with the staff or students on the first floor of Thompson Hall. By keeping to the shadows, I was able to avoid people and arrive at the lab unaccosted.

Things, however, changed one fall day. I had taken my usual route through the woods to the Puddle and began to travel across toward Red Oak Lane. It was a beautiful evening. The sun had set, the evening was crisp and the fall colors were abounding. As I headed along I heard a voice curse, "Damn it! Where are they?"

I had no idea what was happening, but, as I gravitated toward the benches along Red Oak Lane, I could see a student, on her hands and knees, on the ground half under one of the stone benches along the lane. She was sweeping her hands around among the leaves, swearing.

I assumed she was looking for something. Sure enough, I spied a set of keys; I assumed dorm keys just out of her reach mixed in the leaves. I was surprised she didn't see them, so I called out, "Look to the right at two o'clock."

I guess she didn't expect my voice because, as soon as she heard my directions, she bolted up and hit her head, hard, on the bench. She yelped, "Ouch," turned in my direction and said, "Thanks a bunch," in a rather indignant tone.

I said I was sorry and, once again, directed her to the keys clearly visible to her right. She bent down, moved her hand as directed, and found the keys. I soon found out what was going on.

As she stood up, keys in hand, rubbing her head, she turned in my direction and, using a whipping motion of her right hand, snapped out a folded red tipped white cane. She was blind.

Without a word of thanks, or introduction, she spun around and, tapping the cane in front of her, stormed off. I didn't bother to say anything. I just assumed she was pissed at having lost her keys and continued on my way to the lab as usual. That, however, would not be the last time I would see her.

Chapter 80

The next day, I made my way down to the lab through my normal route. As I came to the area of Red Oak Lane, I spied a person sitting, comfortably, on the same bench from yesterday's altercation. It was the same student. This time I planned to pass on by without communicating, but I was not given the chance.

I tried to pass silently but, as I crossed her path, she suddenly sat upright and said, "I'm sorry about yesterday."

I was caught off guard, thinking, "How did she know it was me?"

I remember stuttering something like, "Its ok, no hard feelings." She countered with, "No, it's not ok. I was rude and you were just trying to help. I'm Cathy; I owe you an apology and a thank you."

"Ok, you're welcome. I'm Robbie, Robbie Mauro."

"Pleased to meet you," she said as she held out her hand in greeting.

I hesitated, perhaps a bit too long, for she soon drew her hand back and said, "OooooK then," drawing out the "o" as if the word were five syllables long, "so much for polite."

"No, no it's not that, you see——" Before I finished my thought, she said, "No, actually I can't see. I'm blind," giving a light chuckle, allowing me to regain my composure.

"Of course, sorry," I stuttered again.

"Don't worry. I'm glad we met, and once again thank you for your help yesterday." With that said she stood up, slashed out her cane, and started moving off.

I was a little shocked at her confidence. I had my own issues, but I could not imagine being blind, and how in the hell did she know it was me? I delayed a second or two and moved off to the lab.

Chapter 81

The next day, I headed to the lab as usual and, once again, as I came to the benches along Red Oak Lane, there she was, as if waiting for me. This time I broke the ice and said, "Hi, Cathy. It's me Robbie."

"I know," she said, "Hi back."

I was stunned and said, "Ok, what's the secret? How did you know it was me?"

I'm blind, not stupid," she said laughing. "They say blind people have a sixth sense that develops to help them compensate for the loss of sight. Well, my senses can tell me, sometimes, who is nearby."

"Really?" I gasped a little shocked.

"No stupid, you have a distinctive voice. Since you said 'Hi" first, I knew it was you," she said chuckling. "I'm sorry I shouldn't tease. Bad habit," she apologized, regaining her composure.

"Where ya headed?"

"I have a lab in the basement of Thompson Hall. I tend to work there nights, it's much quieter and I like the quiet."

"What are you working on?"

"I am completing my doctorate on avian virus serotyping," I said, trying not to sound too pompous. "What are you studying?"

"I'm a junior in the psychology department. I am hoping to do research or teach. Maybe get my Masters later."

We chatted a little more about this and that, and then I said, "I really gotta get going," so I excused myself and headed to the lab.

"See ya around," she called after me, laughing again.

I was really amazed how comfortable she was with her disability. With my life so screwed up, I thought, if she could do it, then so could I. I felt much stronger and more confident as I passed through the basement door for another late night in the lab.

I saw Cathy almost every day after that, at the same place and time. It was uncanny. I would come down from the loft, through the woods, and there she would be sitting as if waiting for me. So one day I asked, "You seem to be a fixture on this bench. What's up with that?"

As usual she laughed and said, "And you seem to take the same route at the same time every day. Are you stalking me?"

I was taken aback at her confidence. So I said, "Guilty, you caught me. I am stalking you."

We chatted some more and she said, "I don't know, sometimes being blind has its issues. It's hard to find someone to talk to and you seem, well, I don't know, different. Like we have a connection. I feel different when we talk, ya know?"

I did and I told her that I actually liked our chats and felt comfortable just chatting, something that I had not felt in a long, long time.

So, once again, we chatted for another hour. It was getting dark and I asked her which dorm she lived in. She told me it was Corwin C in the first horseshoe. I told her that the back entrance to Corwin C was just a short walk past my lab, so I asked her if it would be ok to walk her back to the dorm.

"Sure, let me get my stuff," she said and gathered her books. She snapped out the folded cane and off we went.

I dropped her off at the back door of the dorm and said, "Good night. " Before she could invite me in, I continued, "I have a bunch of work to do in the lab tonight, so I better get going."

"Oh, of course," she said with a little disappointment in her voice. "See ya around," and up the back stairs she went.

I'm sure she wanted more, but I wasn't ready. I still had major problems around people, but around Cathy it was different. I was comfortable. I didn't feel a jolt when she brushed by me, nor was I shocked when I accidentally touched her. In fact, I felt nothing at all. Maybe, I was getting better.

Chapter 82

Cathy

Most of the guys I met at school were jerks. They were either uncomfortable with a blind girl, or thought, as a blind girl, I would be "easy." In the end they were jerks, but not this one guy, Robbie.

I met him about two months ago, a fiasco actually. I had lost my keys, a disaster for a blind person. I was searching for them under a bench, when he seemed to just be there behind me. He startled me and I hit my head on the bench. I was more than a bit rude, as I sarcastically thanked him and turned away.

The next day, I screwed up the courage to try and apologize, so I sat back on the same bench hoping he would come by again. I had no reason to think he would come by again, just a strange feeling that he would. Sure enough he did.

I felt strange, however, like I could feel him coming before I actually heard him. In fact, I didn't hear him coming at all. I just knew he was there and I blurted out a lame apology. Strangely, I was right. We chatted a few minutes and introduced ourselves.

He stopped and we talked a little. During our conversation, I "felt" him talking rather than "heard" him talking. It was as if he were talking directly into my brain. It was really weird. I can get that way sometimes; being blind makes things feel different. I sometimes feel I have a sixth sense, which allows me to feel more than usual. I can't explain it since I don't really understand it myself.

Anyway, almost every day, I would sit on the same bench and, at about the same time every day, he would come by and we would chat. I found out he was a graduate student, working on some avian virus. He seemed shy and relatively quiet. I can't explain it, but I could feel an energy emanating from his direction whenever we chatted. It was as if he had an almost palpable aura. I learned, in one of my psych classes, that parapsychologists believe we all have a life energy, some stronger than others. People claim that we can feel these life forces. Maybe being blind helped me feel this energy. Whatever it was, Robbie's was strong.

We would have these little chats by the common, and then he would say he had to go to the lab, and I would head back to the dorm. One day, we chatted for a much longer time, and I sensed it was getting late. He asked me if it was ok to walk me to the dorm. I had told him I lived in Corwin C. He said that it was actually on his way to his lab in Thompson Hall so we gathered our things and headed to my dorm.

When we got to the back door, I was going to ask him to come up for a soda or something, but before I could say anything, he said he had to head to the lab and that he was already late. I was a little disappointed, and I guess he must have sensed it because I could "feel" his energy level change a little.

He took off for the lab and I headed back to the dorm, shaking my head saying, "Men can be such boys."

Chapter 83

I now added a new event to my daily routine. I would leave the loft, travel down the path to Passion Puddle, and spend an hour or so chatting with Cathy. I found myself looking forward to our near daily chats. Cathy was comfortable to be around. I opened up to her. We chatted about growing up, I in Brooklyn, she in a small town in New Jersey. We talked about my research, and her interest in psychology. I spoke mostly about the past and she mostly about the future.

I found myself looking forward to seeing her. One day, I came down and noticed she wasn't at the bench. It wasn't too unusual for her to miss a day from time to time; after all she was busy with classes of her own. I didn't think much of it, that is, until she missed five days in a row. That was unusual. I started to wonder if something happened.

The next day was a Saturday, a bright, clear, warm late October day. It was also All Hallows' Eve or Devil's Night. As usual, I headed to the lab, via my usual route. The evenings were now darker as the days were getting shorter. I could see from a distance that the bench was once again empty. I somehow felt something was wrong; Cathy never missed six days in a row. I was determined to find out what it was. I screwed up my courage, gathered all my energy, and traveled passed my usual side entrance to Thompson Hall and continued on to the back door to Corwin C.

I was a little panicked. I didn't know what to expect. Would I be considered an intruder? I really had no right to barge in on Cathy; after all we were nothing more than friends, or maybe just mere acquaintances. I almost turned around and minded my own business when I felt a pull toward the door. It was strange as if there were something urging me on.

So, I passed through the door and into the dorm. Now, the Corwin dorms were some of the oldest dorms on campus. They were built as individual three story houses. On the first floor was a small kitchen in the back and a common living room in the front. In the middle were two dorm rooms, one on each side of a staircase leading to the second and third floors. There was also a common bathroom and shower on each floor.

I stood there for a minute in the kitchen, alone. I was drawn into the hall and toward the room on my right. No one was about, I was all alone. On the door was a small name plate with the name Cathy Towers. This must be her room.

I was about to knock when I heard a voice from within, say "Come on in Gloria, the door's open." It was Cathy.

I hesitated and called out, "Umm... ah... it's not Gloria, it's... ah.... Robbie."

"Well, don't just stand there, come on in!" So, I did.

The room was dark. There were no lights on. Cathy was sitting at a well-appointed student desk strewn with books. The room had a single bed positioned along one wall, an open door which led to a closet, crammed with clothes. There was a four shelf bookcase loaded with books and papers. Prominently displayed in the middle of the room was a Bentwood rocker, just like the one in my loft.

"Hi, stranger, what brings you here?" she said, turning away from her work.

"I hadn't seen you for a coupla days, and I was wondering if you were all right."

"Glad to know I was missed. I've been buried with a psych paper and was going to use the weekend to catch up. Gloria and I were going to work on it together. Why don't you hang around and you can meet her?"

"No, no that's ok. I just wanted to make sure you were ok. You know me, I am at the lab every night, and I am making great progress, so I really got to go."

"Oh, bummer," she said. I could tell she was disappointed that I was leaving.

"OK then, back at the bench soon I hope," I said, preparing to leave.

"Of course, I'm looking forward to it."

"Good night," I said and, once again, passed through the door and out the way I came. I was glad she was all right. I headed back to the lab and another full night of work.

Chapter 84

Cathy

I was buried with work. I had a psych. paper due, an English reading assignment in Olde English by Chaucer, and a test in sociology to study for. My plate wasn't full; it was overflowing. I hadn't left the room, except for class and meals, for days. I needed a break, but I committed to knuckle down and get this done.

Gloria Jennings lived across the hall from me. She was the dorm moderator, or Dorm Mother, we liked to call her. She and I had become fast friends. We had many of the same classes, so we often studied or commiserated on how much work we had to do. We had planned to work on the psych paper together, since we were lab partners, we only had to turn in one paper. She was supposed to be on her way over when I heard someone outside my door.

I called out, "Come on in, Gloria, the door's open."

A voice replied, "Umm... ah.... it's not Gloria, it's ...ah.... Robbie."

Unexpected, but perfect I thought. If Robbie was here and Gloria was on her way over, I could introduce them and then she could give me a complete rundown on what he looked like. Perfect. So, I told him to come in

Shy, as always, Robbie told me he was concerned that he hadn't seen me in a few days, so he wanted to make sure I was all right. I thought, "How sweet!"

We chatted a few minutes. I told him all was well and I was buried in work. I could tell he was uncomfortable being alone in my room, but I had to keep him there for a few more minutes. Gloria would be here any second. I was thinking, "Gloria, girl, where are you? I need you here NOW! He is panicking and getting ready to leave."

I felt he was itching to go, but I invited him to stay awhile to meet my friend Gloria. That caused him to panic more and he bid a quick, but courteous, farewell and beat it out the door.

Not three seconds later, Gloria walked into the room and said, "Hi, kiddo. What's up?"

"Well, well, did you see him? What's he look like?" I excitedly hit her with a barrage of questions.

"Whoa, girl. Slow down. What's who look like?"

"Robbie, of course. He was just here in my room. You had to have seen him walk out the door. He was just a second or two ahead of you. You had to have passed him in the hall. Tell me, what did he look like?"

"Calm down, Cath," she said putting her hand on my shoulder. "I didn't see anyone. I came straight across the hall and into your room. The back door was closed and there was no one in the kitchen. The front door is locked and we are the only two people on this floor right now. So, sorry, I didn't see anyone.

"Damn," I whispered. "I was sure you would run into him in the hall. I just wanted to know what he looks like."

"Ok, well, I have an idea," Gloria continued. "You know I work part time in the registrar's office."

"Yeah, sure."

"Well, this week, when I am out there, I can look him up and get a copy of his student ID photo and I can tell you what he looks like. Ok?"

"Great," I said with a little more enthusiasm than I expected. "I just want to know what he looks like."

"OK then. What's his full name?"

"Mauro, Robbie Mauro."

"Monday, I will check him out and give you a full report. Now, let's get this damn lab paper done so we can have some fun tonight."

So we settled down to work, but my mind drifted, from time to time, toward imagining what Robbie really looked like. I would learn more than I bargained for soon enough.

Chapter 85

Monday night, Gloria came running into my room all excited. "Cathy, you gotta see this. I found out something about Robbie, and you're not going to believe it."

"Slow down. Have a seat, and take a breath. What did you find that was so exciting?"

"As I told you, I could get into the registrar's files at work, so I looked up Robbie Mauro. At first, nothing. Then I thought, "That's not his full name," so I started to look up possible other spellings and boom I came up with Roberto Mauro, aka Robbie."

"Terrific," I said excitedly, "so what did you find out?"

"Well, that's the strange part. There is no Roberto Mauro currently enrolled in the graduate school."

"What? That's not possible. There has to be something wrong." I was a little frightened. Was this Robbie a stalker preying on the fact I was blind? I couldn't believe I could have been taken in by some asshole. I was getting really pissed.

"Hold on, I did find something else," Gloria replied. What she said next was impossible.

"There is, or rather there was, a Roberto Mauro at the University, studying avian viruses under Dr. Grun, but that was a long time ago. Dr. Grun lived on a small farm at the north end of campus."

"What do ya mean? That makes no sense, that can't be right. Maybe you have the wrong first name. It's obviously not possible that the grad student you found could possibly be Robbie." I was rambling, frightened, and confused.

"Well, I thought about that, so I looked up every name I could think of that ended with Mauro. There was one other, but I didn't have the time to dig deeper."

"So, what do we do now?" I asked.

"There is one way we could find out for sure," Gloria said in a conspiratorial tone.

"Don't like the sound of that, but I'm listening."

"Well, he dropped in on you the other day, right?"

"Yeah, so?"

"Well, one good turn deserves another! We drop in on him!"

"I don't know," I replied with some caution.

"What could go wrong," she said trying to convince me this was a good idea. "What's the worst that could happen?"

Not fully convinced I said, "Ok. He told me he lives in a loft apartment over a carriage house on the north end of the campus. I have no classes tomorrow. We can go then. Deal?"

"Deal," she said.

Little did we know what a mistake that was.

Chapter 86

The next day was a rather bright warm day for December. Winter Break would start soon. My classes were over, so I was free. Gloria stopped by before lunch, ready for our adventure. We decided to walk beside Passion Puddle and through the woods along the path Robbie usually takes. I thought, maybe we could run into him along the way and our stealth visit to his loft would become unnecessary. But, no such luck. We made it all the way through the woods and the beginning of the agricultural station where Robbie was supposed to live.

Gloria followed a map of the Cook College campus, since we are not familiar with this area of the University. According to the map, ahead of us would be the location of the farm where Dr. Grun lived. We followed the path a little further and came to a white building that looked like what once could have been an old farm house.

"I don't see any other buildings around, so this must be the right place," Gloria said, taking my hand and leading me toward the front steps.

"Hold on," I said, coming to a stop and pulling my hand back. "Where are we going? We can't just barge into someone's house."

"Well, from the sign on the front that says Grun Administration Building, I don't think anyone actually lives here anymore," Gloria said and grabbed my hand once again, leading me toward the front entrance.

The front door was open and, indeed, it was no longer a home but had been converted into an administration building with a front receptionist and offices to the rear.

"May I help you?" asked the receptionist in an overly friendly tone.

Gloria piped up and said, "We hope so, we were looking for a Robbie or Roberto Mauro. He is a graduate student under Dr. Grun."

The receptionist was taken aback as if shocked by Gloria's query. She nervously replied, "Ladies, I am afraid you must be mistaken," and proceeded to tell us the story of Dr. Grun. When she was done, Gloria and I were shocked.

I stood there incredulous. What we just heard can't be right. There had to be another explanation. So I asked "Excuse me, but is there a carriage house near this area? Maybe we have the wrong place."

Again the receptionist looked dismayed but replied, "Well, yes, there is, or rather there was, a carriage house outside the front door to the left about 50 yards up the path.

We thanked her for her assistance, and, still confused with what we learned, we headed toward the carriage house. "There has to be some mistake," I said to Gloria as we headed toward the carriage house. I soon found out there was no mistake and things began to fall into place.

Chapter 87

The next time I saw Cathy at the bench, I had the feeling things were different. I really had no idea what happened but she seemed a little nervous and more inquisitive. She asked me question upon question about my past, where I grew up, what I was doing in grad school, personal stuff, some of which I felt uncomfortable with .

She said she wanted to get to know me better, but it felt more like the third degree. I was a little uncomfortable, to be honest, but I took the high road and tried to answer her questions without getting too personal. I tried to turn the tables a few times by asking some questions of my own, but she deftly was able to deflect my efforts and returned to her interrogations.

At some point I had to stop. I asked her "What's with all the questions?"

"Nothing really, I was just trying to fit a few things together," she stammered. "Sorry if I was rude."

"That's OK," I said, "but I better get goin', I have work to do."

"Sure, I get it. Thanks for filling in some of the blanks."

"What a curious response," I thought, as I headed to the lab. "What was that all about?"

Chapter 88

Cathy

My latest conversation with Robbie confirmed some disturbing conclusions I was coming to. I knew I needed to confront him, but I was ill prepared for an intervention. I needed to do some research. So, I spent the weekend in the library preparing. I studied about dealing with denial, moving on, and post-traumatic stress. I read everything I could find on the subject and how to develop a proper and safe intervention. I read scholarly works and some schlocky work as well. I wanted to have both sides of the issue. I knew this wasn't going to be easy and could actually be dangerous. I knew, however, I had to do this alone, so I decided not to tell anyone my plans, especially Gloria.

Gloria also had the registrar's file converted to braille so I could review, on my own time and in depth, what she found out about Robbie. I also did an internet search on Roberto Mauro, and confirmed that most of what Robbie told me was true, except for one crucial point. A point I knew was the source of his denial. If I was going to help him I needed to be prepared.

I knew I didn't have much time. Winter Break was about to begin and the university would be on holiday soon. I would have to leave the dorm in three days, so I had to act quickly, ready or not.

I decided that tomorrow night, Sunday, December 21, the winter solstice, would be the perfect day. Now, all I had to do was make sure Robbie was ready.

Chapter 89

It was a crisp Sunday evening, the longest night of the year and the start of winter. I felt strong and unusually happy. Being a creature of habit, I woke up late and, as evening approached, I headed, once again, through the woods to my lab. I was looking forward to seeing Cathy again and chatting awhile.

As I approached the bench, I could tell from a distance that the bench was empty. I was instantly disappointed. I continued slowly down the path and around Passion Puddle, hoping that if I delayed, Cathy would show up. She didn't, but I did notice something odd attached to the bench.

As I got closer, I saw that there was a sheet of paper taped to the back of the bench. It was a note. The note said, "Robbie, I have something very important to show you. Please come to my room tonight after nine. Cathy"

That's odd, I thought. What could she have to show me that was so important? I had no idea, so I guessed I would just have to go and find out. It was a little after 8, so I had an hour to kill. I headed to the lab, but couldn't concentrate on my work. I kept thinking, "What did she have that was so important? I soon found out.

Chapter 90

Cathy

I was as ready as I would ever be. I did my best to prepare, but I knew a hundred things could go wrong. I had no choice. It was now or never. I headed early down to the bench on Red Oaks Drive and attached a note telling Robbie I had something important to show him. I told him that he needed to come to my room after nine tonight. I had no idea if he would get the note, but I had hoped he would, so I waited

As I waited, I prepared the room to be soothing and comfortable. I had most of the lights off, as usual, but, to set the mood, I lit white vanilla fragranced candles and placed them on a table in the middle of the room. Between the two candles I lit a lavender incense stick. The smell of vanilla and lavender slowly filled the room in a calming fragrance of spring. I had a chair on one side of the table and another on the other side.

As a precaution, I even saged the room. This was something I read in one of the schlock papers. Burning sage was supposed to have a calming effect and also to provide protection. I needed all the help I could get so, since I had the time, I thought I would give it a try. I lit one smaller votive candle and put it in front of the mirror. A lit candle in front of a mirror is supposed to protect you from spirits coming or going through a mirror. I was taking no chances.

The stage was finally set. It was nearly nine o'clock. There was nothing else to do but wait. I sat down at the table and waited. Promptly at nine, I heard someone at the door.

I called out, "Come on in, Robbie. I was expecting you"

Chapter 91

Once again I came through the door and stopped. I looked around and thought, "Not again!"

As I entered, I could smell the sweet perfume of sage. The room had been smudged. The room was dark, lit by a pair of scented white candles on a table in the middle of the room. On one side of the table, seated behind the candles, obscured by smoke from an incense burner, sat Cathy, dressed in a black turtleneck and black slacks. Around her neck was a gold cross, a symbol of her faith. There was an empty chair on the other side of the table.

Cathy said, in a quiet, soothing voice, "Please sit down."

I replied, "Ok," but held my ground.

Cathy took a deep breath and let it out with a sigh. "Robbie, you're my friend, and I want to help you. You've told me a great deal about your past, but I think there is something you're holding back. I really feel we need to explore that."

"I really don't know what you are talking about," I lied.

"Well, let's start with your birthday. Your twenty-fifth birthday to be exact."

"What do you mean? Nothing happened on my birthday," I replied a little defensively.

"Robbie, listen. You once told me you had an accident on your birthday, that you were injured. Tell me more about that. What happened that day?" Cathy said in a soothing voice.

"I don't really remember."

"Try, Robbie. Humor me. Tell me what happened on June eighteenth, the day of your twenty-fifth birthday."

"Well, my best friend, Mark came to visit. It was unexpected, but I was glad to see him, "I started, and then hesitated.

"Good, what happened then?"

"We sat around, reminiscing about this and that then I took him for a tour of the campus and to my lab. That's all," l said, hoping not to continue.

Cathy was relentless, however. She wouldn't let me stop there. "Now, Robbie, that's not all that happened, was it? Didn't you and Mark do something else, something you two always did when you were kids? Come on, Robbie, tell me more"

"Yeah, I remember now. We played some handball."

"Good, great. What happened next? Try to remember."

"I fell and hit my head. It was nothing. Just a good knock on the head. It hurt like hell, but I was all right," I said, trying to make light of my accident.

"Ok, Robbie, that's enough of that for now. I want to ask you about Dr. Grun."

"What about Dr. Grun?" I stammered, a little concerned where this was going.

"Gloria and I took a walk to the far north end of campus; you know where Dr. Grun has his farm and your carriage house loft apartment."

"Why would you do that?" I said, feeling a little invaded.

"I'm sorry if that upset you, I really am, but we had to check out a few things. When we went up to the farmhouse, we found out Dr. Grun doesn't live there anymore, does he?"

"No. he's taking a sabbatical for two years before he retires. The university wanted to expand to the north and Dr. Grun gave the farm to the university as part of an endowment when he retires. You can check it out," I said

"We did," she said. "And all of what you said is true. The problem is not what happened, it's when it happened.

"What do ya mean?" I said, more concerned where this was going.

"We'll get back to that in a minute. Robbie, tell me a little more about your accident. What happened? How long were you in the hospital?"

'I told you already," I said in a voice bordering on angry.

"Calm down, Robbie. I am only trying to help. I need to hear from you what happened. Only then can we move on. So tell me, please, what happened after the accident?" she said once again. I felt compelled to go on.

I couldn't stop myself. I told her about the head injury and that is was actually much worse than I led on. In fact, I told her I was in a coma for a long period of time and that I could hear people and sounds around me but I couldn't respond. I opened up and told her everything. Why? I don't know. Once I started, I couldn't stop.

"That's good, Robbie. That's just perfect. Now what happened after you came back from your injury?" she asked.

"What do ya mean? I don't understand," I stammered.

"You went back to the loft, right?"

"Right," I replied.

'What happened then?"

"I told you. I didn't have any more classes. Dr. Grun was away, so I spent most of my time in the lab finishing my research," I said, matter of factly.

"And you worked mostly at night?" she queried.

"Yes."

"Why?"

"Because I told you, the light causes me to feel sick. I don't like to be around people and my lab is most quiet at night so it worked out best for me," I told her.

"Ok, good," she said. "Do you know what Gloria and I found out when we went to see Dr. Grun's farm?"

I said reluctantly, 'No, what?"

"Well, first, the nice receptionist told us that Dr. Grun had passed away many years ago. Then, we asked her about the carriage house. She told us where it was and Gloria and I went out to see it. Do you know what we saw?" she asked.

I was silent. After a moment she continued. "The carriage house, the one with the loft that you live in, burned down nearly twenty-five years ago. There was nothing left, except a foundation and a pile of rubble."

My silence was like a scream. She continued, "Robbie, I want you to know I only want to help, but you have to want help. " She hesitated, and then continued. "Robbie, the accident on your birthday, June eighteenth, the day you turned twenty-five. You died."

I was stunned. I remained silent. I could feel the atmosphere in the room change. It became oppressive, yet she continued. "Robbie, you were indeed born on June eighteenth, but the year was 1893. Your twenty-fifth birthday was June 18, 1918, nearly 100 years ago. Robbie, you have passed this mortal plane, but you have not moved on. It's time to move on," she said with compassion. 'I am here to help you, Robbie. Will you let me help you?"

I wanted to scream, "NO NO NO, none of this is true," but I couldn't. I was stunned into silence. After a minute she asked me again if I wanted her help. All I could do was whisper, "Yes."

Chapter 92

Cathy took a deep breath and, once again, let out a sigh. "Robbie, I am so glad you will let me help. I know it's for the best."

I remained silent.

Cathy continued, "Ok, then let's start. Robbie I want you to know that there are those on the other side who are waiting for you, your mom, your dad, and others. They will help you move to the other side. Ok?"

"I hope so," was all I could muster. I felt the energy drain from me. I felt weak.

"I want you to look at these candles and see the bright white flame there as it burns with purity from the white candle. Can you do that for me?" she asked.

"Yes." I said without emotion.

"OK, good. Now I want you to imagine the light getting brighter and brighter. It surrounds you. The bright light is everywhere. It is pure, it is good. Can you see the light?" she asked hopefully.

"Yes," was all I could muster. I felt weaker still.

"Ok, Robbie, that's good. Now, I want you to see that, in the light, there is a doorway. The door is opening and beckoning you towards it. Can you see that, Robbie? Can you see the door?"

Again, all I could say was, "Yes."

"That's good, we're almost there. Now, I want you to move toward the door."

"No," I shouted, feeling some strength return. "I'm afraid."

"No, Robbie, no no. There is nothing to fear," she said, soothing my fears and trying to move me to the door. The door opens to a place where there is no fear, no reprisals, only goodness."

I could hear her Catholic upbringing urging me on. "Move toward the light, Robbie. That's where you belong. Your time here is over. It has been over for a long time. Now, go, Robbie. I'll miss you, but it's time to go."

Without a reply, I went through the door. Cathy never saw me again.

Epilogue

In truth, there was no light. There was no door. In fact, there was nothing. The door I went through was the door to her room. It was indeed time to go. So I went, never to return.

I once told you that I would endeavor to tell you the truth, and so I did. Every word about my life story was true and was told exactly as it happened. Cathy was right about one thing, however. I did die on my twenty-fifth birthday, but I wasn't ready to be dead. Let me explain.

When we die, our body, the blood, and muscles and bones, die. The energy, the spark of life or the soul, if you need to believe in that sort of thing, doesn't. The essential essence of our life is energy. Our brain communicates to the rest of our body through a sequence of nerves that transmit signals through tiny sparks of energy. All told, the brain consumes about twenty percent of all the energy produced by the body. The rest is what we are made up of. It is the essential difference that separates from what is "alive" and what is not.

This energy, this essential spark of life, is all around us in one form or another. The first law of thermodynamics says that "energy cannot be created or destroyed, only altered into one form or another." It is also believed that all the energy in the universe, that which exists now and all the energy that has ever or will ever exist, was created in one stupendous moment of the "Big Bang."

Therefore, the energy that makes us who we are is a product of the creation of the universe. We are stardust. We have always been and will always be, until the end of time.

We only borrow this energy for a period of time; then, we have to return it. When our corporeal body dies, our energy remains. It is at this time each of us has to make a choice. We can return our borrowed energy to the center of the universe; some call this moving on. Our other option is not to return our essential energy, but to hold on and stay within the earthly realm.

I chose to stay. I am not ready to be dead. I know this is selfish, but I was too young to be just plain dead. I want more. And, so I stay. How long I will stay is a matter of conjecture. I have met others who can "see" me and for a time we are "friends." But it always ends the same; they want to help and so I move on. I know that someday I will give up and move on. I will return to the universe the energy that was me, but not yet. I'm still not ready.

So, if you hear a voice in your head, or a bump in the night, it may be me or someone like me, not ready to be moving on. Allow us to share this plane with you. Talk with us and perhaps we can be friends. Until then, I bid you, adieu.

November 2, 2014

Made in the USA
Middletown, DE
30 May 2016